THE KADE FAMILY SAGA

VOLUME 3

Between Two Shores

LAUREL MOURITSEN

STRATFORD
BOOKS

ISBN: 0-929753-10-0
The Kade Family Saga, Volume 3: Between Two Shores

Stratford Books
Eastern States Office
4808 37th Road North
Arlington, VA 22207

Stratford Books
Western States Office
P.O. Box 1371
Provo, UT 84603-1371

Rewritten and reformatted for the *Kade Family Saga* series. *Between
Two Shores* was originally published as *For Love and Zion* in 1997.

Between Two Shores
First printing: September, 2005

Printed on acid-free paper in accordance with the guidelines
of the American Library Association

Dust jacket painting: *Shall We Not Go On in So Great a Cause?*
by Clark Kelley Price.
© by Intellectual Reserve, Inc. Used by permission.

Printed in the United States of America

*"We started west in the spring
with an old wagon, one yoke of oxen,
one cow and all the things we could load
in the wagon. We felt to rejoice that we
escaped with our lives."*

MARIAH PULSIPHER
LATTER-DAY SAINT PIONEER

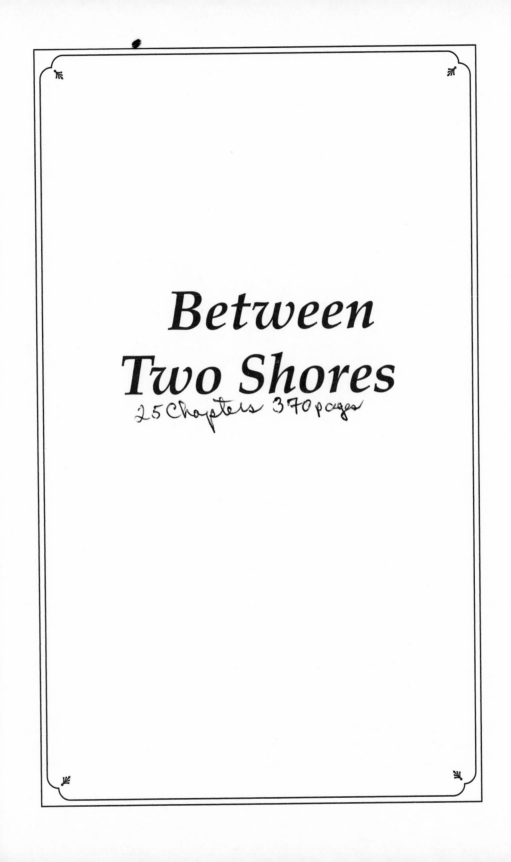

Between Two Shores

25 Chapters 370 pages

CHAPTER ONE

"*Mama?*"

Lydia looked up from her sewing at the sound of Elizabeth's voice. Elizabeth was standing in the doorway of the parlor of the Kades' brick home on Durphey Street. Lydia watched her daughter shift nervously from one foot to the other. Whatever Elizabeth had in mind to say wasn't going to be pleasing—Lydia could see that from her daughter's tense expression. "Elizabeth? What is it?" she asked.

Elizabeth drew an audible breath. "I'm not going, Mama."

Lydia stared at her. "What?"

"I'm not going out west with you. Alexander has asked me to marry him, and we're staying here."

Lydia rose from her chair, stunned by Elizabeth's announcement. The stocking she'd been darning slipped from her lap onto the floor. "You can't be serious," Lydia gasped.

Elizabeth straightened her shoulders. "Yes, Mama. I am."

At that moment, Christian entered the parlor. He paused, sensing the tension in the room.

Lydia stumbled to her husband's side. "Elizabeth just said she's planning to marry Alexander Scott and stay in Nauvoo," she told him in a choked voice.

"Is this true?" Christian asked, turning to his daughter.

"Yes. Alexander and I are going to be married, Papa."

Christian's jaw tightened. "Now, wait just a minute . . ." he began.

"No, Papa. You listen to me. I'm grown now—nearly eighteen. I have my own life to lead." Elizabeth paused, and when she spoke again her voice quavered. "Alexander and I don't believe Brigham Young is God's spokesman, and we won't follow him to some wild place in the mountains."

"You don't realize the implications of this decision," Christian said in a quiet voice.

"Yes, I do, Papa. I've thought about this for a long time."

"If you think your mother and I will agree with this notion of marriage to Alexander Scott, you're mistaken, Elizabeth. The man has earned himself an odious reputation."

"You dislike Alexander solely because he's not a member of the Church," Elizabeth lashed back. "Don't try to pretend there's any other reason."

"The man is without principles or scruples," replied her father firmly. "But the important issue here is your welfare. Choosing this course is a mistake, Elizabeth, a mistake that could ruin your life."

"Ruin my life?" Elizabeth sputtered. "How in heaven's name can you presume to know that?"

"Elizabeth, listen to your father," Lydia pleaded. "He's offering sound advice."

"He's not my father!" Elizabeth cried. "My father is lying in the cold ground of Green County. I have no father!"

"Are you all right, Mother?"

Lydia, immersed in her thoughts, hadn't noticed James approach her. He put an arm around her shoulders and smiled into her face.

"Yes, son. Just a little weary."

"Come ride in the wagon. At least until the afternoon heat subsides."

Lydia shaded her eyes with her hand and looked up into the still sky. The sun was a brilliant ball of fire overhead. In its blazing light the painful memory of the scene with Elizabeth began to burn away. She shook her head and smiled. "I'm fine. Would you find your brother? I'd like him to climb in the wagon and rest for awhile."

"Zachary is up by the Parkers' wagon with Roxana and Milly. They've been playing tag among the wagons all morning."

"That child is going to be worn out long before supper. Please fetch him for me, James."

He nodded and trotted up ahead, disappearing among the wagons lumbering their way along. Lydia sighed and glanced up briefly again at the sky. The expanse of blue was broken by only a few high, wispy clouds. The sun beat down relentlessly on her shoulders, and the trail ahead shimmered in the summer heat. Lydia wiped her brow with her sleeve. Her neck and face were gritty with dirt, and dust clung to her body like a pair of close-fitting long johns. It invaded her nostrils, coated her lips, and stung her eyes. Sometimes the trail was so dusty that she couldn't see the next wagon.

But soon they would be out of the dust and the heat. The mountain country ahead would be a welcome relief from the unvarying scenery of the plains. She was so tired of the lifeless sagebrush and greasewood, the irksome mosquitoes, the deadly rattlesnakes, and the ever-present dust.

She tucked a straying strand of auburn hair under the brim of her sunbonnet, then squinted ahead at the long line of wagons stretched out over the prairie. They looked to her like a great, undulating snake. Their canvas tops, clean and white when they left Illinois, were now smudged with dirt and streaked with dusty rain. The blue paint on their own wagon was blistered and peeled, and its shiny red wheels were caked with mud.

It had been more than two years since they left their beautiful city of Nauvoo in February of 1846. Those first few weeks on the trail seemed almost a blur in Lydia's mind. They had made their first camp at Sugar Creek in Iowa territory, then moved on to Garden Grove, Mount Pisgah, and Kanesville. The last months of that year were spent at Winter Quarters, where Roxana had fallen ill with the "black canker" and nearly lost her life. She was confined to bed for weeks, and her illness prevented the family from continuing their journey west until the summer of 1848. They traveled with a company of over 600 persons and 226 wagons, under the leadership of Heber C. Kimball.

The camp followed the broad, sandy banks of the Platte for two hundred miles, a muddy, yellow river which the Saints described as "too thick to drink and too thin to plow." They kept to the north bank to avoid the heavier traffic of the Oregon Trail on the south side. The Oregon Trail had been traveled since the 1830s by trappers, traders, and immigrants making their way west to the Willamette valley of Oregon or the lush country of California. Occasionally, they spotted Indians. Once, a group of Pawnee came into camp to barter for food and blankets. The children had been terrified at first by their fierce appearance. Dressed in animal skins, with painted faces and shaved heads except for a single scalp lock, they were quite unlike any Indians either she or Christian had ever seen.

They left Pawnee country near Loop Fork. From this point, great buffalo herds became a common sight. Thousands and thousands of the beasts roamed over the prairie. Sometimes a herd was so large that it darkened the ground for miles. The men hunted enough buffalo to satisfy the needs of the camp, but to kill them for sport was strictly prohibited. Lydia enjoyed the fresh buffalo meat, and she and the other women dried the remainder for future use. The camp also ate fish from the streams and wild herbs that grew along the road.

Zachary suddenly came bounding into view. He dashed to Lydia's side and grabbed her hand.

"Guess what, Mama?" he cried excitedly.

"What?" Lydia returned with as much enthusiasm as she could muster.

"Sarah Parker found an arrow, with feathers tied to the end!"

"She did?"

"Yes, over behind some bushes. She showed it to me. She said it probably came from some Pawnee chief."

"More than likely it belonged to a Sioux warrior. We're in Sioux country now."

Zachary's eyes widened. "Sioux? Are they meaner than Pawnee?"

Lydia could feel a smile twitching at the corners of her mouth. "I don't know if they're meaner, but they're certainly better dressed."

She heard her husband's chuckle coming from the wagon seat. She looked up to see Christian grinning at her. His face was brown and lined from constant exposure to the sun, and his hands roughened from the weather. He'd grown a beard which hid his chin.

She smiled at him, then glanced down into Zachary's face. It was scrunched up in thought—the identical expression Christian wore whenever he was mulling over something perplexing. Zachary had his father's soft brown hair, and eyes that were clear and expressive.

"Zachary, I'd like you to climb into the wagon now and rest."

"Now? But, Mama, I'm not tired."

"Yes, but you will be. Do as I ask, please."

Zachary's mouth drooped, but quickly perked up again. "Can I sit with Papa for a few minutes first?"

"If I let you sit up front with Papa for five minutes, will you promise to take a nap afterward?"

"Oh, I promise," Zachary answered.

"All right." Lydia kissed him, and then he was off, clamoring up the tailgate of the wagon. He scooted through the interior and emerged at the front end.

Christian smiled at his exuberant arrival. He glanced over at Lydia, and with a wink he asked, "Did you say Zachary could skip his afternoon rest today?"

"Not skip it, just postpone it," Lydia replied, feigning sternness.

"That's right, Papa," Zachary said soberly.

"In that case, you take over the reins while I rest awhile." He lifted Zachary onto his lap and put the reins into the boy's small, pudgy hands, then covered them with his own.

"Look, Mama!" Zachary shouted. "I'm driving the oxen! Gid up, you slowpokes. We'll never reach the mountains at this rate."

"You tell 'em, Zach," Christian smiled.

Zachary snapped the reins over the oxen's broad backs, though they scarcely took note of it. One of the beasts raised his head as if to comment that he wouldn't be hurried by anyone, least of all a seven-year-old boy.

Zachary laughed and shouted exultantly, "I'm a wagon master. Look, Mama, I'm driving the wagon all by myself!" He shook the reins with glee, and leaning over the side of the wagon, called down to Lydia, "Are you looking, Mama?"

"I'm watching, Zachary. You'd better pay attention to what you're doing. If you're not careful, you'll fall right out of that wagon and break your neck, young man."

Zachary grinned and gave another yank on the reins. "Gid up, you old oxen."

Lydia shook her head and smiled. In the distance, about six or seven wagons ahead, she saw Millicent and Roxana running toward her. They arrived at her side, panting and out of breath.

"We found an Indian arrow," Milly said excitedly.

"I know, Zachary told me."

"It had yellow feathers," Roxie added.

"My goodness."

"I hope there was no Indian on the end of it," Christian remarked, his eyes crinkling in amusement.

"No, Papa, it was just lying there in the bushes. Some Indian must have dropped it," Roxana observed.

"Or shot it out of his bow," Millicent said, nodding her head vigorously.

"Ohhh, they got me . . ." James stumbled into view beside the wagon, clutching at his chest. He staggered and fell dramatically to the ground.

"Oh, James, don't be silly," Roxie said, her chin lifted in sisterly scorn.

James kicked his heels once for effect and then scrambled to his feet, grinning at his sisters. "Scared you for a minute, didn't I," he said, chuckling.

Lydia smiled as she listened to their banter. The children were doing remarkably well on the trail. They'd adjusted quickly to the inconveniences of camp travel, and there was little serious bickering among them. A pang of sorrow assailed her as she thought again about Elizabeth. Her eldest child should be with them now, laughing and joking with the rest of the family. Lydia wondered how Elizabeth was getting along in Nauvoo—if she and her husband, Alexander, were happy. Even after all the Saints had suffered at the hands of their enemies in Illinois—the loss of their homes, their properties, and their beloved prophet, Joseph Smith—Lydia's greatest trial had been her separation from Elizabeth. She mourned her daughter's decision to remain in Nauvoo, alienated both physically and spiritually from the Saints. As she trudged beside the wagon, Lydia offered a silent prayer for her daughter's well-being.

Lydia's chin drooped onto her chest and her head nodded. She tried to keep her eyes open, but she was bone tired. So tired that she didn't even mind the bumping and jarring of the wagon as it lurched along the rocky trail. Since they'd left the vicinity of Ash Hollow, the terrain had steadily become more broken and rugged. It was cooler now, too. The canvas cover on the wagon was rolled back and bunched to catch the breeze. She felt Christian sitting next to her in the wagon seat, his arm brushing up against hers as he deftly handled the ox team. She slipped in and out of consciousness, the hilly ground transforming itself into the shapeless mass of her dreams.

She didn't know how long she'd been dozing when she felt Christian gently nudge her shoulder.

"Would you take the reins for a minute, Lydia?"

When she glanced up at him, he was staring out across the hills. She took the reins from his hands, and then he crawled into the wagon bed, returning in a moment with his sketching pad and a pencil. He peered again toward the horizon and began making long, sweeping lines on the paper, steadying the pad upon his knee.

Lydia looked in the direction that held his interest. At first she could see nothing out of the ordinary in the landscape, so she shaded her eyes and again scanned the horizon. There in the distance, shrouded in haze, sat an unusual rock formation. It began at the bottom with a wide base and rose to a slender point.

Lydia looked from the stone mountain to Christian's paper. An exact replica had taken shape on the page, complete except for the slim pinnacle. Christian was in the habit of sketching anything that caught his fancy while they journeyed west, and he had quite a portfolio of drawings by this time. He had captured the grace and strength of the buffalo on the plains, the beauty of wild sunflowers, and the grandeur of such natural features as Ancient Ruins Bluff and Courthouse Rock. The sketches would be precious keepsakes for their children.

Lydia yawned and covered her mouth with her hand. Perhaps she should give in to her body's insistent demand for rest and lie down in the wagon for awhile. She had been up most of the night with Sister Kendall, whose husband had died at Winter Quarters, leaving her with two small children and several months pregnant with a third. Last night the child had been born, and Lydia had been summoned to help with the difficult birth. Lydia did not know the woman well, for Sister Kendall and her children kept to themselves, and their wagon was near the end of the long train, quite a distance from Lydia's own rig. She intended to walk back to the widow's wagon a little later in the day and check on her and the baby. But right now, overcome with fatigue, it was all she could do to keep the reins from slipping out of her hands.

At last, Christian finished his drawing and put away the paper. He took the reins from Lydia's hand and gave them a shake to urge the oxen forward. "That's Chimney Rock, Lydia," he commented. "It's probably the most famous landmark on the entire Oregon Trail."

Lydia glanced again at the odd-shaped rock. It spiraled upward almost to a point. "How tall is it, do you suppose?"

"I don't know. Maybe 200, 250 feet."

"It's certainly aptly named. It looks like a factory smokestack."

Christian nodded. "The maps show the distance from Winter Quarters to this point as 425 miles."

"And I've felt every inch of it," Lydia smiled.

"You can rest at Fort Laramie. It's not far. Meanwhile, why don't you climb back in the wagon and get some sleep. You look exhausted."

"I am." She sighed and stifled another yawn with her hand. "Maybe I will sleep for a little while."

"I'll keep an eye on the children."

Lydia nodded and crawled into the shade of the wagon. It was fairly cool inside. The days were warm, but the nights now were a pleasant temperature. She felt some apprehension about reaching the Great Basin before the first snows of winter, not wishing to be caught out on the trail in a blinding blizzard. As she lay back on a makeshift bed of blankets and shut her eyes, she saw the tapering peak of Chimney Rock silhouetted against her closed lids. They had come such a long way, yet they still had hundreds of miles to go. And the most difficult part of the journey lay ahead of them.

Restless with fatigue and uncertainty, Lydia turned onto her side and stared at the canvas wagon cover. It was stained and patched, and numerous pinpoint holes were beginning to wear themselves into the fabric. She forced herself to relax and put her anxieties out of mind. The next thing she became aware of was an image of Zachary climbing the slopes of Chimney Rock. She kept calling to him to come down, but he only grinned at her and continued to climb. At last he reached the pinnacle and teetered perilously on top. She shouted a warning to him, but it went unheeded. Suddenly he lost his balance, and an instant later began tumbling down, down the steep side of the rock. She screamed, watching in helpless terror as he fell. Then she heard the terrible thump as his little body slammed against the base of the rock.

Lydia awoke with a jerk, the dream vivid in her mind. She sat up quickly and rubbed her eyes, exhaling slowly as the hideous vision grew fuzzy and then faded altogether. She realized that the wagon had ceased its motion, and the camp was bustling with activity. Evidently she had slept until the bugle sounded for the train to make camp. She quickly smoothed back her straggling hair and climbed down from the wagon box.

Zachary and the girls were standing near the wagon, feeding sagebrush to a struggling fire. She couldn't see Christian or James—probably bedding down the stock for the night, she thought. Not only did the men have their teams of oxen to care for, but they were also responsible for the many cattle, horses, mules, and chickens traveling with the camp. For safekeeping, all of the animals were brought into a corral created by the wagons forming a circle.

Lydia hastily began preparations for supper. She sent Roxana down to the stream near their encampment for water, and set Millicent to mixing the johnnycake. Then she opened a covered bucket tied to the side of the wagon and scooped out a generous portion of butter. Each morning, fresh milk was poured into the bucket; and by the time evening arrived, the milk had been churned to butter by the lurching and jogging of the wagon. The meal was soon ready, and the family assembled around the campfire to eat.

After supper, while Lydia and the girls washed the dishes and put them away in the wagon, Christian left to make his rounds of the ten families for whom he was responsible according to Brigham Young's instructions for organizing the wagon trains. When the evening's chores were done, Lydia watched James quietly slip away. He walked past several fires burning in the camps and came to a stop near one almost directly across from the Kades'. He lingered at the edge of the fire for a moment and then strode into camp.

Lydia smiled to herself. She knew exactly what he was doing there. Etta Stanton. The oldest of Brother Stanton's seven children, Etta was a pretty, dark-haired girl with lively blue eyes and a ready smile. Lydia had watched her nineteen-year-old son furtively eyeing Etta for weeks now. She turned back to the mending in her lap. James and Etta; it was a nice combination. If they decided to marry, Lydia would be pleased with the match. Brother and Sister Stanton were fine people, devoted to the gospel and striving to live its principles. Lydia decided to make it her business to get to know Etta Stanton better.

The sweet strains of a hymn started from the wagon next to them. Lydia closed her eyes and softly hummed along with the melody. It was one of her favorites. "The spirit of God like a fire is burning, the latter day glory begins to come forth . . ." The family inside the wagon sang sweetly and confidently. Lydia could plainly hear the father's clear tenor and the children's buoyant tones, rising in a crescendo as they approached the swelling chorus. "We'll sing and we'll shout with the armies of heaven, hosanna, hosanna to God and the Lamb . . ."

The hymn concluded and was followed by a second, then silence enveloped the wagon and Lydia knew the family knelt in prayer. Her eyes involuntarily turned heavenward. The night sky was alive with stars. Overhead, a full yellow moon hung as if suspended on an invisible thread. She put her sewing aside and leaned back against the wagon, her mind crowded with thoughts. A few moments later, Christian joined her. He sat down on the ground next to her and rested his hand on her knee.

"Tired?" he asked.

She shook her head. "Not much. I had a long nap, I'm afraid. You should have wakened me."

"You needed the rest." He yawned and rubbed his bearded chin between his fingers.

She watched him silently in the flames of the dying fire. His shirt was open at the throat, and his worn felt hat rested at an angle on his head. His leather boots reached almost to his knees. She thought he cut a strikingly handsome figure as he sat there beside the fire.

"Where's James?" he asked sleepily.

Lydia pointed in the direction of the Stantons' wagon.

"Again?"

"Yes."

Christian smiled slowly as he watched two shadowy figures standing close together at the edge of the Stantons' campfire. "Well, Mrs. Kade, how do you feel about losing your eldest son to that pretty young woman?"

"If he's half as lucky in marriage as I have been, I won't begrudge it a bit."

Christian looked up at her, his dark eyes lost in shadow. He took her hand and squeezed it. "I love you, Lydia."

"I love you, too, Christian."

Neither of them spoke further as they sat contentedly side by side, watching the prairie moon travel across the sky.

CHAPTER TWO

At five o'clock the following morning, the bugle sounded to bid the Saints arise and tend to their morning devotions. Then came the hurry of breakfast, breaking camp, and returning to the trail. The Saints would travel until noon or so, stop for their afternoon meal, then push on again until evening. After supper there would be visiting or dancing. The men brought out their fiddles and their mouth organs, and soon the camp was merry with music. Lydia was always amazed to see how quickly music could revive the sagging spirits and bodies of the trail-weary Saints. She especially liked to watch the young people frolic to a quadrille or a fast-paced Scotch reel. The dancing was often interspersed with songs or recitations. Afterward, families gathered in their wagons for prayer and scripture reading before retiring for the night.

The routine seldom varied, except on the Sabbath, when the Saints rested and spent much of the day in worship. Occasionally the schedule was interrupted by tragedy. Sickness and death were no strangers to the camp. A few weeks earlier a young girl picking wildflowers along the trail had been bitten by a rattlesnake. She died the following day, and her parents laid her body in a sandy, forlorn grave. There were grave markers scattered all along the trail, grim reminders of the dangers and vicissitudes of the journey.

But there were also births, and these were joyous occasions in the camp. As Lydia scrubbed the last of the breakfast dishes, she thought again of Sister Kendall's new baby. She must surely see Sister Kendall this morning. She decided to pay her a visit right after the wagons pulled out for the day.

The morning, however, started out badly. Milly tripped on a sharp rock and cut her ankle. James cleaned and bandaged the wound for her, but she needed Lydia's soothing words and reassuring presence. In the early afternoon, it began to rain heavily. The downpour continued throughout the day, making the road almost impassable. The animals slipped and slid on the unstable ground, and several wagons became mired down in the sticky ooze. Christian and the other men worked to free the wagons in a torrent of driving rain. They covered barely five miles before it was time to make camp. It was still raining and impossible to keep a fire going, so the Kades huddled in their wagon and ate a cold supper. It was a thoroughly miserable day. With the evening came cold temperatures, and Lydia had to unpack all the extra blankets for their beds.

The next morning, the sky had cleared but the ground was saturated. Little pools of muddy water lay at almost every step. The animals slogged over the soft ground, their hooves sinking into the mire. Even the air smelled rank and foul. In spite of the unpleasant weather, Lydia was determined to visit Sister Kendall. She pulled on a pair of Christian's tall boots, hitched up her skirts, and started off down the long column of wagons. It took much longer to reach the Kendalls' wagon than the last time she'd come; every step she took was a struggle in the deep mud. Finally, she reached the widow's rig. Sister Kendall's young son was up front handling the team.

"Hello, son. How is your mother this morning?" Lydia asked him as she endeavored to keep up with the pitching wagon.

"All right, I guess," came his mumbled reply.

Lydia glanced toward the wagon's rear opening. There was no sign of activity inside. A small girl with disheveled hair and a dirty face appeared at Lydia's side; the boy on the wagon seat gruffly told her to get back inside the wagon. She looked grudgingly up at him and then did as she was told.

"Would you mind if I poked my head inside and said hello to her?" Lydia asked the boy.

He shrugged his thin shoulders and darted a sidelong glance at her.

Lydia fell back a few paces until she was even with the tail of the wagon. Then she called softly, "Sister Kendall, it's Lydia Kade. I've come to see how you and the baby are doing."

Several seconds passed before there was any answer. Then she heard Sister Kendall reply in a faint voice, "We're fine, Sister Kade. Please don't trouble yourself on our account."

"I'd like to come inside, if you don't mind."

Another long pause. "I don't really feel well enough to visit, Sister Kade. Perhaps in a day or two."

Something in the tenor of the woman's voice caused Lydia's throat to constrict in alarm. "If I just stayed a moment, Sister Kendall . . ."

"No, please. Go away." Lydia heard a shuddering sob come from the depths of the wagon.

"Sister Kendall, I'm coming inside," Lydia insisted as she secured a footing on the wagon.

The first thing that struck Lydia as she entered the Kendalls' wagon was the foul odor inside. It was almost overpowering. Sister Kendall lay on a bed of ragged blankets, her eyes glassy in a pallid face. She held her baby, wrapped tightly in a quilt, close to her bosom.

"Go away," Sister Kendall pleaded. "Leave us alone." She clutched the baby tightly to her chest.

"Sister Kendall, please, let me help you . . ."

The woman began sobbing and moaning. Lydia quickly went to her side. The widow's eyes grew round with fright as she pulled away from Lydia's outstretched hand. "No," she wailed. "No!"

"Whatever the problem is, let me help," Lydia said anxiously.

"You can't help. You can't help."

"Let me hold the child so you can rest."

"No! Please go away."

The odor was stronger now, and with a start Lydia identified the source of it. "Let me take the baby for you. Please," she said quietly.

Sister Kendall looked down into the tiny bundled face. Tears streamed down her cheeks and she groaned aloud. Slowly she handed the infant to Lydia.

Lydia's fears were confirmed in an instant. The child was dead—and had been for some time. "Oh, Sister Kendall. Dear Sister Kendall, I'm so sorry."

The woman looked at her with pain in her tear-filled eyes. From the corner of the wagon, the little girl Lydia had seen earlier poked her head above a crate filled with crockery and cooking pots. She'd evidently been hiding behind the crate since Lydia had entered the wagon. Her heart went out to the child, who was obviously frightened.

"How long has the baby been dead?" Lydia asked softly.

The woman looked up into Lydia's face with fear and uncertainty. "She never saw morning."

Lydia's breath felt trapped in her throat. "Let me take her for you. I'll see that she gets a proper burial."

"No!" Sister Kendall rose up in bed, terror flashing across her face. "No. I won't leave my baby for wolves to ravage. I won't leave her, do you hear me!" Exhausted by the outburst, she sank back down. Her eyes quivered and closed. "I won't leave her," she whispered.

The little girl crept from her hiding place and went to her mother's side.

"I promise you she'll be buried in a safe place," Lydia assured her. "The men will dig a deep grave. I give you my word." Lydia glanced from Sister Kendall's tortured face to the little girl's. The child must have been only four or five years old.

"I won't leave her out there all alone," Sister Kendall murmured.

Lydia stroked the woman's feverish brow. "God will watch over her, Sister Kendall. She won't be alone."

Sister Kendall looked up at her. A flicker of hope passed over her face.

Lydia covered the woman's hand with hers. "I'll see the baby is taken care of. You have my promise."

The widow caressed the blankets swathed around the infant. She nodded weakly and turned her head away.

Lydia gently took the lifeless child from its mother's arms and, clutching the baby, prepared to leave. She felt the little girl's eyes on her. "I'll be back," she whispered. "Everything's going to be all right now. You stay with your mama. She needs you."

The girl looked down at her mother and began to tenderly smooth her hair.

Lydia climbed out of the wagon with the baby's body in her arms. The boy watched her from the wagon seat. His eyes grew big when he saw the still, bundled form she carried. She spoke a few reassuring words to him, realizing that he was just as confused and concerned as his sister, though he hid his feelings more successfully.

She made her way back in the sucking mud, the over-sized boots sticking to the ground with each step. When she reached her wagon, she called James to take the reins while she spoke privately with Christian. He took the dead child from her arms and left to contact Brother Kimball and the other Church leaders traveling with the train.

After he'd gone, Lydia found she could barely stand, for her legs were shaking uncontrollably. What a terrible ordeal for Sister Kendall—nearly three days of carrying her dead child in that wagon. Three days, and no one knew it. She must have pretended all was well when callers came, and allowed no one inside the wagon. Lydia's heart ached for the woman.

A short time later, the wagons halted. A tiny grave was dug on the side of a rocky hill several yards off the trail. The men laid the baby inside the grave and covered it with mud and wild sagebrush. Then they piled rocks and small boulders atop it to protect the grave from wild animals. Lydia silently watched the proceedings from her wagon. She wondered if Sister Kendall was watching, too.

The Saints rested for a few days at Fort Laramie before moving on. The fort belonged to the American Fur Company and was comprised of a few houses and a central yard. Near Fort Laramie the Black Hills jutted to the banks of the Platte, making it impracticable to continue on the north side of the river. The camp ferried their teams and wagons across the river and took up their journey on the Oregon Trail.

The road became much more difficult now. In the rough and broken terrain, the oxen often had to pick their way over solid rock. They camped one night at Heber Springs near Horse Shoe Creek. Its green meadows were a welcome break from the rocky bluffs and hills they had been traveling. At a point dubbed "Last Crossing," they left the Platte River behind. After ferrying their wagons across the river, they resumed their way until reaching the Sweetwater. Unlike the muddy, meandering Platte, the Sweetwater River was clear and gentle. Lydia heard the river had earned its name after a pack mule loaded with sugar had fallen into it—a rather fanciful explanation, she thought.

Now that they were traveling the Oregon Trail, the Saints frequently had contact with fellow travelers. They met trappers, traders, and groups of immigrants in prairie schooners bound for Oregon or California. Christian enjoyed talking with the wayfarers and hearing about their experiences. He continued to sketch interesting or novel landmarks along the trail. He was fascinated by the uniqueness of Devil's Gap and took careful pains to render it exactly. A natural opening between the hills called Emigrant Gap likewise captured his attention, as did humped Independence Rock.

The Saints made camp at the foot of Independence Rock in the tall prairie grass. After supper, Christian, James, and Zachary climbed the huge outcrop and carved their initials on it. Lydia sat outside the wagon listening to the wind whispering through the grass. It was a lonesome sound and brought on a spell of melancholy. She felt more longing for Elizabeth than she had in weeks.

They would follow the Sweetwater for some ninety miles, with frequent crossings, to South Pass. Lydia was concerned about the road to South Pass, the high point of land at which the rivers flow in one direction to the Atlantic and the other to the Pacific. She asked Christian about it one afternoon as they sat together in the wagon.

"Will it be a difficult climb to South Pass?" she queried.

Christian took off his hat and wiped his brow with his sleeve. "I understand it's a gradual ascent and, in fact, difficult to determine exactly when you've reached the summit. I don't think we'll have much trouble. It will be more mountainous west of the pass."

Lydia's brow furrowed in thought. "Will there be many streams to cross, Christian?"

He nodded.

"The rivers cause me the most worry. I'm always nervous about the crossings."

If the rivers were shallow enough the Saints forded them; if not, they built a ferry to float their wagons and teams across. Lydia was frightened of the swiftly moving water and the inherent dangers in crossing. There was the hazard of being swept downstream by the current or of the oxen bolting in mid-river. Lydia had seen wagons capsize and carried away for a mile or more, and children tumbling off the wagons into the turbulent waters.

Christian covered her hand with his. "We'll be all right."

She felt comforted by his reassuring words.

He leaned over and kissed her cheek. "You've come nearly 1100 miles; don't get faint-hearted now," he said, grinning at her.

"Who would ever have imagined we'd be coming all the way out here to live," Lydia remarked, shaking her head.

"Are you sorry?"

"No. Are you?"

"Not in the least. In fact, I've come to quite enjoy the rigors of trail life. It certainly beats sitting in a newspaper office all day."

"You can't fool me, Christian Kade. I know you'd jump at the opportunity to write for a paper again. You'll probably start up your own newspaper once we reach the Basin. Let me see, what can we call it? How about the *Rocky Mountain Rattler*?"

Christian broke into a gale of laughter.

"What's so funny?" asked Milly as she walked briskly beside the wagon.

"Your mother. She has a marvelous imagination."

"Oh. I guess I didn't know that."

Lydia smiled in amusement. "Apparently, your father is the only one who thinks so."

"Mama, can I ride in the wagon for awhile? I'm so tired, and my feet hurt."

Lydia scooted to the edge of her seat. "Give me your hand, sweetheart. Up you come."

Christian slowed the oxen so Millicent could climb into the wagon. She sat behind the seat, her head poking between her parents. The three of them chatted for awhile and then Christian began whistling a tune. Millicent joined in, singing in a lively soprano. "I've got a mule and her name is Sal, fifteen miles on the Erie Canal . . ."

Soon Roxana came alongside the wagon and added her voice. She preferred the mournful strains of a song they'd sung back home in Nauvoo. "Oh, Shenandoah, I long to hear you—away, you rolling river; oh, Shenandoah, I long to hear you—away, I'm bound away, across the wide Missouri."

They sang together, moving on from one song to another and ultimately singing the songs they loved the best, the songs of Zion—"This Earth was Once a Garden Place," "O God our Hope in Ages Past," "The Spirit of God Like a Fire is Burning," and a new hymn recently written by Brother William Clayton entitled, "Come, Come, Ye Saints." Lydia didn't know the words to the new song well, but the feelings which came into her soul as she listened to Christian's strong voice carry the melody convinced her that this hymn would become one of her favorites.

CHAPTER THREE

Near South Pass, Christian became ill. At first he refused to let either Lydia or James handle the team for him, but after a day and a half he felt considerably worse and was forced to lie down in the wagon. James took over the oxen and most of Christian's other responsibilities in the camp. Christian had been pushing himself too hard, and Lydia was worried about him. Working outdoors in inclement weather and seeing to the welfare and safety of others, he had neglected his own health.

Lydia sat next to James in the wagon seat, with Zachary on her lap. The girls walked beside the wagon, talking between themselves. Christian had slept off and on all morning, occasionally calling out to Lydia for a report on their progress. Lydia retied the strings of her bonnet snugly beneath her chin and looked out over the broken ground.

"How much further to Fort Bridger, do you suppose, James?" she asked.

"I don't know, Mother. Maybe a hundred miles. I heard some of the brethren saying that we shouldn't expect much at Fort Bridger; it's nothing more than a few log dwelling houses."

"At least we'll be able to stop and rest for a day or two. That will be good for your father."

"Will Pa be well by the time we reach Fort Bridger, Mama?" Zachary asked.

"I hope so, son." She exchanged a wordless glance with James, who had kept close watch over his father's condition. Although he could not pinpoint exactly what ailed Christian, he had at least ruled out the more serious maladies. While in Nauvoo, James had gained some medical training and experience by working alongside Dr. James C. Bennett; and now he had become somewhat of the camp physician. There were no regular doctors traveling with the train, and although James' medical knowledge was limited, he was often called on to diagnose a case or consulted about a remedy. Lydia placed great faith in his abilities in that regard, and she was comforted in having him near Christian's side.

"I want Pa to go with me to catch lizards. He said he would," Zachary pouted.

"He will—just as soon as he feels better. Don't bother him with that now," answered Lydia.

Zachary frowned and folded his arms across his chest in a huff. "I want to now."

"Keep still, Zach," James told him in a kind voice. "I'll take you lizard hunting myself as soon as I can."

"You promise?"

James nodded.

"When? When will we go?"

"Maybe this afternoon. We'll see."

"Yippee! I'll catch a million of those old lizards."

James smiled and reached over to tousle his little brother's hair.

"Cut it out," Zachary complained, shoving James' hand aside.

"You pipe down now, so I can talk to Mama."

Lydia smiled at the little boy and gave him a kiss on the cheek. "Hop down and walk with the girls for awhile."

Zachary scrambled down the wagon and jumped to the ground.

"Stay close to the wagon, Zachary. Don't wander off the trail."

Zachary skipped over to Millicent and Roxana's side and wormed his way between them. They loudly protested his rough intrusion and tried to elbow him out of the way. Zachary stuck out his tongue and pulled a face at them.

"Zachary!"

The boy looked up sheepishly at his mother. "Sorry, Mama."

Lydia gave him a stern look. The wagon bumped and jostled along the rough trail. The wheels rolled over sharp rocks and patches of dried brush, often tipping the wagon precariously to one side. Lydia had to hold on to the edge of the wagon to keep her seat.

"Gid up, there," James cried to the oxen, snapping his whip in the air over their heads. The grueling pace was telling on the animals. Lydia had watched them stumble and strain under their heavy load. One of the wagons in their camp had lost an ox a few days before. The poor beast had just fallen dead in its yoke. The family had to hitch one of the camp's mules to its wagon after that.

"Don't drive them too hard," Lydia cautioned her son.

James didn't answer. Instead, Lydia saw that his attention was riveted on something ahead. She followed the direction of his stare and saw a great cloud of dust hanging over the trail in the distance.

"What is it?" she asked. "Another wagon train?"

"Yes, I think so. But they seem to be traveling off to the side of the trail. Look there . . . a rider is motioning our wagons to go on ahead."

Sure enough, thirty or forty yards in front of them, a hatless rider was gesturing to the wagons to move steadily forward. Both Lydia and James watched in silence, waiting for some word of explanation.

As they drew near the column of wagons slowly traveling to the left of the trail, one of the brethren in camp came riding up beside James. "Keep on going," he said, waving his arm. "They've cholera among them."

Lydia clutched James' arm. The word elicited a chilling fear inside of her. A cholera epidemic could wipe out an entire wagon train. She watched in macabre fascination as their wagon crawled past the long column. She could see men and women peering from their wagons, their faces grim and haggard.

"What's wrong?"

Christian's sudden voice from behind startled Lydia. She turned around to find him leaning up in his bed, his face flushed and glistening with fever.

"It's all right, sweetheart. We're overtaking another wagon train, that's all."

"Oh." He lay back down and pulled the quilt up around his neck.

Lydia climbed into the back of the wagon and covered him with an extra blanket. He murmured a thank you and closed his eyes. She stayed next to him for the rest of the day, leaving him only long enough to prepare supper and help the younger children to bed. James fed and bedded the animals, put up the tent for the night, and then came inside the wagon to check on his father. Lydia could see he was concerned by Christian's condition, although he didn't comment on it. He stayed near the wagon that evening instead of going for his usual visit to the Stantons' camp. A fear began welling up in Lydia's heart. She had already tasted the bitter loss of one companion. She prayed the Lord would spare her from experiencing it a second time.

The next morning, Christian wasn't any better. While James drove the team, Lydia tended to her husband. The jarring and bouncing of the wagon caused him discomfort, and he slept little through the day. They forded the Sweetwater three times that day as it looped back and forth across the trail. Christian rode in the wagon, while Lydia and the children waded through the river.

James handled the team almost as expertly as Christian. The other men in the camp treated him as an equal when they sat around the campfire in the evening, discussing the next day's ride. James also saw to the care of his father's company of ten wagons, reporting night and morning to the captain of fifty. Lydia was grateful that he shouldered the additional responsibilities without complaint, leaving her free to care for Christian.

The following day, the sky was overcast and gray. Rain threatened, and the air was much cooler. Christian was able to sit up to eat his breakfast, which consisted of a few mouthfuls of cornmeal mush. Then he slept through the morning.

Lydia rode beside James for a few hours in the afternoon. They chatted about the scenery they passed, and about their anticipation of reaching the valley of the Great Salt Lake. The girls picked sunflowers and put them in their hair, while Zachary romped along the trail beside them.

Before long, Zachary tired of racing up and down beside the wagons and began teasing his sisters. He slipped up behind Millicent and tugged her long red braids, then he flipped the sunflower out of Roxana's hair.

"Mother, make Zachary stop it!" Roxie cried impatiently.

Zachary grinned and ran in circles around his sisters. "Crybaby, crybaby, cryin' away all day," he shouted in singsong fashion.

"Zachary, stop bothering the girls," Lydia instructed.

"I'm not hurting 'em." With an impish grin on his face, he picked up a handful of sandy dust and let it slowly filter out of his hand over Milly's head.

"Oooh, Zachary, I'm going to spank you if you don't stop it," said Millicent, stamping her foot.

"Mo—ther," Roxana said pointedly.

"All right, Zachary. You come sit up here with James, and I'll walk with the girls," Lydia said.

"Okay," Zachary answered happily.

Lydia climbed down from the wagon seat, and Zachary scampered up in her place. He grinned at James and leaned back in the seat, his feet resting atop the footboard.

"You sit still, Zachary. The road is bumpy."

Zachary waved a confident hand at his mother in reply.

"Mama, sometimes he can be so *impossible*," Millicent said with a perturbed sigh.

"Just give him a few years, and he'll outgrow most of his mischievousness," Lydia answered, taking Milly's hand in hers.

"I hope so," said Millicent, rolling her eyes.

Lydia smiled. Ten-year-old Milly was fast developing into a young woman. She was nearly as tall as Roxana now, but the two of them were as different as night and day. Milly was gregarious, impetuous, and full of energy. A host of red freckles splashed across her nose, and she wore her thick copper hair bound in braids. Like Millicent, Roxana generally confined her dark hair in two long braids that reached to the middle of her back. She was more decorous in her conduct, and more timid. She was also the most tender-hearted of the children; the slightest injustice would bring tears to her eyes. At twelve years of age, Roxie already exhibited traits of dependability and responsibility.

"Mama?"

"Yes, Roxana?"

"When we reach the valley, will Papa build us a house like we had in Nauvoo?"

"Well, not right away. It takes time to build a nice home."

"Do you think there will be a letter from Elizabeth when we get there? I miss her."

"So do I, sweetheart. I hope there's a letter waiting for us. I'm anxious to hear how she's getting along."

"And Alexander," said Milly, wiggling her red brows up and down meaningfully. "I think Alexander is sooo cute."

"Maybe Elizabeth and Alexander will come out west to visit us some day," Roxana said wistfully.

"That would be nice, wouldn't it?" Lydia's heart ached as she thought about her absent daughter.

"Mama."

"Um?"

"I'll be glad when we get to the Salt Lake. I'm so tired of walking. I hope I don't have to ever walk anywhere again," said Millicent with a pouting frown.

Lydia put her arm around Milly's shoulder. "I know you're tired. Both of you. You've been little soldiers through this whole trip. When we get to the valley, you will have earned a well-deserved rest."

"Have I been a good soldier too, Mama?" asked Zachary. He leaned over the edge of the wagon to look down at his mother, an impetuous grin spread across his sunburned cheeks.

Lydia looked up just in time to see the wagon tip suddenly and violently to one side as it rolled over a large rock in the trail. The lurching wagon threw Zachary from his seat, and the boy's innocent smile abruptly changed to an expression of panic. He flailed his stubby arms wildly in an attempt to regain his balance, failed, and toppled over the edge of the wagon. James made a grab for him, but Zachary was beyond his reach.

The girls screamed, and Lydia watched in stunned horror as the wagon's front wheel rolled over the midsection of Zachary's body. He cried out and thrashed briefly on the dusty ground, and then, stillness.

James yanked the oxen to a stop and leaped to the ground. He bent over Zachary and gently lifted his head. Lydia was beside him in an instant. Zachary's face was streaked with dust, but otherwise appeared calm and reposed as if in sleep. A thin trickle of blood oozed from beneath his shirt.

Lydia screamed his name and clutched Zachary's limp body to her bosom. Her tears fell on his face, turning the dust on his cheeks into a muddy smear.

"Mama," James said in a choked voice. He put a shaking arm around her. Roxana and Millicent stood staring over their mother's shoulder, their eyes wide with terror.

"He's gone, Mama," James whispered, fighting back tears.

"No! Do something, James. You must know of something you can do for him!"

James' hands went over the boy's body, feeling for any sign of life. He laid his ear against the spreading stain on Zachary's chest and listened. Then he looked up despairingly at her. "I'm sorry, Mama. There's nothing I can do."

To their rear came a shuffling sound and then a startled gasp. Lydia looked up to find Christian, pale and trembling, grasping the back wheel of the wagon. His face was contorted in a look of horror and disbelief.

James immediately went to his father's side, putting an arm around him to support him. Christian took a step or two toward the still, small body lying in his mother's arms, and then his eyes rolled in their sockets and he crumpled against James.

Lydia couldn't remember what happened after that. She must have fainted because when she came to her senses again she was lying in her wagon, with Sister Stanton hovering over her. Sister Stanton gave her a sip of tepid water and murmured kind, sympathetic words in her ear. For an instant, Lydia couldn't recall the reason why she felt so numb and desolate. Then Zachary's lifeless form leaped into her consciousness. She cried out and bolted upright in her bed.

"There now, Sister Kade. Lie down and rest. Your boy's being taken care of. Try to rest for a few moments."

Lydia burst into tears. She sobbed so fiercely that her throat felt like it was being wrenched apart. Sister Stanton clasped Lydia to her bosom and stroked her hair, as if comforting a frightened child.

"Go ahead and cry. You just cry as long as you like." Sister Stanton continued to smooth Lydia's hair and rub her back. Her touch was comforting and reassuring, and with each pass of her strong, gentle hands, Lydia felt control seeping back into her mind and body.

When at last she was able to speak, she asked about Christian. Sister Stanton assured her that he was resting in one of the other wagons. Several of the brethren were with him. The children, likewise, were being cared for. Lydia closed her eyes and wept silently. Zachary. Her Zachary dead.

Sisters in the camp prepared Zachary's body for burial, dressing him in a clean white shirt and trousers, and carefully combing his dark, curly locks into place. James made a headstone with Zachary's name, age, and date of death printed on it, and he was buried that evening on a little knoll overlooking the trail. Christian could barely stand for the service. Weak from illness and the shock of their loss, he stood propped up against James while one of the brethren read from the twenty-third psalm.

As the mourners started back to their wagons, someone began reverently singing the first few bars of a hymn. Lydia paid little heed to the soulful strains of the song as she stumbled, grief-stricken, at Christian's side. Soon others joined in, mingling their voices in sorrowful tones. As the hymn progressed toward the chorus, the voices swelled in hope and prayerful supplication. The words of the final verse rang in Lydia's ears—"And should we die before our journey's through, happy day! All is well! We then are free from toil and sorrow, too; with the just we shall dwell!" Her heart was touched by the inspirational words, and her soul comforted. In a trembling whisper, with tears trickling down her cheeks, she united her voice with the others in the closing words of the hymn—"All is well, all is well."

*"If the Lord should say by his revelation
this is the spot, the Saints would be satisfied
if it was on a barren rock."*

BRIGHAM YOUNG

CHAPTER FOUR

"James, put a log on the fire, will you?" Lydia asked.

James set aside the harness he'd been repairing and walked over to the hearth. He picked up two short logs and started to toss them into the low-burning fire.

"Just one, son."

James turned to glance at his mother.

"Just use one log for now," she directed in a quiet voice.

James nodded. He did not need to inquire why his mother wished to use only a single log. He understood the reason well enough.

"Christian. Girls. Come to the table, please. Breakfast is ready," Lydia called.

James seated himself in the usual place, between his sisters, Roxana and Millicent. Christian held a chair for Lydia to sit on. When everyone was seated, Christian bowed his head in preparation for the blessing on the food.

James folded his arms and closed his eyes tightly while his father pronounced a prayer. It was one of appreciation— for the family's safe arrival in the valley, for their shelter, for their food. He asked for the Lord's blessings to be with Elizabeth and Alexander. He thanked God for Brother Brigham, the Prophet, and for all the leaders of the Church. His "amen" was echoed by those seated around the table.

Lydia spooned out the cornmeal mush into individual bowls and handed them around the table one by one. James would have liked a little sugar to sprinkle on his mush, but the family's supply of sugar had long since been depleted. He scooped up a spoonful of thick, pasty mush and put it into his mouth.

"How was your meeting with the brethren last night?" Lydia asked, turning to her husband.

"It went well. Brother Brigham informed us that there are over five thousand Saints in the valley now. He hopes to see many thousands more come in the spring."

"That's good. The Saints always seem to flourish once we're gathered together," Lydia replied.

Christian nodded as he swallowed a mouthful of cornmeal.

"I guess I was already asleep by the time you returned home," Lydia commented.

"Yes, you were. Otherwise, you would have heard the ruckus outside the fort," Christian answered with a grin.

"What ruckus?" asked James. He hadn't heard anything out of the ordinary either the night before.

"A couple of gold seekers had a rather loud disagreement last night. It took several of the brethren to calm them down."

Lydia glanced up from her breakfast with a frown, but she made no comment. James knew his mother was disturbed by the presence of the gold miners, as many of the Saints were. She didn't appreciate the fact that scores of them were wintering in the Great Salt Lake City, waiting for the snows to melt before continuing on to the gold fields of California. James would have liked to hear all about the "ruckus," but he kept his curiosity to himself out of respect for his mother's feelings.

Millicent, however, was not so reticent. "What happened, Father?" she asked. "Was there a fight?"

"Eat your breakfast, Millicent, and keep still," Lydia told her.

Millicent obeyed, but she was itching to hear what had taken place. She squirmed in her chair and swirled the mush in the bowl with her spoon. Roxana gave her younger sister a sharp look. The unspoken communication passing between them was plain enough for James to read—"Don't give Mother and Father any trouble," Roxana's look said.

Good advice, James thought to himself. There were difficulties enough already. Ever since his family had arrived in the valley of the Great Salt Lake nearly four months ago, food and fuel had been in short supply. When the Kades left Winter Quarters in June of 1848, their company, under the leadership of Heber C. Kimball, was well stocked with seeds, cattle, flour, bacon, blankets, and tents. They pulled into the valley on September 24, trail-weary and in low spirits over Zachary's death. Soon afterward, James and his father set about building the family an adobe home within the confines of the fort. The fort was comprised of three sections, and built as a protection against the Indians. James hadn't seen any Indians, however, since he'd been in the Great Basin.

His first impression of the valley had been favorable. The soil was fertile, and when irrigated with water flowing from the mountain streams, was capable of producing a bountiful harvest. But a late frost and then a horde of large black crickets had destroyed most of the crops in the months preceding the Kades' arrival. Since then, food had been scarce. The valley population of Saints had been swollen by the arrival of non-Mormons on their way to the gold fields of California. Many miners, arriving late in the season, chose to winter in the Salt Lake valley, and this put additional strain on the already scant supplies. Church president Brigham Young counseled the Saints to share what they had with those in need, but the presence of the miners was causing tension.

James finished his meager breakfast. He was still hungry; the hollow gnawing in his belly never seemed to go away completely. "That tasted real good, Mother," he said.

Lydia flashed him an appreciative smile.

"James, we won't be hunting this morning," his father said. "Some of the brethren are going up into the canyon to cut timber. I told them we'd come along to help. All right with you?"

"Sure. I'll get my coat." James stood, then reached for his heavy woolen coat which was hanging on a peg beside the door. The adobe cabin his family occupied consisted of a single room. The fireplace, table, and chairs were at one end, and the beds on which the family slept at the other.

"I wish I could go up into the mountains with you," said Millicent. "James gets to have all the fun."

"What fun is there in going outside to work in this bitter cold weather?" Roxana asked. She shivered and hugged her arms against her body.

Milly gave her sister an impatient look. "You may be content staying indoors, but I love to see the snow piled on the ground like mounds of soft cotton. Can I come with you, Father? Please?"

Christian tugged one long, red braid. "Not today, Milly. You stay inside to help your mother, and I promise I'll take you for a ride into the mountains in the next day or two."

Millicent's brows rushed together, and she slumped unhappily in her chair. James chuckled at his sister's display of temper. Milly's disposition was as vibrant and fiery as her red hair.

Lydia began clearing the dishes from the table, and Roxana rose from her chair to help. "I'll fetch the hot water for you, Mama," she said.

James pulled on his coat and jammed an old felt hat on his head.

"Don't forget your muffler, James," his mother said as she deposited an armful of dishes into a wooden bucket to be washed.

James walked across the one-roomed cabin, covering the distance in a few short strides. He planted a kiss on his mother's cheek. "You remind me to put on my muffler every time I go out the cabin door, do you know that?" he told her with a sparkle in his brown eyes. "And I'm nearly twenty years old."

"Then you're old enough to remember to dress warmly when you go outside," Lydia replied. She smoothed his dark, wavy hair away from his forehead. The top of her head barely reached his shoulder.

James grinned at her. "No matter how old I get, you're still going to remind me to take care of myself, aren't you?"

"That is a mother's prerogative," Lydia answered with a smile.

James wound his red woolen muffler around his neck and started for the cabin door. "I'll go hitch the horse to the sled," he told his father.

"I'll come help you," Milly volunteered. She flew from her chair and scrambled into her coat. James held open the door for her.

"Come on, then," he said, putting an arm around her shoulder.

The cold air snatched James' breath away the moment he stepped outside. He began trudging through snow which came nearly to the top of his knee-high boots. Ever since the beginning of December, frequent snowstorms and biting wind had pummeled the valley. James glanced over his shoulder at the little adobe cabin floundering in the deep snow. The sod roof lay buried under a thick layer of white flakes. The Kades' cabin was similar to the others squatting together in a row within the fort walls. Some cabins were constructed of wood, but most were built of mud and straw adobe bricks.

"Have you ever seen such deep snow?" Millicent asked, as she traipsed along at James' side.

"No, I haven't. We're really in the tops of the mountains here."

"Oh, I like being here, don't you?" Millicent chirped. "The mountains are so grand. I can't wait until spring, when all the mountain flowers come into bloom."

"I thought you liked the snow," James replied.

"Oh, I do! I love it. But won't the flowers be breath-taking, and the grass will grow up to our ankles."

James laughed. "You're never satisfied with the moment, Milly. You always want tomorrow."

Milly didn't reply. She was too busy dancing and whirling in the pristine snow. She dashed ahead of James, swooping like a bird over the vast field of white. Her red braids trailed from beneath her bonnet, and her coat billowed out like wings.

James smiled at her exuberance. She had more energy than any ten-year-old he had ever encountered. Had Roxana been with him instead, she would have walked primly by his side. His thoughts shifted from his two younger sisters to his elder sister. The family had received one letter from Elizabeth since arriving in their new home; she had sent the note with an acquaintance who was traveling to Oregon. The letter contained a recital of Elizabeth's activities in Nauvoo, references to her husband, Alexander, and a glowing report concerning the prosperity that Alexander's sawmill was enjoying.

James frowned as he contemplated his relationship with his sister. As children, they had enjoyed a close association, though Elizabeth was two years his senior. But as they grew older, their differences began to divide them. Their feelings concerning their stepfather was a case in point. James and Elizabeth's natural father, Abraham Dawson, had died when they were young children living in Green County, Illinois. Elizabeth had always dwelled on her loss, and when her mother married Christian Kade, she never completely accepted him as her father. All through her growing-up years, she was in conflict with Christian. She refused to submit to his parental authority, and showed increasing hostility toward him and toward her activity in the Church.

Elizabeth's rebelliousness, and her decision to stay in Nauvoo, widened the gulf between her and the family. She and Alexander Scott married the week before the Kade family left to take up their journey west. The ceremony took place at the Kades' home on Durphey Street. Even though Lydia and Christian were opposed to the marriage, once Elizabeth determined to go through with it, they gave her their support. James knew they were not happy about the union; both of them disliked Alexander because of his unscrupulous character and his proud heart. But they kept their feelings to themselves and saw to it that Elizabeth enjoyed a wonderful wedding day.

James missed his sister more than he was willing to admit. Elizabeth had always been stubborn, more than ever over the issue of going west with the Saints. James had hoped up to the last minute that she would relent and travel to the Great Basin with them. Now that she was married, it was out of the question. Alexander would never leave his thriving lumber business to go west. At every opportunity, he openly displayed his antagonism and disdain for the Church. James wished he and Elizabeth had been closer. It hurt him to leave her with hard feelings between them.

Reaching the corral where the animals were kept, James opened the gate for himself and Millicent to pass through. Near the gate stood the big, dappled gray horse owned by the Stanton family. He patted the animal's rump, then gathered up his tack and began hitching his father's chestnut mare to one of the flat sleds the brethren used to haul logs down from the mountains.

Millicent stroked the mare's velvet nose. "What sort of ruckus went on between the gold miners last night, do you suppose?" she asked.

James shrugged his shoulders. "I don't know. Maybe a fight. A couple of the miners probably got liquored up and had a quarrel."

Millicent wrinkled her nose. "I wish they'd go away to California."

"You and a lot of others wish that same thing," James replied, buckling the leather harness strap underneath the belly of the mare. The horse snorted and stamped her feet.

Millicent petted the horse's neck. "Is there a lot of gold in California?" she asked.

"I suppose so."

"Are we going to California to get some of it?"

James glanced at his sister. "No, we're not. Father would never allow it. And besides, President Young and the other brethren said we shouldn't go chasing after riches."

"But wouldn't just a little gold be nice, James?"

A picture skittered across James' mind—an image of himself with a fine brick house, a splendid horse and carriage, suits of fine linen. He reluctantly blanked the image out. "Brother Brigham said this is the place God has appointed for his people, and the quicker we can purge ourselves of gold fever, the better off we'll be."

"Do you think Brother Brigham is right about that?" Millicent asked.

James looked into his sister's face. Her expression was innocent and trusting. "Yes, I do, Milly. I think if we concentrate on agriculture and industry, and building up the Church here in the Great Basin, we'll prosper. Father says if we do that, we'll be more successful than twenty miners put together. And I believe that."

"So do I!" said Millicent vigorously.

"Then let's have no more talk about gold. Here, take this strap and help me harness the horse to the sled."

The ride up the canyon was miserable. Blowing snow stung James' face, and his ears ached from the chill, driving wind. He pulled the brim of his hat down, trying to shield his face against the onslaught of cold and snow. His father was handling the reins, urging the horse up the steep canyon trail. The sled bumped across the uneven surface of snow, following in the wake of the two sleds up ahead. Christian flapped the reins against the mare's thin back and shouted, "Gid up there!" The sled lurched forward over the deep snow.

At last the lead sled stopped in the midst of a stand of tall, straight lodgepole pines. Three brethren, bundled in coats and low-fitting hats, climbed down from the sled. The brethren in the second sled also pulled to a stop, and Christian reined in his horse. Grabbing two axes and a saw from the bed of the sled, James followed the other brethren into the forest of towering pines. He counted seven men who had come on this excursion to obtain fuel for the settlers in the valley. He knew only two of them well—Brother Royce and Brother Babcock. Both men had been in the same wagon company as the Kades on their trek to the Great Basin. Both were around forty years of age and had large families. Brother Royce was a lanky fellow with a shock of red hair that seemed to grow upright from his head. Brother Babcock was shorter, and portly. He puffed and grunted as he swung his ax at the base of a tall pine.

"Let's start on this one over here," Christian said to James. "Hand me an ax, son."

James did so, then followed him to a straight pine a few feet from where Brother Royce and Brother Babcock were working. The snow was much deeper here in the canyon than it was in the valley. It spilled over the tops of James' boots as he tramped to the tree his father had selected.

"You take this pine, James, and I'll work on the one next to it."

"All right," James answered. He rubbed his cold hands together and then gripped the handle of the ax. Taking a wide, deliberate swing, he delivered a sharp blow to the base of the tree. The blade bit into the pine, making a deep gash in the bark. He swung the ax again and again, each time chipping his way deeper into the trunk.

The dull thud of metal striking wood punctuated the stillness of the canyon. Occasionally the men talked and jested with one another, but the exertion of working in such biting cold tempered their conversation. James found his own breath coming in short little puffs. His feet were growing numb from the cold, and his stiff fingers couldn't keep a tight grip on the ax handle. After a few more blows, he felt the tree shudder and begin to give way. "She's coming down," he shouted in warning to his companions. With one more strike of the ax, the pine creaked, swayed, and came crashing down. A spray of snow arched into the air where the tree came to rest.

"Good job, James!" shouted his father.

A couple of the other men glanced at him, nodding their heads in approval. A moment later another warning was called out, and a huge pine a few yards from where James stood toppled to the snowy ground.

The work went on for almost an hour. Some of the men continued to cut trees, while others sawed off branches and loaded the heavy trunks onto the sleds. Although it was bitter cold, James was perspiring from his labor. His hands were sore from wielding the ax, and the muscles in his arms ached.

"She's down!" James heard the warning. He turned to watch as a wide-girthed pine Brothers Royce and Babcock had been cutting together wobbled and started to fall. Brother Royce stepped out of the way of the falling tree. Brother Babcock, too, started to move aside, but his boot slipped on an icy patch of snow. James watched as Babcock sprawled onto the ground. In the next split second, James saw a tall, thin shadow lengthening out on the snow. Babcock saw it, too. He tried to scramble out of the path of the falling tree, but he couldn't get a foothold on the icy ground.

James watched the scene in horror. The tree seemed to fall in slow motion while Babcock squirmed desperately on the ground. James lunged forward in an effort to reach him, but the knee-deep snow hampered his movement.

He couldn't have reached Babcock soon enough, even without the snow impeding his way. The tall pine slammed to the ground. Babcock screamed. For one terrifying moment, James stood rooted to the spot, unable to move or to speak, then he frantically began wading through the deep snow to Babcock's side. He dropped down next to the writhing man, his breath frozen in his throat. The trunk of the tree had missed striking Babcock by a fraction of an inch, but its heavy, bushy boughs lay across his body. Babcock cried out in pain. Christian and the other men clustered around him, anxious to offer aid.

"Quick, let's get him in the wagon," one man shouted.

"No, don't move him," another exclaimed. "He may have broken bones."

"How did this happen?" Brother Royce moaned as he knelt beside his friend.

James watched the clean white snow around Babcock's leg turn red with blood. The patch of scarlet grew wider and wider. The men's frenzied voices blurred and faded from his ears as the man lying on the ground became a small boy—a small, dark-haired boy with a red stain spreading on his clean white shirt. Zachary. Zachary!

James' brow became drenched in perspiration. It took every ounce of control he possessed to erase the image of his brother and concentrate on the man lying in the snow. "Don't move him. Not yet," he said as hands reached out to Babcock's limp body.

"Can you do something for him, James?" came Christian's tense voice in his ear. "He's bleeding to death."

James blinked and ran a shaking hand across his brow. He willed himself to focus on Babcock's wounds. "You men move that tree aside," he commanded in a trembling voice.

"You're interested in medicine?" Dr. McCaffrey asked. He looked intently into James' face. He was a man of generous size, with a drooping gray mustache and gray, shaggy brows.

"Yes, sir. Very much."

Dr. McCaffrey nodded. He glanced at his patient, then back at James. "You know, if you had tied the tourniquet any tighter, that fellow lying there would have lost his leg. As it is, he should recover without too much difficulty."

James swallowed. He was glad he'd taken the correct action.

"It takes a clear head to act appropriately in an emergency." Dr. McCaffrey tugged at his mustache. "Mr. Royce told me you reacted calmly and with efficiency under very difficult circumstances."

James gave the doctor a wry smile. "Brother Royce was mistaken if he thought I was calm. I was scared to death."

"But you reacted with clear reason. A very good quality for a physician to possess—especially a young one." McCaffrey walked across the room to a large, glass-fronted cabinet and placed inside it the unused portion of a roll of cloth bandages, along with a pair of long-handled scissors. James noticed a contingent of stoppered bottles lined up on the cabinet shelf. Most contained powders; a few held colored liquids. He would have liked to examine the bottles more closely.

McCaffrey closed the cupboard door. "How would you like to apprentice with me, James?" he asked.

Christian and Brother Royce lifted the trunk of the pine, while the other men grasped bushy branches. When Babcock's body was free of the heavy boughs, the extent of his injuries became apparent. His trousers were in tatters, and blood poured from a gaping, jagged tear in his left thigh. Other cuts and scratches crisscrossed his legs and body, but the wound in his thigh required immediate attention.

James quickly unwound the woolen muffler from his neck. His fingers were shaking with cold and fear, but he forced himself to remain calm. He scooped away some of the bright red snow underneath Babcock's injured leg and slipped the muffler under the leg. He wound it around Babcock's thigh and knotted it. No! That was too tight! It would cut off the circulation to the leg completely! With numbed fingers, James loosened the knot. As he worked, the men surrounding Babcock waited in silence; James could hear their ragged breathing. Babcock wasn't moving, and his face looked ashen.

"What can we do to help?" asked Christian.

"Press your hand over this wound to stop the bleeding," James directed.

Christian put the heel of his hand over a deep cut just below Babcock's shoulder and applied a steady pressure.

"That's good. Hold it tight," James murmured to his father.

"I'll get the sled and bring it over," one of the other men volunteered.

"One of you quickly burn a piece of cloth or wood, and give me the ashes to put in these wounds. It will help to control the bleeding," James instructed. He labored over Babcock for the next several minutes, keeping his eye on the shallow rise and fall of the man's chest. With each breath Babcock drew, James grew a bit more hopeful for the man's life.

Brother Royce, kneeling at Babcock's head, gently wiped the snow from his friend's brow. "Help me here, brethren, to give him a priesthood blessing," Royce said in a strained voice. Two of the other brethren knelt by Royce's side. James closed his eyes and bowed his head as Royce offered an impassioned prayer.

At last, James felt satisfied with the assistance given the injured man. But if Babcock was to survive, he needed attention from a physician as quickly as possible. "All right, let's lift him into the sled. Gently now," James said. "Any movement is going to start those wounds bleeding worse."

A dozen hands carefully lifted Babcock into the waiting sled. James followed behind the men. His legs felt weak as he stumbled through the snow. When he reached the sled, he was grateful for his father's strong arm in helping him climb up into the seat. Christian shook the reins and the horse started forward. Throughout the ride down the canyon, James kept his gaze fixed on Babcock's still body.

CHAPTER FIVE

Dr. McCaffrey rinsed his hands in a washbowl sitting beside a pitcher on a small, square table. James watched the clear water turn red with Babcock's blood.

"What did you say your name was, son?" McCaffrey asked.

"James Kade, sir."

"Well, James, your quick action saved Mr. Babcock's life." The doctor shook the water from his hands and reached for a towel. "How did you know what to do?"

James glanced at Brother Babcock, who was lying on the bed next to the table. His wounds were freshly dressed and his breathing was rhythmic. James drew a deep sigh of relief. "I studied for a time with a physician in Nauvoo, Illinois," he replied.

"What?" James exclaimed, unsure if he had heard the doctor correctly.

"I've been looking for a young man to take over my practice. I'm thinking of retiring soon, going back home to Vermont to live out my days in the company of old friends and family. The West is a rugged place." He smiled ruefully. "I'm willing to teach you what I know. If you prove receptive and responsible, I'll turn my practice over to you when I retire."

James stammered and stuttered, trying to articulate his thoughts. "Dr. McCaffrey, I don't know what to say. Thank you. Yes, of course! This is more than I ever hoped for." James grasped the doctor's hand and pumped it up and down. "I'll be an attentive pupil, Dr. McCaffrey. You won't be sorry. It's been my desire to become a physician for as long as I can remember."

McCaffrey nodded. "Come to my office tomorrow, and we'll discuss the proposition further. You can look in on your friend then. See how he's doing." McCaffrey nodded toward the sleeping figure on the bed.

"Yes, sir. I'll do that," James replied. "I'll certainly do that. And thank you, Dr. McCaffrey. Thank you very much." James began backing out of the room as he spoke, when suddenly he bumped into the bedside table. The washbasin and pitcher sitting on the table swayed crazily. James grabbed the pitcher as it teetered on its edge. He set it back in place with trembling hands. "I'm sorry, sir. I'll be more careful," James mumbled, his face burning.

Dr. McCaffrey's shaggy brows twitched with the onset of a frown. "I'll see you sometime tomorrow," he said. He turned and bent over his patient lying on the bed.

James left the doctor's cabin. His father had gone out ahead of him and was waiting in the sled. The other men had already left for their homes after learning that Brother Babcock would recover.

"Ready to go?" Christian asked him.

James climbed into the sled beside his father. His spirit was soaring.

"What is it, James? Is something wrong?" asked Christian.

"You're not going to believe what just happened, Father," James began breathlessly. "Dr. McCaffrey invited me to apprentice with him."

"He did? That's excellent news, James! What an opportunity for you." Christian clapped him on the back.

"He took me completely by surprise. I had no idea he was interested in training someone." James went on to relate his conversation with Dr. McCaffrey. Christian listened intently as he reined the horse toward the stockade.

"I thought I'd never get another chance to study medicine," James remarked.

"Opportunity favors the prepared mind," replied his father. "And you've been preparing for this opportunity for years. I'm very proud of you, son. I know your mother will be, too."

"Thank you, Father. Your support means a lot to me. I give you my word that I'll study diligently and learn all I can. I intend to be the most conscientious medical student Dr. McCaffrey has ever seen."

James shoved his hands into his coat pockets as he slogged through the deep snow to Etta's cabin. He hardly felt the cold, for his body and mind were burning with thoughts of working with Dr. Jacob McCaffrey. He'd been able to think of nothing else all day. The near tragedy in the canyon had miraculously turned into the opportunity of a lifetime. James had met Dr. McCaffrey only once before today. He knew the doctor was not a Latter-day Saint. He had arrived in the valley with a wagon train making its way to California, liked what he saw, and decided to stay. He practiced homeopathic medicine. Beyond that, James knew nothing else about him.

The Stantons' log cabin suddenly loomed before him. James knocked at the door. A young boy, chubby and towheaded, undid the latch.

"Hello, Martin," James said. He bent down and rumpled the boy's hair. "Is your sister at home?"

"Yep. She's helping Mama with the mending. You can come in, Brother Kade."

James stepped into the cozy cabin. It was much like the Kades' own cabin, except it was built of logs instead of adobe. It consisted of one large room. A curtain hanging from the ceiling rafters divided the room in two, closing off the sleeping quarters during the day.

"Hello, Brother Kade," Mrs. Stanton greeted him. She and Etta were seated beside the hearth, darning stockings. James whisked off his hat.

"Evening, Sister Stanton. Good evening, Etta."

Etta peeked up from her darning, and James saw her cheeks grow rosy in the light of the fire.

"Come sit down, Brother Kade," Mrs. Stanton invited. She glanced at the corner of the room where Martin and two of his younger brothers were standing, staring at James. "Don't you boys have something to do?" she asked them. "If not, I'll find something for you."

The boys instantly dashed behind the curtain.

James pulled a chair closer to the fire. Mrs. Stanton smiled at him and kept on with her sewing.

James twisted his hat in his hands. He always felt a little uneasy calling on Etta in the cramped quarters of her family's cabin. He would have preferred taking a walk with her, or a buggy ride, but the wintery weather hindered any such activity. He cleared his throat nervously. "I think it's going to snow more tonight," he said.

Etta glanced out the cabin window. "Yes, I believe it does look that way." Her eyes went back to her sewing. James noticed her fingers trembling slightly under his gaze.

James loosened his collar with the tip of his finger. The fire in the hearth was blazing brightly, and he was beginning to feel uncomfortably warm. "Have you heard about the accident Brother Babcock had this morning in the canyon?" he asked Etta.

She looked up at him. "Yes, we did. One of the brethren told us about it. Is Brother Babcock going to be all right?"

"Dreadful," Mrs. Stanton murmured. "Absolutely dreadful. That poor man was nearly killed."

"Dr. McCaffrey thinks his injuries will heal without too much problem."

"I'm very glad to hear that," Etta replied.

James watched her darn the stocking. Her white, narrow hands maneuvered the needle and thread expertly through a gaping hole in the heel; James couldn't help imagining it was his stocking sitting in her lap, receiving her attention. For the hundredth time, he imagined himself to be Etta's husband. Etta, with her smooth, dark, shining hair and luminous brown eyes. When she glanced up suddenly at him, he saw the undisguised affection in her eyes. He felt a stab of guilt. He knew he should ask her to marry him. She would be the perfect wife—beautiful, mild-mannered, kind and loving. Why was it when he tried to picture himself married to her, the image in his mind crumbled to pieces? He loved her. Or at least he thought he did. And she loved him. She'd never spoken the words, but she didn't have to. Her eyes betrayed the desire and longing she felt for him.

He dropped his gaze, fidgeting with the hat in his hands. He should ask her to be his wife. He should ask her tonight.

"We also heard you were responsible for saving Brother Babcock's life," Etta said quietly.

James looked up at her. Her gaze met his, and he fumbled for words. "I did what I could for him, but it was Dr. McCaffrey who saved his life."

Etta's gaze lingered on him. Her eyes were pools of liquid brown. James felt himself toppling into the depths of them.

"It was a good thing you were there to help Brother Babcock," Mrs. Stanton said firmly.

The older woman's voice broke the spell under which James had been falling headlong. His eyes shifted from Etta to her mother. "I had a talk about that with Dr. McCaffrey," he said. As he recalled their conversation together, James felt excitement course through him. He turned eagerly back to Etta. "Dr. McCaffrey invited me to apprentice with him. He's offered to teach me what he knows about medicine."

"Oh, James, that's wonderful!" Etta put down her sewing and leaned forward in her chair. "That's exactly what you've wanted, isn't it?"

"Yes, it is. It's what I've always dreamed about." James' heart was pounding.

"I'm so proud of you, James," Etta said. "I know you'll make a fine doctor."

"It won't happen overnight. It will take hard work and diligent study. I hope I'll be equal to the challenge."

"Of course you will. You'll learn what you need to know quickly. You're so bright, James, and so caring. You'll have more patients than you can handle." Etta laughed lightly. The sound of it was like the tinkling of a bell.

"Congratulations, Brother Kade," Mrs. Stanton said. She patted James' knee. "It looks as if you have your feet firmly planted on the path you intend to trod. A fine young man you are, James, from a good family. And now you have a profession, too. I suppose there's nothing now to hold you back from getting on with your life."

Etta's cheeks bloomed a bright pink. She picked up her sewing and bent over it. James felt his own face flush at the blatant insinuation behind Mrs. Stanton's remark. He was more embarrassed for Etta's sake than for his own. Etta's needle flashed in and out of the woolen stocking, and he thought he saw her lip quiver.

James cleared his throat. "Uh, yes, I suppose so," he mumbled. Etta wouldn't lift her eyes to look at him. Mrs. Stanton's remark hung in the air between them like a noxious perfume. James felt miserable; he couldn't think of anything to say to cover the odor of the words. Mrs. Stanton expected James to ask Etta's hand in marriage. Her allusion to that fact had spoiled their conversation and ruined their evening together. He saw no sense in trying to carry on a visit that was now strained and awkward.

"Well, I guess I'd better be getting on home," he stammered. He stood up from the chair, clutching his hat in his hands. "Good night, Mrs. Stanton. Etta."

Etta nodded, but said nothing.

"It's always nice to see you, James," Mrs. Stanton smiled.

"Thank you."

"Just let yourself out." Mrs. Stanton gestured toward the door.

James started for the cabin door, paused, and turned around.

"I'll see you again soon, Etta," he offered.

Etta didn't reply or look up from her sewing.

James' shoulders sagged. He walked slowly to the door and out into the cold night.

CHAPTER SIX

"All right, James, let's begin by having you tell me exactly what kind of medical experience you've had." Dr. McCaffrey was seated on a stool in the front portion of his adobe home, which doubled as his office. James sat on a chair opposite him. In back of the chair, behind drawn curtains, Brother Babcock lay recuperating from his injuries.

James nervously rubbed his hands together. "Well, sir, I've read quite a bit on the subject of medicine. The physician in Nauvoo, Dr. Bennett, gave me access to his library. I worked with Dr. Bennett for a few months whenever I could spare the time, mostly for a few hours after school."

"Did you assist Dr. Bennett in caring for his patients?"

"Some. I helped him set broken bones a time or two, bandaged wounds, mixed a few compounds. That sort of thing. Mostly I just watched what he did." James fidgeted in his seat. He felt self-conscious and unsure of himself under McCaffrey's watchful eye.

"Did you observe any surgeries? Amputations of a limb, or the removal of growths, perhaps?"

"No, sir." James shook his head.

Dr. McCaffrey leaned back and folded his arms. He regarded James gravely. After a few moments of silence, he continued. "You mentioned having read a bit about medicine. What books have you studied?"

James was quick with his answer. "I've read Benjamin Rush's *Medical Observations* and *The Progress of Medicine.* Also a number of medical journals."

Dr. McCaffrey nodded. "Then you have your knowledge on good authority. What kind of medicine did Dr. Bennett practice, James?

"What kind, sir?" James asked, not sure what McCaffrey was driving at.

"Yes. Did he subscribe to the Brunonian theory of medicine? Or lean toward some other method? You are familiar with the Brunonian, or Cullenian, theories of medicine, are you not?"

"Yes. I am. I studied about Dr. John Brown, the Scottish physician. Brown considered disease to be an imbalance of excitability in the body. I suppose Dr. Bennett relied upon that theory to some degree. He often prescribed calomel, laudanum, and quinine."

Dr. McCaffrey shifted his weight on the stool. "Are you familiar with homeopathy, James?"

"To some extent, sir."

"Homeopathy embraces some of the practices and methods of the Brunonian theory of medicine. Brown felt that good health was maintained by keeping a balance between stimuli producing excitability and the body's ability to compensate for it. Some disorders require treatment to reduce excitability, such as the use of opiates, aromatics, or bleeding. Other illnesses use cathartics or sweating to help the body regain its natural balance."

James nodded. He was familiar with the things Dr. McCaffrey was rehearsing.

"But the homeopathic practice of medicine does not rely on sweatings, bleedings, or some of the other cures Brown recommended," Dr. McCaffrey continued. "Homeopathy cures disease by prescribing medicines which cause symptoms similar to those produced by the disease itself. Given in small doses, homeopathic medicines stimulate a person's innate healing powers."

Dr. McCaffrey stood up and walked to a case which held ten or twelve well-worn books. His finger traveled over the books, pausing at a thick volume with a brown leather cover. He removed the book from the case, rifled through its pages, then handed it to James.

James scrutinized the title, *Organon of the Rational Art*, written by Samuel Christian Hahnemann. He opened the book and glanced over its first few pages.

"This will be your bible, James. Read it. Reread it. Commit its precepts to memory."

James looked up into Dr. McCaffrey's face. He swallowed, self-conscious under the doctor's solemn stare. "I will, sir. I'll make myself completely familiar with it."

"Good. Then we can begin in earnest."

James nodded.

"I think that will be all for now, James. When you come next time, I'll introduce you to the various medicines and compounds we use to cure imbalances in the body. If you'd like to look in on Mr. Babcock before you go, you're welcome to do so."

"Thank you, Dr. McCaffrey, I will. And thank you for the book."

"You're welcome."

James got to his feet and lifted aside the curtain that provided a measure of privacy for the patient. He stood beside Babcock's bed for a few minutes, watching the sleeping man's chest rise and fall.

"You missed that magpie by a mile, James."

James lowered his rifle and squinted into the distance. "Are you sure?" he asked his hunting companion.

"Of course. I saw the magpie wing serenely off into the horizon," Lars Johanssen replied with a grin.

"You're sure he didn't just fly to the next bush?" James asked, raising an eyebrow. "You tend to wax lyrical now and again, Lars."

Lars laughed. He pushed his straw-colored hair off his forehead and started to tramp ahead in the snow. "They'll be other magpies, James. Don't fret."

James hoisted his gun over his shoulder and followed Lars through the deep snow. Lars seemed to know exactly where he was headed in the vast snow-covered hills outside the fort. He and James had been hunting for most of the morning. They'd seen a bobcat and two foxes, but hadn't been close enough to bring them down with their rifles. Lars had shot a raven, and James had almost felt sorry for the loss of the beautiful bird. Its glistening black wings had shone in the winter sun as it cut through the air like an arrow. But the raven would help sustain some hungry pioneer family. Any bit of meat the men could bring home to their families was welcomed. To help bolster the food supply and protect their stock from predators, the High Council was sponsoring a hunt. Two teams had been formed, one under the leadership of John D. Lee and the other captained by John Pack. The deadline for the contest was February 1, two weeks from now.

"I don't know, Lars. If our success is any indication, Brother Lee's team won't have a chance of winning the contest," James lamented.

"There it is." Lars stopped and shaded his eyes with his hand.

"There *what* is? Do you see a deer or something?" James asked. He scanned the empty wilderness stretching before them.

"That hollow over there. Look at it, James. Look at the snow dressing those willows. Here, hold these for me." Lars passed his gun and the burlap sack containing the dead raven into James' hands. Then he reached into the pocket of his trousers and withdrew a bit of paper and a pencil. He bent down, balancing the paper on one knee, and quickly started to sketch the snowy scene before him.

To James' eyes, the snow-filled hollow looked no different than any one of a dozen others the pair of them had waded through that morning. But something about this picture arrested Lars' attention. Perhaps it was the way the sunlight filtered through the close-growing willows. James watched Lars' drawing come to life on the paper. He marveled at his friend's talent for capturing the inanimate and breathing life and motion into it. Neither of them spoke as Lars quickly sketched the scene.

"There, I'm finished." Lars stood up and held the paper out at arm's length, eyeing it critically.

James looked over his friend's shoulder. "That's very good, Lars. I'm impressed."

Lars frowned. "I didn't quite catch the grace and feeling of it like I wanted to." Lars turned the paper to one side and then the other, closely examining the lines of the drawing.

"No, it's an excellent job. You ought to become a professional artist, Lars."

Lars folded the paper in two and slipped it into his pocket along with the pencil. "You're beginning to sound like Inger. She keeps suggesting that I pursue a serious study of art."

"Inger's right. You should listen to your sister."

Lars retrieved his rifle and the burlap sack from James. "I don't know. I'm not sure that's the direction I want to take with my life. I'm not like you, James. You've always known what you wanted."

"I've been lucky," James replied with a smile. The two of them started walking back toward the fort.

"How are your studies coming along with Dr. McCaffrey?" Lars asked.

"Well, I've been to his office every day for a week now. I'm not sure if he's pleased with me or not." James gave his friend a wry grin. "I like the work, though. It's exhilarating and satisfying all at the same time. It's like a miracle, you know, Lars? Helping people get well. Repairing a wound, or setting a broken bone."

"Like Brother Babcock's injuries?"

"Yes. That's just what I mean. Dr. McCaffrey dressed his wounds and set his broken leg, and now Brother Babcock is up moving around. A miracle." James shook his head in awe.

"Have you done any actual doctoring yourself?" Lars asked as they climbed up a snowy embankment.

"Yes. Dr. McCaffrey is adamant about giving me practical experience. It frightens the daylights out of me! He examines the patient first, then turns him over to me. He asks for my opinion on a diagnosis, and what remedy to prescribe for it."

"That is a staggering load."

"I worry about making mistakes, but it's marvelous training. Yesterday I stitched up a laceration without his help."

"You were born to the profession, James," Lars remarked, clapping his friend on the back.

"Time will tell," James replied.

"You know, I wish Inger would come in to see you. She's been bothered with a fearsome cough, and pain in her chest. But you know how stubborn she is. She'll just wait it out until she gets better."

"Too many people do the same thing—they go to a physician only as a last resort. I'd like to see that attitude change. Tell Inger she should come by the office to see Dr. McCaffrey. Her symptoms could indicate serious illness."

"I'll tell her, but it won't do any good. With just Inger and me at home now, my sister does pretty much as she chooses."

James summoned a mental picture of the Johanssens' adobe cabin situated at the far end of the fort. Twenty-one-year-old Inger and eighteen-year-old Lars shared the cabin. Their two older sisters, Johanna and Kirstine, were both married with families of their own. None of them knew where Jens, the oldest boy, was living; he'd broken away from the family years before, and there had been little contact with him since. The Johanssens' parents, Neils and Gerda, had been friends with James' mother when both families lived in Green County. They had both passed away since, however.

"Hold up!" Lars exclaimed. "There's another magpie, on that bush over there."

James stared in the direction Lars pointed.

"Go ahead, James. Get him," whispered Lars.

James wordlessly raised his percussion-lock rifle to his shoulder and aimed down the long barrel. The magpie was perched on the branch of a barren tree not more than fifteen yards from him. James carefully sighted along his weapon and squeezed the trigger. A blast roared in the stillness.

"You got him!" Lars whooped. Lars ran toward the branch, which was still bobbing in the air from the magpie's fall.

James grinned as Lars picked up the limp bird and held it out for him to see.

"Well, I won't be going home empty-handed after all," James said with satisfaction.

Lars came to his friend's side and dangled the dead bird in front of his eyes. "Do you know what you ought to do with this magpie?" Lars asked cheerfully. "Give it to Etta Stanton's mother for her cooking pot. That ought to ingratiate you with Sister Stanton."

James took the bird and dropped it into the burlap sack Lars held open for him. "I don't need to impress Sister Stanton any more than I already have," he said, a frown wrinkling his brow.

"What do you mean by that?" asked Lars.

The two of them started walking again over the snow-covered ground. James was silent for a moment as he tried to shape his thoughts into words. "Sister Stanton already expects Etta and me to marry," he said at last.

Lars peered into his friend's face. "You don't sound very happy about that."

"That's just it. I don't know if I'm happy or not about the prospect of marrying Etta," James replied miserably.

"Now, hold on here," Lars said, taking James by the arm. "Are you trying to tell me that you're not in love with Etta Stanton. I thought you were crazy about her."

"I am fond of her."

"*Fond* of her?" Lars repeated with one raised brow. "That doesn't sound like something a lovesick young buck would say."

"I don't know what to do, Lars. I think I'm in love with Etta. Whenever I'm with her, my heart starts racing. I enjoy her company. But I'm just not sure I'm completely smitten with her, you know?"

Lars strode through the snow at James' side without saying anything for some moments. "Does Etta know how you feel?" he asked finally.

James shook his head. "I know she's expecting me to bring up the subject of marriage . . . it looms between us like a shadow. But how can I ask her to marry me if I'm not sure that's what I want myself?"

Lars clamped a hand on James' back. "Do you want to know what I think?"

"Sure. Tell me."

"If you don't hear a symphony playing every time that girl looks at you, then you're not in love, my friend."

James paused in his stride, considering Lars' word of advice. As much as he hated to admit it, he knew in his heart that Etta's presence didn't provoke such a response in him. "That's awfully poetic, Lars, but not very realistic, I'm afraid," he replied in a deceptively light tone.

"It's real enough," Lars responded, striding past him. "Love is the music of the heart." He glanced over his shoulder at James, who was still standing motionless in the snow. "Come on," he said, grinning. "It's still a long way back to the fort."

James shook away his gloomy thoughts. He caught up with Lars and playfully shouldered him aside.

"Hey, do you want a punch in the nose?" Lars returned jokingly.

"Not unless you want a broken arm," James grinned.

Lars shrugged his shoulders. "Well, I know a good doctor who could mend it."

CHAPTER SEVEN

With February came a break in the harsh weather, allowing the valley settlers a burst of activity. James and his father helped commence construction of a gristmill on City Creek. A flour mill and sawmill were started as well. Work began on a public building, to be called the Council House, which would be used for meetings and other Church and city functions. The February thaw also caused the eroding of some of the adobe cabins within the fort; the blocks in James' own family dwelling began to separate and collapse. Repairs on the cabin and work at the gristmill kept James from pursuing his labors with Dr. McCaffrey more than he liked. Still, he managed to spend two or three afternoons a week at the office.

In addition to the time he spent with patients at the office, or accompanying Dr. McCaffrey on house calls,

James put in many long hours studying the books and medical journals McCaffrey gave him to read. He had read all of Hahnemann's book, an exposition on the subject of homeopathic medicine. He agreed with many of the precepts he learned from the book, but he had slowly come to the realization that homeopathy was not, strictly speaking, the kind of traditional medicine he had intended to pursue.

The medical field was rife with all kinds of theories and practices—homeopathy, hydropathy, herbal medicine, Thomsonism or botanic medicine, dietary reform, patent medicine healers, and so on. Each of these espoused a different theory regarding the origin and treatment of disease. The more James read, the more confused he became about which one of the conflicting theories was most correct. In his book, Hahnemann taught that disease is a general derangement of the vital principle which keeps the entire body in balance. There are three chronic "miasmas" which cause imbalance, Hahnemann declared. The disordered vital principle can right itself under normal conditions, but needs assistance when disarranged by abnormal miasmic imbalance. The process of re-establishing harmony within the body is initiated by minute doses of drugs which produce symptoms similar to the disease. This stimulates the vital principle to greater effort, thus helping the body to heal itself.

James agreed in principle with this interpretation, but he questioned the theory behind it. What if disease was not caused by an imbalance, but by something completely different? No one seemed to know for a fact the answer to that question. And so, for now, James accepted the theories which homeopathy embraced. He studied diligently, learning which combinations of drugs to prescribe for any particular ailment. The drugs were compounded from plant, animal, or mineral substances and prepared in the form of tinctures and powders, which then were diluted into different strengths. Doctor McCaffrey kept his compounds in glass bottles with cork stoppers. Some were lined up on the cabinet shelf in his office, but most were housed in a square wooden case which could be carried with him on house calls. The case held nearly eighty bottles of different compounds. James struggled to learn the kinds and amounts of compounds to use.

One afternoon in late February, as James sat cleaning surgical instruments in Dr. McCaffrey's office, he heard a light tap at the door.

"I'll get it," Dr. McCaffrey said.

James watched as the doctor stepped to the door and opened it.

"Good afternoon, Doctor," came a woman's voice. "Am I disturbing you?"

"No, not at all. Come inside." McCaffrey ushered the woman into the room. She was bundled in a long woolen shawl, and a bonnet with a wide brim hid most of her face, but James recognized her immediately.

"Hello, Inger," he said, setting aside the instruments he'd been cleaning. He rose from his chair and went to her side.

Inger Johanssen glanced up at him. "Why, hello, James. It's nice to see you."

"Here, let me take your wrap." James held out his hand to receive Inger's shawl, then carefully laid it and her bonnet across a chair.

"Lars told me you were working with Dr. McCaffrey," Inger said with a smile.

"That's right. Dr. McCaffrey has been kind enough to let me associate in his medical practice."

"There's nothing kind about it," McCaffrey said, gesturing for Inger to take a seat. "James is a capable young man. Now, what can I do for you, Miss . . . ?"

Inger supplied the name. "Johanssen. Inger Johanssen."

"All right, Miss Johanssen, tell me what's been troubling you."

James lingered beside Inger's chair, anxious to hear the explanation of her malady.

"Well, it's probably silly of me to bother you with this . . ." Inger began hesitantly.

"Matters of health are never silly, my dear young woman," Dr. McCaffrey assured her.

Inger glanced down at her hands, which were clasped together in her lap. "Ever since the beginning of January I've suffered from a recurring cough, and a tightness here." Her fingers fluttered toward the bodice of her plain blue cotton dress. "Some days, I can barely draw a breath."

James frowned and leaned forward slightly.

"How often does the cough occur?" Dr. McCaffrey asked.

"Many times a day. Some days, I'm worn out with coughing." As if to validate her words, Inger suddenly hunched over in a spasm of coughing—deep, racking coughs that made her shoulders shudder and her eyes fill with tears.

Dr. McCaffrey folded his arms and eyed her intently.

"I'm sorry," Inger gasped. She put a handkerchief to her mouth and coughed into it a time or two more.

When the spell of coughing had passed, Dr. McCaffrey leaned forward in his chair and asked, "When you cough like that, do you expectorate any mucus or blood?"

Inger's eyes darted to James. He saw fear and concern reflected in their blue depths; he put a reassuring hand on her shoulder.

"Once in awhile, yes. A little phlegm," Inger answered in a small voice.

"I'd like to examine you, if I may, Miss Johanssen. Do you mind if James attends?"

"No, that would be fine." Inger looked up at James again. He thought she looked very much like a child with her wide, frightened eyes and wan cheeks. All the color seemed to have fled her face. He noticed that her flaxen hair, wound into a braided bun at the nape of her neck, accentuated the paleness of her complexion.

"Everything will be fine, Inger," he whispered in her ear.

She nodded without speaking.

James watched as Dr. McCaffrey proceeded to examine his patient. He had already guessed what was ailing Inger, but he paid strict attention as the doctor carried out his inspection. When he finished, he invited James to conduct his own examination. With gentle hands and a studious eye, James repeated the doctor's actions. He smiled at Inger when he'd completed the exploration.

"What is your opinion, James?" asked Dr. McCaffrey.

Inger sat upon her chair, twisting the handkerchief in her hands.

"A persistent cough, fever, general weakness— I suspect Miss Johanssen is suffering from inflammation of the lungs due to an onset of winter fever."

Dr. McCaffrey nodded. "I concur with your diagnosis." He turned to Inger. "Now, Miss Johanssen, James is going to compound a drug for you that will relieve your symptoms and get you feeling better. But you must do your part. Get plenty of rest. Stay warm and avoid drafts. Try to expel as much of that phlegm as possible. I know that doesn't sound very ladylike, but the more mucous you can expectorate, the faster your lungs will return to normal."

"All right," Inger replied in a small voice.

"Get lots of rest. That's most important," James reiterated.

"Yes, I will."

While Dr. McCaffrey continued to speak with Inger, James began mixing the compound. He knew just which herbs and medicines to use, and the proper dilutions of each. In a few moments' time he was finished.

"There you are," he said, handing the medicine to Inger. "Mix this powder with half a glass of water and repeat the medication four times a day."

"Thank you, James," Inger replied, giving him a grateful smile.

"If you're not feeling better within ten days or so, come back to the office and let us check you again. But you should be fine," said McCaffrey.

"I appreciate your help, Doctor." Inger stood and reached for her shawl and bonnet. "How much do I owe you?" she asked the doctor.

"That will be three dollars, Miss Johanssen."

Inger's eyes widened. "Oh, dear, I'm afraid I don't have that much money with me. Can I give you one dollar now and bring the rest to you in a week?"

"Of course. That will be fine," McCaffrey replied.

A quick frown creased James' brow. He knew Inger and Lars had little money. The doctor's fee would be a considerable hardship on them. Back in Nauvoo, James had never seen Dr. Bennett charge more than two dollars for an office visit and prescription. He deliberately smoothed the frown from his face as Inger turned to bid him goodbye.

"Take care," James said in parting.

Inger wrapped her shawl around her shoulders and left the office.

"That's the sixth case of winter fever I've seen this month," Dr. McCaffrey said casually as he began putting away the instruments he'd used in Inger's examination.

"Yes. It seems to be a common malady."

"Exactly. Any doctor can more or less predict what his seasonal practice will be. Winter fever, colds, whooping cough, diphtheria during the winter months. Dysentery, summer complaint, cuts, bruises, injuries from accidents in the spring and summer. In the autumn you generally see chills and fevers, ague, and gout. At least once a year you can expect an attack of malaria, sometimes yellow fever, too. Then there's always cholera. A cholera epidemic can ravage whole cities."

McCaffrey ticked off the diseases with a curious detachment. The list sent shivers down James' spine.

"Well, James, I believe I'll close up shop for the evening. I have a few calls to make, and an errand or two to do."

James quickly put away the surgical instruments he'd been cleaning before Inger's visit. Then he reached for his coat and put it on. "I'll see you tomorrow afternoon, Dr. McCaffrey," he said.

"Yes. Tomorrow we'll make the rounds among our bedridden patients."

James nodded. "Good night, then, sir." He let himself out the door and stepped into the street. It was late afternoon, and the shadows were falling across the roofs of the houses in the fort. Smoke curled from every chimney, and the smell of supper roasting tickled his nose.

As James made his way through the slushy snow toward home, his thoughts were filled with the day's activities at Dr. McCaffrey's office. In addition to treating Inger Johanssen, he and the doctor had seen several other patients. One woman had come in complaining of stomach cramps and fever. Another had badly cut her hand on the blade of a cooking knife. A small child, ill with whooping cough, was brought in by his anxious mother. Dr. McCaffrey had allowed James to treat nearly all the patients who came into the office that afternoon. James was gaining a tremendous amount of practical experience, which he supplemented with his reading and studying. His mind swirled with the details he'd memorized concerning treatments, diagnoses, compounding drugs, and dispensing advice. He felt deeply satisfied with his endeavors, and eager to learn and accomplish more. When he went to call on Etta Stanton this evening, he decided, he would tell her about his experiences of the day.

A quick frown ruffled James' forehead as he thought of Etta. The last few times he had kept company with her, she'd seemed unusually quiet and withdrawn. He hoped she wasn't falling ill. Perhaps he should inquire about her health during his visit this evening. He felt a sudden headiness in realizing he could probably treat Etta for any malady from which she might be suffering. His steps were light as he hurried through the snow to his cabin.

Although the inviting smell of supper cooking over the hearth had beckoned James, when he reached home he found only the usual poor fare of fried johnnycake and a bit of salted pork.

Lydia portioned out the food onto plates. "How was your afternoon at Dr. McCaffrey's?" she asked as she handed him a plate.

"Fine. Inger Johanssen came into the office."

"Inger?" Lydia's brow lifted in concern. She glanced at James as she filled Millicent's plate. "Is Inger ill?"

"Yes. She says she hasn't been feeling well for some time. But I gave her some medicine that should make her feel better."

"How do you know which of those medicines to give people?" Millicent wanted to know. She sat at the table next to James.

"That's what I'm learning how to do, Milly. It's really interesting."

"No more talk now until after the blessing on the food is said," Lydia directed as she sat down at the rough wooden table. "James, will you offer the prayer, please?"

James nodded and bowed his head. His prayer was short, but sincere. When everyone at the table had added their "amen," James picked up his knife and sliced off a wedge of johnnycake.

"When will Father be back?" asked Roxana.

"Probably not until late," replied Lydia. "He's helping one of the brethren shore up the roof on his cabin."

"I heard some of the brethren talking about moving out of the fort as soon as the snow melts, and begin building homes on the city lots," James commented.

"Oh, I hope so," Millicent squealed. "Can we build a great big cabin, Mother, with flowers growing around the door?"

Lydia smiled at her youngest daughter. "No reason to build a house bigger than to suit our needs, Milly."

"Will we be able to plant all the vegetables we want, Mother?" This time the question came from Roxana.

"Yes, we'll clear a large garden plot, Roxie. I think most of the vegetables we enjoyed eating back east will also grow well here."

"I'm going to grow my very own pumpkin," Millicent announced. "The biggest, orangest pumpkin anyone ever saw."

"And I'll grow turnips. Elizabeth loves turnips. I'll have some nice plump ones for her when she comes to visit," added Roxana.

James saw a sadness creep into his mother's eyes. "I don't know if Elizabeth and Alexander will be able to come for a visit this summer, Roxie. It's a very long way to travel, you know."

"If not this summer, then perhaps next," James put in quickly.

Lydia glanced at him and smiled.

"Well, I shall grow turnips just the same, in case Elizabeth does come," Roxana replied stoutly.

James listened to his sisters' conversation while he finished his supper. When he was through, he pushed his plate aside and rested his elbows on the table. "If you don't need me here tonight, Mother, I think I'll go visit Etta," he said.

Lydia nodded. "On your way there, would you take some flour over to the Bentons for me?"

"Of course. But, Mother, will that leave enough for you?" James knew his mother had only a few pounds of flour left in the bottom of the flour barrel, and there wasn't much prospect of getting more anytime soon. All the Saints were low on foodstuffs, especially flour and meat. James hadn't tasted a vegetable in months, or a piece of fresh fruit. The family had resorted to eating boiled sego lily roots, cowslip greens, and thistle roots to supplement their meals.

"The Lord won't let us starve, James, and the Bentons have eight children to feed. I'll get the flour."

While Lydia scooped the precious flour into a cloth, James changed into a fresh shirt and combed through his hair. His hair had grown longer over the course of the winter; he wore it parted and combed back off his broad forehead. His eyes were nearly the same shade of brown as his hair, and his cheeks were ruddy from the winter's cold touch.

"You look very handsome," Lydia said as she handed him the coarse cloth tied up at the corners and filled with flour.

"Thank you. I hope Etta thinks so as well."

Lydia smiled. "Tell Etta's mother hello for me."

"I will."

"And don't forget to deliver the flour first, before you call on Etta."

"I won't."

"Oooh, kissy, kissy," Millicent giggled, screwing her lips up as James walked past her toward the door.

James paused, grabbed Millicent, and began tickling her ribs. "This will teach you to keep quiet," he growled playfully.

Millicent wriggled and squirmed as she hooted with laughter.

"Are you ready to eat those words?" he asked.

"Never!" Millicent screamed.

James gave her another round of tickles, then patted her head. "You'd better pipe down," he said to her affectionately. Then he leaned toward Roxana and kissed her cheek. "You, too," he added sternly.

"Me? I never said anything," Roxana protested.

James grinned at the pair of them and left the cabin, shutting the door behind him.

Etta's expression was solemn, and her voice quivered as she invited James inside. The only person in the cabin besides them was Etta's younger brother, Martin. The boy sat on a bed, idly watching the two of them.

"How are you this evening, Etta?" asked James as he took a seat. He noted at once her grave demeanor.

"I'm well, James. And you?"

"Fine, thank you."

An uncomfortable moment of silence ensued. "Is your family away?" James finally asked, seeking a topic of conversation.

"Mother is with a neighbor, and the boys are outside somewhere. Except for Martin." She glanced at her brother.

Martin quickly dropped his gaze, pretending to be interested in his own activities rather than in eavesdropping on his sister's conversation.

James shifted in his chair. He knew Etta was disturbed about something, and he was fairly sure that it had to do with him.

"How is your family?" Etta asked quietly.

"Everyone is fine—anxious for spring to arrive so we can build a proper house outside the fort." James colored suddenly as he realized his comment could be misconstrued to mean marriage and setting up housekeeping with Etta. "Mother asked me to tell Sister Stanton hello for her," he said quickly.

Etta nodded.

The tension between them was building, and it made James' skin prickle. Finally he could bear it no longer. "Something's wrong, Etta. What is it?" he blurted out.

Etta's eyes lowered, and color blossomed in her cheeks. "I'm glad you're here, James. I've been wanting to speak with you."

James braced himself for the blow he knew was coming. "Yes?" he asked hoarsely.

Etta looked up at him for a moment, then dropped her eyes again.

"Go on, Etta. Tell me what's wrong."

"You and I . . ." she paused, clasping her hands together tightly.

"Yes? What about you and me?"

"From the first time I saw you, on the trail west, I knew you were an extraordinary young man, James." The words fell reluctantly from her lips. "We became friends, and then after the tragedy of your brother's death . . ." She stopped, and sudden tears filled her eyes.

The vivid scene leaped into James' mind—Zachary lying still and white on the prairie grass with blood soaking his shirt. His father's horrified look. His mother's terrible scream. James struggled to block out the image.

"After Zachary's passing, we seemed to mean more to each other. Or at least I thought so." Etta's hands fluttered helplessly in her lap. "This is very difficult for me," she murmured.

"Then let me help you," James returned in a brusque voice. He felt furious with himself for causing Etta this grief—for making her have to say these hard, hurtful words. "I've given every indication that I intended to ask your hand in marriage. Yet I've postponed doing so. I'm sorry, Etta." James' glance flickered to the young boy sitting on the bed. Martin's eyes were wide, his expression bright with interest.

"Please, don't, James," Etta whispered.

"Let me finish. I've been a fool, Etta. I should have asked for your hand months ago. I love you. I love you, Etta." James spoke the words tenderly, but with great urgency.

"Please don't say anymore. It will only make things that much harder." Etta turned away from him and covered her eyes with her hands.

James' stomach began churning. He feared Etta was going to tell him she no longer cared for him. He felt suddenly desolate, desperate. His forehead broke out in perspiration. "Etta, I . . ." he began feverishly.

She cut him off with a raise of her hand. "No, James. Let me speak now."

The tears were gone from her eyes, and for the first time since their conversation began, James saw the firm set of her jaw.

"It's true that I did hope we would marry. I kept waiting for you to broach the subject, but you never did."

James' stomach twisted into a knot. "I know that, but . . ."

"Please, let me say what I must before I lose courage." There was a look of desperation in her eyes.

James nodded. He was feeling sick to his stomach.

"I'm not blaming you, James. It's just that I grew tired of waiting, of not knowing how you really felt. I didn't know if you loved me enough. If you'd ever love me enough. That's why I accepted Franklin's proposal of marriage."

James' jaw dropped. "Franklin? Who's Franklin? What are you saying?"

"Franklin Metcalf. I met him about eight weeks ago. He's from Virginia. He's spending the winter here." She paused, dropping her gaze. "He's a gold miner."

"A gold miner!" James exploded. "Etta, this is incredible. I can't believe what I'm hearing. You're going to marry some gold digger from Virginia?"

Etta's eyes were steady when she lifted them. "Yes, James. That is what I'm going to do. Franklin asked me to marry him more than a week ago, and I accepted. I've just been trying to work up the courage to tell you."

"But, Etta, you can't! I love you!" James exclaimed.

"I don't think you really mean that," Etta replied softly.

James jumped up from his chair and began pacing the room. He saw Martin staring open-mouthed at him, but he didn't care if the boy witnessed his passionate outburst. "Etta, you can't be serious. Even aside from the fact that you've decided against me, how can you marry a man who is not a Latter-day Saint, and one whose priority is seeking riches?"

Etta's face hardened. "I really think you're saying things you know nothing about. Franklin is a member of the Church; he was baptized three weeks ago. And his priority is not simply to seek riches. He wants to make a better life for himself—for us."

James was stupefied beyond words. He just stared at Etta. "What does your mother say about all of this?" he finally blurted in exasperation.

Etta's face lost some of its color. "Well, she wasn't pleased in the beginning, but she's accepted it. She had hoped you and I would marry."

James bent down so that his face was only inches from hers. "Are you sure this is what you really want? Because if you don't, I'll ask you this very minute to marry me and . . ."

Etta stood up, facing him. "This is what I want, James. I'm sorry."

James searched her eyes. They seemed like a closed book. He shook his head. "I don't know what else to say."

"Perhaps that's best," Etta returned quietly. "Some things are better left unsaid."

James stared into her face. It was expressionless. She looked like a beautiful marble statute he had once seen pictured in a book belonging to his father. "Well, then, at least let me wish you and Franklin every happiness," he said stiffly.

"Thank you."

"Goodbye, Etta."

She didn't speak as he stepped through the door. When he'd closed it behind him, he let out his breath in an audible groan. He walked away from Etta's door with his stomach writhing. Tears burned in his eyes. He hastened his step, closing the distance between Etta's cabin and his own in long, silent strides. He lashed himself for letting Etta slip away. Self-recrimination and self-ridicule filled his heart. He remembered thinking to himself that Etta might be ill, and how he possessed the skill to cure her. What presumptuousness on his part! What stupidity! He had totally bungled the most important decision of his life.

Suddenly, the door to the family cabin confronted him. He jerked it open and crossed the room in three long strides. His mind registered the fact that Millicent and Roxana were sitting beside the hearth, but he ignored them.

"Oooh, kissy, kissy," Millicent cooed as he walked past.

He heard Roxana giggle.

The teasing was almost more than he could bear. He went to his bed, which was nestled against the cabin wall, and stretched out upon it. He flung an arm over his eyes to stop the tears.

CHAPTER EIGHT

"I heard the symphony," said James as he strained to lift the crossbeam above his shoulders. Lars held the other side of the heavy log, and the two of them hoisted it into place.

"What are you talking about? I thought you and Etta were through," Lars replied. He ran a hand across his forehead, brushing the hair away from his eyes.

"That's what I'm saying. I heard the symphony you were telling me about. When Etta told me she was going to marry that gold seeker, the music came crashing down around my ears. And all the notes were sour ones."

Lars climbed down the ladder he'd been standing on. "I'm sorry it didn't work out between you and Etta. Who would ever have guessed she'd want to marry someone like that?"

"Not me, that's for sure," James replied bitterly. He glanced at the crossbeam. Its notches fit snugly into the logs supporting it at either end.

"Not you what?"

James turned at the sound of Inger's voice. He hadn't heard her enter the log house he and Lars were in the midst of building. "Morning, Inger," he said as he followed Lars down the ladder and stepped onto the dirt floor. "Lars and I were just making small talk."

"Yeah. James was telling me about a music lesson he just had."

James shot his friend a crooked smile, then he turned to Inger. "What do you think?" he asked, indicating the partially-constructed cabin.

"Inger's eye roved over the structure. "It's going to be a wonderful house. Thank you so much for your help, James. Lars and I will be perfectly content here."

"You have a choice lot. The sun will warm your porch all morning, and Lars said he's going to plant a big sycamore tree to shade it in the afternoon."

Inger clapped her hands together. "I can hardly wait. And you, James, will be our first guest in the new house."

"Is that a promise?"

"An absolute promise." She was about to say something more when she was seized with a violent cough. It was a deep, hoarse cough that shook her slim shoulders.

James eyed her anxiously. When she'd quieted he asked, "Are you taking the medicine Dr. McCaffrey prescribed for you?"

Inger's smile was apologetic. "Yes, I'm taking it. But it doesn't seem to be doing me much good."

"Lars told me that you were feeling better," James replied, frowning.

"Truthfully, I am. I'm not coughing nearly as often."

"But you still don't feel well?" James pursued.

"I'm fine, James. Really. Your medicine was a great success. Does that make you feel happier?" she asked, laughing lightly.

"I am interested to hear if the compound helped you, Inger. But I'm more concerned about the status of your health."

"And I'm concerned about you spending too much of your time here, helping Lars build this house. You should be studying your medical books," she scolded.

"She's right," Lars confirmed. "Let's call it a day. I know you have things of your own to do."

"No, I can give you another hour. I'm not due at Dr. McCaffrey's office until after lunch. We can get a couple of these roof beams up before I go," James answered.

"If you're sure you can spare the time, then I accept your offer," Lars replied. He picked up a log that had been split lengthwise.

"You let me know if you're not completely well in the next couple of days," James told Inger sternly.

"Don't worry about me, James. I'll be fine. But if it will make you feel better, I promise to let you know."

"Thank you."

"You're quite welcome." Inger flashed him a mischievous grin. "Now stop standing around and get back to work."

"You're a hard taskmaster, Inger Johanssen."

"Grab hold of the end of this log, will you, James?" Lars asked as he started up the ladder to fix the beam into place.

James gripped the unwieldy plank. "Have you enough split logs to finish the roof?"

"I think so. If not, we'll have to wait until I can get some more. I'm glad to see the snow melting like it is, so we can be building on the city lots outside the fort."

Inger watched the two of them maneuver the beam into place, then she gazed about the log house with a pleased smile on her face. James heard her begin to hum a sprightly tune.

"Is this house going to meet with your approval, sis?" Lars asked her as he hammered the beam onto the log frame.

"I'm going to sew sunny yellow curtains for the window, Lars, and make a cozy rag rug to set before the hearth. You can whitewash the walls, and I'll embroider a sampler to hang above the door. Then we'll plant a lovely little flower garden beside the porch." Inger twirled around the spot where she stood, trying to see every corner of the structure at once.

"Hold on a minute, sis. I haven't even got the place built yet."

"But you will, my darling brother. And then we'll be as cozy as two little peas in a pod."

James chuckled at Inger's words. As he glanced down at her from where he stood on the ladder, he noticed that the March sunshine streaming through the open roof had set Inger's yellow hair aglow. The braided bun at the nape of her neck glistened. His eyes lingered on the pretty picture Inger made standing in the ribbon of sunlight.

"With all your planning and daydreaming, I hope you remembered to bring lunch for us," Lars said to his sister.

"That's one of the reasons I came," Inger replied. "The picnic basket is in the buggy."

"That's good to hear. I thought you drove out here just to see if James and I were working hard enough."

"That, too, of course," Inger grinned. "I'll get the lunch basket."

James watched her walk out to the buggy, parked beside the house, and return with a wicker basket. The basket was covered with a cheery red and white checkered cloth.

"I'll set it here, and you boys can eat when you're ready," Inger told them. She put the luncheon basket on a stump of wood.

"Thanks, Inger," said James. He felt reluctant to take his eyes off her. Her flaxen hair, and the way her skirt hugged her narrow waist, held his gaze. After a few moments more of conversation between the three of them, Inger left in the buggy to return to the fort.

Lars began preparing to hoist another split log to the roof. James stepped to his side. "Tell me the truth, Lars. Is your sister feeling any better at all?"

"Yes, I think she is. Like she said, she's coughing less, and she seems to have gotten her strength back."

"I'm glad to hear it. Winter fever is nothing to snicker about. It can be deadly serious."

"Spoken like a true physician," Lars replied, grinning.

"I don't know, Lars. Maybe I wasn't cut out to be a doctor after all."

"What's that supposed to mean?" asked Lars. The grin dissolved from his face.

"Things haven't been going too well at the office lately."

"What happened?"

"What *hasn't* happened would be more correct," James answered glumly. "I misdiagnosed a patient, for starters."

"That's to be expected. You're just learning the trade, James."

"Yes, but it was an obvious mistake. I overlooked a glaring symptom."

"Ah, that's not so bad," Lars replied.

"Then, yesterday, I made a mistake in mixing the compound for a patient. It could have killed the patient if he had ingested it."

"That is bad," Lars conceded.

"Yes. It was a stroke of luck that Dr. McCaffrey caught my mistake and corrected it. He was furious with me. After the patient left, he let me know in no uncertain terms how careless I'd been."

Lars didn't reply, but his expression was sympathetic.

"That incident could have been disastrous." James shook his head. "I got so puffed up with my knowledge and my burgeoning skills . . . . Perhaps I should give up the idea of becoming a physician."

"Listen to me, James." Lars put a hand on his friend's shoulder. "Don't let this destroy your confidence. You're going to make a fine doctor. And we need doctors badly here in the valley. Just think about Inger. You helped her, didn't you?"

James shrugged. "I don't know. Maybe I don't have the intellect for doctoring."

"You're upset over this thing with Etta Stanton. It's got you a bit rattled. But you'll sort that out, and then you can concentrate on your work. Both Inger and I have full confidence in you."

James gave his friend an appreciative glance. In spite of Lars' show of support, James' confidence was shaken. He'd set high expectations for himself, and he'd fallen short of them. Part of him wanted to give up, set aside his desires and ambitions. The critic within him berated his lack of education, his native intelligence, and his ability to perform the duties required of a physician.

As he helped Lars nail the beams onto the log frame, a struggle raged within him. Should he abandon the profession before he got into it any deeper, or forge ahead with greater effort? Perhaps he couldn't win back Dr. McCaffrey's confidence in him. What if the doctor decided not to turn his practice over to him after all?

"James?"

James' head came up with a start. "Yes?"

"You going to hand me another board, or are you just going to keep pounding nails into that one?" Lars asked.

"Oh. Sorry. Here it is." James hoisted the end of another log up to Lars.

"Once we get this roof in place, we'll really have something to show for our efforts," Lars said as he fit the log against the crossbeam.

"Yeah, that's right," replied James absently.

"James?" This time Lars' voice summoned him out of his reverie.

"What?"

"Quitting isn't in your nature. You wouldn't be here in the valley if you were a quitter."

James looked into his friend's face. Lars' steady gaze lifted his spirits. He smiled ruefully. "I'll try not to lose sight of that fact."

Lars' comment about quitting imbued James with fresh resolve. That afternoon, after he'd finished helping Lars with the house, he went back to his own cabin. Finding himself alone, he poured out his heart in prayer. He thanked God for all the blessings he'd received. He rehearsed his hopes and dreams of becoming a physician, his gratitude for the opportunity to apprentice with Dr. McCaffrey, and his personal fears and concerns over his inabilities. He prayed with singular purpose and an unflinching faith that God would hear and answer his pleas. He must have prayed for an hour or more, although he wasn't aware of the passage of time, and when he was through his heart felt lighter. A few moments later he put on his coat, strode through the cabin door, and walked resolutely toward Dr. McCaffrey's office.

That afternoon at the doctor's office proved to be difficult. Dr. McCaffrey was still aggravated over what he referred to as James' "ineptness." Several patients came into the office to be treated, and McCaffrey watched James closely as he examined, diagnosed, and prescribed treatment for them. James felt ill at ease and insecure, but he doggedly kept at his task. He painstakingly considered every option before making a diagnosis, and he mixed the required compounds with utmost care. He was relieved when the afternoon wore itself out and it was time to leave the office.

"Before you go, James," the doctor said, "I'd like you to make a list of the medicinal solutions we're running low on. I know we need to obtain more tincture of Belladonna and more arsenic salts."

"Yes, sir. I'll do that right away."

"I have one house call to make; I believe I'll do that now. Just lock the door when you leave," McCaffrey instructed.

After the doctor left, James sorted through the various bottles of liniments and medicines that McCaffrey kept on the shelf of the small, glass-fronted cabinet. Then he checked the bottles stored in McCaffrey's felt-lined medicine box, lifting each bottle from the chest to inspect its contents. Some of the compounds were scarcely used, others were nearly gone. James wrote down on a sheet of paper which medicines needed to be replenished.

When he finished his task, he closed the lid on the medicine chest and sat staring at it for a long moment. He thought about Inger Johanssen's comment concerning the compound he had prescribed for her. She seemed to think the compound hadn't helped her malady at all. He drummed his fingers on the top of the medicine box. If the compound hadn't helped Inger, then it shouldn't be prescribed for patients in the future, James reasoned. But what if it had helped other patients? Could the compound have been effective for some patients, but not others?

James stood up and began pacing the floor. In order to answer that question, he told himself, an accurate record needed to be kept. It was necessary to know what medicines were prescribed for which illnesses, and to keep a follow-up report of the results. He knew Dr. McCaffrey kept no such records. Most doctors didn't; they simply treated illnesses according to what they'd studied and learned about disease, and from their own experiences with the practice. But the knowledge one doctor gleaned from years of experience was of little worth to the medical establishment as a whole if he did not pass it on to others. Medical journals were helping; in the last few years, several of them had begun regular publication. But even that was not enough. Physicians still lacked reliable medical statistics, and without them it was impossible to establish relationships between the treatment of an illness and its result, or to check the accuracy of medical theories.

James returned to his seat and took up his pencil again. He smoothed out a clean sheet of paper. Across the top he wrote six headings, or categories, and underlined them in bold strokes. He tapped the paper with the point of his pencil, thinking over what he'd just written. Then he made his first entry.

Patient's Name—"Inger Johanssen"

Approximate Age—James frowned, trying to recall Inger's age. He knew she was a year or two older than he. He entered the information. "21 years"

Symptoms—"Recurring cough, difficulty in breathing, fever, chills, body aches, general weakness"

Diagnosis—"Inflammation of the lungs"

Treatment Prescribed—"Second dilution of Aconite, second dilution of Bryonia, third dilution of Phosphoric Acid"

Results of Treatment—James paused, recalling Inger's explanation of her condition and consolidating his own thoughts. Then he quickly, but carefully, wrote out his conclusions.

He'd just finished with the entry on Inger and begun the next one on a patient he'd seen earlier that afternoon, when a tap sounded at the office door.

James laid aside his pencil and hurried to the door. A blond-haired young man, cradling his left arm against his side, stood anxiously in the doorway. James saw at a glance that the man's forearm was seeping blood through the makeshift bandage tied around it.

"Come in. Let me have a look at that arm," James said briskly.

"Thanks, doc. I ripped it open on the teeth of a saw."

James helped the man into a chair. Then he carefully removed the stained cloth covering the wound. A jagged cut ran across the man's forearm, and it was bleeding profusely.

James quickly took a clean cloth bandage from the shelf and held it tightly over the oozing wound. "You were right to come here directly. This wound will need to be cleaned and stitched up."

The man grimaced.

Upon closer observation, James saw that the man was older than he'd first thought—perhaps in his early thirties. Fine lines creased his brow and the corners of his eyes, and his face was hard and lean. The man's tangled yellow hair hung over his shirt collar. "What's your name?" asked James as he pressed the cloth over the jagged cut.

"Metcalf. Frank Metcalf," the man replied, keeping his eyes glued to the blood leaking through the clean white bandage.

James' whole body suddenly went limp, as if someone had pulled a plug and drained all the strength out of him.

The patient, Metcalf, must have noticed the slackening of pressure on his arm, for he shot a glance at James.

James held the bandage in place with numbed fingers. Franklin Metcalf. Here before him sat the gold digger Etta intended to marry! Anger and resentment sprang up inside him, threatening to overwhelm him. He renewed the tension on Metcalf's arm, willing his hands to perform contrary to the raving fury of his thoughts. He forced his attention back to the wound, making himself see it through the eyes of a physician instead of a man racked with jealously.

"You think it will be all right, doc? I mean, I won't lose the strength in my arm or anything, will I?" Metcalf asked.

A bead of sweat broke out on James' forehead. He wiped it away with the sleeve of his shirt and struggled to answer Metcalf in an even voice. "I won't know how severe the injury is until I can get a clear look at it." He drove his eyes to Metcalf's face. "Keep applying pressure to this wound while I get some disinfectant."

James went to the cabinet containing the surgical instruments, bandages, and liniments. He moved slowly, for his legs felt weighted. He took a clean cloth and a bottle of whiskey from the shelf and returned to Metcalf's side.

The man watched him with a nervous stare.

"Let me see that wound now," James said in a flat voice. He removed the blood-soaked cloth. The wound continued to ooze blood, but the flow was much reduced. James poured whiskey from the bottle onto the clean cloth. "This will sting some," he said to Metcalf without looking at him.

Metcalf's sharp intake of breath greeted James' first application of disinfectant to the injury. "Holy Moses, that hurts!" Metcalf gasped, blowing out his breath.

James continued to dab the injury with the alcohol-laden cloth as he wiped away the blood and cleansed the wound. Metcalf's arm shook involuntarily with each fresh application of the cloth.

With the blood cleaned away, James could better see the extent of the injury. The gash along Metcalf's arm was long, and the skin had spread apart, but it didn't appear to be too deep.

"I don't think you've severed any muscle," James said as he studied the injury. "I'll sew it up for you, and you shouldn't have any lasting ill effects."

"I'm glad of that."

James heard the relief in Metcalf's voice. Somehow it cushioned the dislike he felt for the man.

James secured the surgical needle and thread, and an empty cup. He poured a quantity of whiskey into the cup and handed it to Metcalf. "Drink some of this. It will help dull the pain," he directed.

Metcalf took a gulping swallow, then another. James saw that the man was accustomed to drinking spirits, and the realization filled him with loathing. He threaded the needle with a trembling hand, endeavoring to keep his emotions in check. He refused to let himself think about Etta and this man . . . . Etta with her gentle manner, her fair skin and raven-black hair.

"You ready?" he asked Metcalf roughly.

Metcalf's reply was another deep swig from the cup.

With deft, sure motions, James began to sew closed the gash in Metcalf's arm. As the operation proceeded, Metcalf alternately drank from the cup and cursed under his breath. His profanities aroused a cold fury within James, but he didn't allow his feelings to show. He concentrated on the task before him, keeping a tight rein on his emotions.

When at last he finished the sutures, he laid the needle and thread aside.

"Is that it?" Metcalf asked.

"Yes. I'm through."

Metcalf uttered a profane phrase to express his relief.

Wordlessly, James wrapped the wound in a clean bandage. Then he said, "Keep this bandage on for three days, then come back to the office and let me look at the wound. If it's healing properly, you won't need to come in again."

"Thanks, doc. I really appreciate your help," Metcalf replied.

"You're welcome," James answered coldly. He began putting the medical supplies back into the cabinet.

Metcalf dug into his pocket and withdrew a roll of paper currency. "How much do I owe you for your work, doc?" he asked as he peeled away several bills from the lot.

"Dr. McCaffrey generally charges four dollars for stitching up cuts. I charge three," James replied brusquely.

"You mean you ain't Doc McCaffrey?" asked Metcalf in surprise.

"No, I'm not. I'm Dr. McCaffrey's assistant. My name is James Kade."

"Kade?" Metcalf repeated. One brow slowly rose as Metcalf digested this information. Then a faint look of amusement crept into his eyes. "So, you're the young doctor I've been hearing about."

The innuendo behind Metcalf's remark was unmistakable, and James felt anger spilling out of him. It took every ounce of control James possessed to keep from clenching his fists. "That will be three dollars," he restated in a low voice.

Metcalf's gaze was insolent. James met his stare, his eyes burning with fury. The two men stood silently for an instant, face to face. Then Metcalf gave him an arrogant grin. He counted three dollars and held the money out.

James took the bills without a word, then turned his back on Metcalf and continued placing the instruments he'd used on the cabinet shelf. He jerked at the sound of Metcalf slamming the office door behind him.

James put his hands on the shelf in front of him and clenched it so tightly his knuckles turned white. He lowered his head and shut his eyes. A low moan escaped his lips. Etta. Etta and this man—this gold seeker with the foul mouth. Metcalf's arrogant smile flaunted itself behind James' closed eyes. He slammed his fist on the cabinet shelf, and the medicine bottles on the shelf jumped with the impact. The sound of rattling glass brought his head up, and his eyes flew open as a frightening thought struck him. With hands shaking, he checked the bottles lining the shelf of the medicine cabinet. If he had cracked or broken any of the glass bottles in his outburst of temper . . . His heart pounded in his chest. Dr. McCaffrey was already displeased with him, and it wasn't difficult to imagine what the doctor's reaction would be if he found his medicines disturbed. Perspiration dotted James' brow as he carefully examined each cork-stoppered bottle on the shelf. When he was finished, he went over the whole process again to make certain his eyes hadn't betrayed him. At last, when he was satisfied that all the medicine bottles were intact, he carefully closed the cabinet door.

He sank down on a chair and put his head in his hands. If he was going to become a physician, he scolded himself, he must be able to control his personal feelings. Today, he had almost let emotion overpower reason. He promised himself that he would never again lose control of his passions when he was acting in a professional capacity. He gave himself a long and severe lecture on that topic. Afterward he felt exhausted, drained.

Wearily, he pulled his chair over to the table where he had been writing before Metcalf's visit. He read over what he'd written on the paper, then picked up his pencil. He paused for a moment, the pencil poised above the sheet of paper. Then he proceeded to write in a slow, clear hand, finishing the entry for a patient he'd seen earlier in the day. He followed that with the case history of another patient. Finally, he wrote the words "Franklin Metcalf" in the column marked **Patient's Name**. He gripped the pencil tighter, forcing himself to write the words in an impartial, clinical fashion. He filled in the information called for under all six headings on his sheet of paper, then laid down his pencil.

He sat for a time, letting his thoughts run loose. Drawing a long, deep breath, he made a silent vow to himself. He, James Kade, would in fact become a physician. Despite his lack of formal medical training, his family's modest means, and his own human frailties, he was determined to become a skilled doctor. He would study, sacrifice his time and means, do whatever was required to become a trained physician. And, with God's help, he would succeed in using that knowledge to ease the suffering and sickness of all those within his reach. He promised himself that.

*"Time was, and that not two years and a half ago,
when every house was full and every farm under cultivation;
now, everything looks forlorn and desolate,
not half the buildings are occupied, . . .
The stores are closed. The farms are running to waste.
The streets are overgrown with grass."*

J. H. Backingham,
a visitor to Nauvoo

CHAPTER NINE

Elizabeth refolded the letter and slipped it into the pocket of her skirt. She paused outside the door of the mercantile, glancing at the rain-slicked, rutted road. Gathering her skirts in one hand, she stepped into the street, carefully avoiding the puddles of muddy water left by the spring rains.

"Mornin', Mrs. Scott," hailed a woman coming from across the street. Elizabeth looked up, planting a quick smile on her face.

"Hello, Mrs. Palmer," she replied in a friendly tone. As soon as the older woman had passed by, Elizabeth frowned. "The old cow," she muttered under her breath. Mrs. Palmer's husband, Nathaniel Palmer, had taken his order for a large delivery of lumber to a mill other than the one owned and operated by Elizabeth's husband. Elizabeth never forgot nor forgave a slight.

Elizabeth continued across the road and onto the plank sidewalk that ran parallel to the many shops bordering Mulholland Street. She patted the pocket of her skirt, making sure the letter from her brother was still safely harbored there. She hurried down the sidewalk, eager to reach her doorstep so she could read James' letter a second time. She'd given it only a cursory glance while inside the mercantile, which also served as the post office, just enough to make sure the letter bore no ill news from the valley.

Elizabeth continued up Mulholland Street until it intersected Camden Street. She nodded at several passersby, most of whom greeted her pleasantly, although the smiles on the faces of a few of the townsfolk were as artificial as Elizabeth's own. These were people who had known Elizabeth's family—known they were Mormons, and hated Elizabeth for it. Elizabeth shrugged her shoulders. She didn't much care what the old cronies thought of her. As long as she and Alexander enjoyed the respect and attention of the wealthier citizens of Nauvoo, Elizabeth was happy.

She drew up in front of the handsome two-story frame home Alexander had built for them. It was constructed in the Greek Revival style and painted a brilliant white. A single slender column flanked either side of the door. Each corner of the house was fitted with a flat pilaster crowned by a Doric column cap. The small-paned windows were equipped with shutters, and fan-shaped ornaments decorated both gables. The classic lines of the house appealed to Elizabeth's aesthetic tastes.

Elizabeth opened the front door and went inside. Laying her cloak aside, she deposited the few packages she'd brought home from the mercantile onto a polished mahogany side table and sank down into her favorite upholstered chair. She withdrew James' letter from her skirt pocket and unfolded it. It was dated the first of March, 1849—little more than six weeks ago. By some lucky stroke, her brother had located a traveler coming east who agreed to carry the letter with him, and upon passing through Nauvoo had deposited it at the post office.

Her eyes passed leisurely over James' meticulous handwriting. The letter consisted of three closely-written pages. James and the rest of the family were well, her brother reported. The winter had been difficult, but now that spring was near, the brethren were busily engaged in clearing ground for their crops and building permanent homes. The family had moved out of the confines of the fort and built a comfortable log cabin with logs hauled from the canyons. James' remark about wishing Alexander's sawmill was closer at hand brought a smile to Elizabeth's lips.

She finished reading the first page and turned to the second. James spoke enthusiastically about his practice with Dr. McCaffrey. He mentioned some of his patients by name, briefly describing their maladies and treatment. He wrote of his association with Lars Johanssen and Lars' sister, Inger. Elizabeth's brow creased at the mention of Inger's name. She had no interest in the plain girl who had once been her childhood friend. She smoothed out the pages of James' letter and read further. The rest consisted mostly of inquiries about herself, Alexander, and the state of affairs in Nauvoo. He concluded with a wish for her continued good health, and expressed hope that she and Alexander might come out west one day soon.

Elizabeth sat staring at the letter after she'd finished reading it. James' words elicited in her an intense longing for her family. She'd once broached the subject of traveling west to visit her family, but Alexander had promptly dismissed the idea. He said he had no desire to travel the great distance required, and he certainly did not have the time to spare from his business. Elizabeth knew better than to ask him again. She'd learned that Alexander could fly into a rage at the slightest provocation.

Her eyes wandered over the pages of James' letter again. He'd written about several friends and acquaintances, but strangely there was no mention of Etta Stanton. Elizabeth thought that was odd. His other letters since arriving in the valley had been filled with Etta's name. And her parents' letters intimated he was quite serious-minded about the young woman.

Elizabeth folded the letter carefully and went upstairs to put it with the rest of her correspondence in the bottom drawer of her bureau. As she wiped away a speck of dust from the bureau, her eye traveled over the contours of the beautiful rosewood chest of drawers with the brass ring handles. Alexander had ordered the handsome piece, along with the matching side table and bedstead, from a furniture dealer in Springfield. Elizabeth's entire house was filled with lovely furniture. Her fine china was stored in a carved mahogany cupboard, with her polished silver service displayed on top. The house and its trappings gave her immense pleasure.

She returned to the parlor and glanced at the tall clock standing against the wall. Four-thirty. Alexander would be home from the mill in less than an hour. She hurried into the kitchen area to start supper. Alexander wanted his supper promptly so he could leave on time for his meeting. Every Wednesday, the Masons met together in the Masonic Hall on Main Street. Elizabeth was aware of the fact that Alexander did not care a whit about the Brotherhood, but his membership in the organization was a good way to rub shoulders with the men in town in order to solicit business for his lumber mill.

An hour later, Elizabeth had a hot supper prepared and waiting for her husband. She set the table with an embroidered cloth and her fine china. She filled a crystal pitcher with water from the pump outside the house and placed it on the table. Then she sat down to wait for Alexander. In a few minutes, she heard the sound of hoofbeats. Pulling aside the lace curtain on the parlor window, she glanced out to see Alexander swinging down from his saddle. She watched him tie the reins around the hitching post at the side of the house; the sight of him made her heart beat a little faster.

She went to the front door and opened it for her husband. He smiled when he saw her.

"Hello, sweetheart," Elizabeth greeted him.

Alexander paused in the doorway to give her a kiss on the cheek.

"Are you hungry?" she asked, standing close to him. She loved the smell of him, and the curl of his mouth when he smiled.

"Starving," Alexander replied.

"Good, because I have chicken and dumplings in the pot."

He took off his hat, brushed the sawdust from it, and hung it on a peg beside the door. Elizabeth closed the door behind him.

"I have to hurry with supper," Alexander said. "I've a meeting tonight."

"I know." Elizabeth quickly dished him a plate of hot food, then she filled a plate for herself and sat down next to him at the table.

"This is real tasty," Alexander mumbled with his mouth full of gravy-sodden dumpling.

Elizabeth smiled at the compliment. "Thank you. Did you have a good day at the mill?"

Alexander shrugged his shoulders as he shoveled another bite into his mouth. "Just business as usual," he said.

Elizabeth ate her own chicken and dumplings in small, slow bites. She watched Alexander enjoy his food.

"So, how was your day?" Alexander asked. He reached for her hand and held it in his for a moment. "What did you do with yourself all day?"

"Well, I purchased a few things at the mercantile. And I stopped at the dressmaker's."

Alexander smiled. "The dressmaker's. Your day wouldn't be complete without stopping at the dressmaker's, would it?"

Elizabeth leaned over and planted a kiss on Alexander's mouth. "I'm having a new dress made for the town picnic this Saturday. You know, the one the Icarians are sponsoring to raise money to purchase the temple block."

"Yes, I know about the picnic," Alexander replied with a grin. "What color is the dress you're having made?"

"Indigo blue. It's beautiful. The skirt is ruffled along the hem, and embellished with a fancy border," Elizabeth answered. "And I'm having a blue velvet bonnet made to match. You're going to like it."

"I'm sure I will. And I hope I'm going to like the price, as well."

"I've given every consideration to your pocketbook," Elizabeth replied, giving him a coy smile.

"Uh-huh," Alexander grunted, taking another bite from his fork.

"Anyway, sweetheart, while I was at the mercantile today I struck up a conversation with a young woman who belongs to that group of French Icarians in town. She was quite friendly. She said more of her people will be moving into Nauvoo this summer."

Alexander nodded.

"They'll need lumber for new homes," Elizabeth continued.

"Yes, they will."

"They're nice people, don't you think? At least the ones I've met seem to be happy about settling in Nauvoo."

"The group's leader, Mr. Cabet, is a smart man. He knows how to get what he wants for his society of friends. They're some kind of communal group, aren't they?" Alexander asked as he finished the last of his chicken and dumplings.

"I believe so. I don't know too much about them yet."

Alexander set down his fork.

"Would you like more to eat?" Elizabeth asked, putting her hand on his arm.

"No, I'm through. It was a good meal, though," he added. "I really need to go now, or I'll be late for the Masonic meeting."

He stood up from the table and started for the door. Elizabeth rose from her chair, too.

"Will you be long?" she asked.

"I don't know, maybe a couple of hours. Sometimes the men get long-winded. I'll get back as early as I can, all right?"

Elizabeth went to his side as he took his hat from the peg beside the door. She leaned on tiptoe to kiss him. He returned her kiss with a hardy kiss of his own.

"Don't wait up for me, in case I'm late." Alexander gave her a quick smile and left the house. Elizabeth watched him mount his horse and ride off down the muddy road.

She watched until he turned the corner and was gone from sight, then she closed the door with a sigh. Alexander always seemed to be in a hurry to get somewhere. He either had a meeting to attend, or an errand to run, or a business appointment to keep. He was seldom home. Elizabeth sighed a second time. She missed his company; the evenings dragged when Alexander was away. Surveying the dirty dishes on the table, she didn't feel inclined to clean them up just yet. She sat back down in her chair at the table and put her chin in her hand. She drummed her fingers on the tabletop and thought again about her brother's letter. She hadn't mentioned the letter to Alexander; he didn't have the best of feelings for James, so she'd deliberately refrained from telling him about the correspondence.

From his words, James had sounded happy and busy. She framed a picture of him in her mind. Dark, curling hair. Serious eyes. Sensitive mouth. The picture she harbored was more than three years old; it had been that long since she had seen James. He would look a bit older now, of course—perhaps taller and leaner. But the image in her mind refused to shape James in any other form than how he had looked the last time she saw him, waving at her with a solemn expression as he trudged behind the rear of their family's covered wagon. She'd held back her tears until the wagon was out of sight; she hadn't wanted her parents to guess how much she was hurting inside at their parting.

Not that she was sorry about remaining in Nauvoo. Or about marrying Alexander. She loved both Alexander and the town. Nauvoo had changed somewhat since that day her family pulled away with their few possessions packed inside the wagon. The beautiful brick house they'd owned on Durphey Street was sold to one of the "new citizens" who flocked to Nauvoo after the Saints' exodus. Many of the vacated properties had been purchased for little more than the payment of back taxes. Some of the homes, however, hadn't found new owners and were falling into disrepair. Town life seemed to be moving away from the flats, where the Saints had settled, to the bluffs above. And it really seemed a better place to build; the ground there was higher and drier than the flat lands. New streets were being laid out, with homes and buildings bordering them. Elizabeth's own pretty home on Camden Street was one of those. Alexander had commissioned the finest carpenters and craftsmen to build their two-story dwelling of sturdy white pine. The house was large and spacious. Alexander's profits from the lumberyard had paid for the new home and the rooms of new furniture within it. His lumber mill had been a fruitful enterprise from the beginning. The mill was located near the river, where raw timber could easily be rafted downstream into Nauvoo. With all the building going on in the city, business was thriving. Alexander had been right about establishing his mill in Nauvoo. It was turning a handsome profit.

But the mill also took Alexander away from home much of the time. He was adamant about overseeing every detail that went on at the lumberyard. Elizabeth knew he was a shrewd and aggressive businessman; and while those qualities disaffected a few of his customers and most of his competitors, she realized they were the very qualities which made Alexander so successful.

Elizabeth idly toyed with a dinner spoon lying on the table. The spoon was of gleaming silver, polished to a high luster. Holding it up to her face, Elizabeth could practically see her reflection in it. Her shoulder-length blonde hair was pulled up at the sides and caught into a mass of golden curls cascading down her back. Her cheeks were rouged to a pink shine. The lace collar of her satin dress fit snugly around her neck. But the eyes staring back at her from the glistening utensil looked a trifle sad.

Elizabeth pushed a lock of straying hair out of her eyes as she stood surveying the crowd of people gathered on the town square. "It looks like everyone in the whole county is here," she commented to the dark-haired young woman at her side.

"I imagine we've raised over a hundred dollars already," the young woman observed. "Have you ever seen so many beautiful cakes and pies all laid out in one place? It's no wonder they're selling quickly."

Elizabeth nodded in agreement. Her eye followed the seemingly endless line of baked goods piled on tables set out on the grassy square.

"This bazaar will be such a big help toward raising funds to purchase the temple lot," Marie remarked.

Elizabeth glanced at the young woman standing beside her. She had become acquainted with Marie Le Sueur, and her husband Emile, only a few days earlier while shopping at the mercantile on Mulholland Street. The two of them had arrived in Nauvoo with the first group of Icarians to come upriver from New Orleans. Marie was twenty-two, a year older than Elizabeth. Elizabeth thought she was a pretty woman; her dark hair and eyes created a compelling contrast against her fair skin. She was slimmer than Elizabeth, and a bit taller.

"It will be nice to see the old temple building being put to use again," Elizabeth commented. "I thought that would be the end of the building after the arsonist set his torch to it last October."

Marie smiled serenely. "Our people can rebuild the burned parts easily enough. It will be a perfect structure for our needs."

A series of gunshots sounding from the street startled Elizabeth. The shots were followed by raucous laughter and the slurred shouts of drunken revelers. It seemed the entire town had turned out to take advantage of the festivities. Women milled around the food-laden tables. Children darted through the crowd as they played a rowdy game of tag, oblivious to the disapproving frowns of their elders. The rougher elements in town were enjoying their whiskey, betting on horse races, or pitting their strength against one another in a series of wrestling matches on the grass.

The weather had given its full cooperation. Although the first few days of April had been rainy, this afternoon was sunny and warm. Elizabeth enjoyed the feel of the sun on her face as she stood beside Marie, watching the crowd. The narrow-brimmed, blue velvet bonnet she wore complemented her ruffled velvet dress. The dress was a perfect fit. Elizabeth was aware of how attractive she looked in her stylish new clothes.

"Is your husband here this afternoon?" Marie asked.

"Alexander is somewhere about," Elizabeth replied. She shaded her eyes with her hand as she gazed at the throng of people strolling about the square. "He's probably racing his stallion. He swears it's the fastest horse in all of Illinois."

Marie laughed softly. "And is it the fastest?"

"I'll put it this way: Alexander always has money jingling in his pocket after a horse race."

"Then the horse is either very fast, or your husband is very shrewd," Marie said, smiling.

"I suppose it is a little bit of both," Elizabeth agreed. Whooping and hollering from the direction of the street, and then a sudden pounding of hooves against the hard-packed dirt of the road, confirmed the fact that the men were running yet another horse race. Elizabeth strained to see through the crowd, searching for Alexander's handsome face.

"Afternoon, Elizabeth."

Elizabeth turned at the sound of the young man's voice.

"Why, hello, young Joseph. Are you enjoying yourself this afternoon?"

"I am, thank you," Joseph answered. "How much would that berry pie be?"

Elizabeth glanced at the pie the youth was eyeing hungrily. "Twenty-five cents. Would you like to buy it?"

"I sure would." Joseph fished into his trouser pocket and withdrew several shiny coins. He counted out twenty-five cents' worth into Elizabeth's hand. She gave him the pie.

"How is Julia?" Elizabeth asked.

"She's fine. Still seeing plenty of her beau, Elisha Dixon. I think they'll be getting married soon," Joseph confided.

"Elisha is a nice fellow. Tell Julia hello for me, will you? I haven't seen her in ages."

Joseph nodded. He was a stout lad with intense dark eyes and dark hair. Elizabeth noticed the beginnings of a scruffy beard on his face.

"What's this?" she asked teasingly, giving his chin a pinch. "You're not old enough to grow a beard."

"I'll be seventeen in November," Joseph returned.

"So you will," Elizabeth said with a grin. "And growing into quite a handsome fellow. Joseph, do you know Mrs. Le Sueur?"

Joseph shook his head.

"Marie, this is young Joseph Smith. His mother operates the Mansion House, and Joseph is her ablest assistant."

Marie smiled at the youth. "I've heard that your mother runs a fine hotel. She's Mrs. Bidamon, isn't she?"

"Yes, ma'am."

"It's very nice to meet you, Joseph," Marie replied.

"Thank you, ma'am." Joseph was rocking on his feet, eager to be off with his pie.

"Enjoy your berry pie," Elizabeth told him as he turned to leave. He waved a hand as he disappeared into the throng.

"That was the Prophet's son?" Marie inquired when Joseph was out of earshot.

"Yes. His oldest son. You've heard of the Prophet Joseph Smith?"

"Oh, yes. I imagine anyone living in Nauvoo has heard about Joseph Smith. He has quite a reputation."

"Indeed," Elizabeth muttered. She was sorry she'd asked the question. She surely had no desire to pursue the topic with Marie.

"Did you know the man?" Marie asked.

"Yes, I did," Elizabeth answered tersely. She busied herself rearranging the pies on the table.

"Really? How fascinating. What was he like? I've heard from some that he was a great scoundrel, and from others that he was a man of God. What was your opinion of him?" Marie's dark eyes flashed with curiosity.

"I didn't know him very well," Elizabeth answered. "I was still quite young when he was killed." Elizabeth hoped that would be the end of Marie's questions. She didn't wish to be drawn into a discussion about Joseph Smith or the Church. And she especially didn't want Marie dredging up the fact that she'd once been numbered with the Saints.

"Yes, murdered. Murdered right in his jail cell, wasn't he? My, what a travesty. Whether he was guilty of crimes or not, it was certainly an injustice to be cut down by a lawless mob," Marie observed.

"Those were troubling times. I think everyone in Nauvoo is glad to see things settle down and return to an ordinary way of life. I know I am." Elizabeth frowned. The tumultuous years she'd spent in Missouri and Nauvoo still caused her nightmares. Some nights, she awoke from her sleep shaken and sweating with fear.

Marie was silent for a moment. Then she asked, "Do any Mormons still live here in Nauvoo?"

Elizabeth avoided the dark brown eyes peering into hers. "A few. Nearly all of them have moved out west."

"Oh? I didn't know that. To California territory?"

"A place called the Great Basin. It's located in the mountains of the Rockies." A sudden image of James flashed into Elizabeth's mind. She saw her brother seated in the parlor of their brick home, eyeing her with a somber expression as she told her parents she wasn't going west with them. She shuddered at the image.

"I suppose they won't be bothered there by their enemies," Marie commented.

"I hope not," Elizabeth replied under her breath. James, Roxana, Millicent—sometimes she missed her family so much the pain was physical in nature. She couldn't think of her mother without her heart aching. Even Christian's memory elicited a sense of melancholy, and that was a contradiction. She had never gotten along well with her stepfather; she had, in fact, convinced herself that she despised him. But time and distance had softened her attitude toward him. The thought made her smile wryly.

"The widow remarried, then? After the Prophet's death?" Marie asked after a pause.

"Emma? Yes. She's married to Colonel Bidamon, a successful storekeeper," Elizabeth said.

Marie fell silent, apparently digesting this last bit of information.

It seemed a good opportunity to direct the conversation into a different channel. "Is your house nearly finished being refurbished, Marie?"

"Emile thinks we will be through by the end of the month. Oh, I do hope so. It will be wonderful to have our own home. Not that the boarding house where we've been staying has been unpleasant. It's very nice. But I shall enjoy having my own place."

"If Emile needs an extra hand, I'm sure my husband would be happy to help," Elizabeth volunteered. She knew Emile and Marie had purchased one of the homes on the flats left vacant by a Mormon family moving west. They'd acquired it for an extremely good price.

"That's very kind, Elizabeth."

Elizabeth nodded graciously.

"I've not yet met your husband. That wouldn't be Alexander standing next to that tree, would it? I've noticed him watching you."

Elizabeth's eyes traveled in the direction Marie indicated. Across the square, leaning against the trunk of a large elm tree, was a man with shaggy black hair and a heavy beard. He had on a pair of worn, brown baggy trousers and a flannel shirt. An old felt hat was jammed under one arm.

"No, that's not Alexander. I've never seen that man before." Elizabeth shot the man a second quick glance. He did, indeed, seem to be staring at her. When her eyes met his, he gave her a slow, deliberate nod.

"Are you sure he's not an acquaintance of yours?" Elizabeth whispered. "Perhaps he's one of your group. He rather looks French."

"No, I don't think so. I know nearly all the Icarians here, and I don't believe he belongs to our society."

"Uh-oh, here he comes," Elizabeth mumbled. The man had moved away from the tree and was walking toward them. As he approached, Elizabeth could see the swarthiness of his complexion and a dull glimmer in his brown eyes.

In another moment he was at her side. He paused, eyeing her boldly.

"May I help you?" Elizabeth asked in a cold tone. She didn't care for the man's audacious stare.

"I hope so. Would you be Elizabeth Dawson?" the man asked in a low, guttural voice.

Elizabeth's heart skipped a beat. No one had called her by her natural father's name since she was a child. "Perhaps," she answered cautiously. "Who wants to know?"

A slow smile flickered at the corners of the man's mouth, then disappeared. "Spunky, aren't you? Like your pa."

Elizabeth's breath caught in her throat. "Did you know my father?" The words came out in a hoarse rush. She was instantly sorry that she hadn't controlled her eagerness.

She felt the soft touch of Marie's hand on her shoulder, as if urging her to be wary.

The man tipped back his head and gave a short, harsh laugh. "Did I know your father? For pity's sake, what kind of man wouldn't know his own brother?"

The words struck her with powerful force. She stared at the man's coal-brown eyes and curly black beard. The visage resurrected memories Elizabeth had long since buried. And the memories filled her with excitement. "What are you saying?" Elizabeth exclaimed, her heart hammering in her chest. "That you are my uncle?"

"Benjamin Dawson, at your service." The man bowed from the waist, sweeping the air with his stained and rumpled felt hat.

CHAPTER TEN

Elizabeth stared, open-mouthed, at the bearded man.

"If you're Elizabeth Dawson, the daughter of my dead brother, Abraham Dawson—God rest his soul—then I'm your next of kin. In the flesh."

"Elizabeth, perhaps you ought to . . ." Elizabeth paid no heed to Marie's murmured word of caution in her ear. Her mind kept racing around the fact that this was her uncle standing in front of her. Her father's brother! She felt like hugging him—would have, in fact, if she hadn't been standing in such a public place with hundreds of people milling around her.

"I can't believe this," she exclaimed. "This is wonderful! I didn't think I'd ever see any of my father's family again. Ever meet them. I can't believe it," she repeated.

Benjamin Dawson slapped his hat against his knee and then plunked it on his head. "For pity's sake, darlin', I'm about as tickled as a polecat up a tree to finally hook up with you."

"How did you find me? How did you even know where to look?" Elizabeth asked breathlessly.

"My brothers and me heard tell that you and your mama took off to Quincy after your pa died . . ." Benjamin Dawson began.

"That's right. Mother, me, and my brother, James. James and I were just children when Papa died," Elizabeth broke in eagerly.

"Yep. You and James would have just been young 'uns," Benjamin agreed, nodding his shaggy head up and down.

"You looked for us in Quincy?" Elizabeth asked.

"Not right off, you understand," her uncle answered hastily. "Things was kind of in an uproar at home at the time. Jeremiah, Nathaniel, and me couldn't get away to come a lookin' for you for a spell."

"Uncle Jeremiah and Uncle Nathaniel. I haven't heard their names in years. How are your brothers?"

"They're good. They'll be real happy to hear I found their little niece, that's for sure."

Elizabeth beamed with pleasure. She wanted to pinch herself to make sure she wasn't dreaming. After all these years, her uncles still remembered and cared about her. She danced on tiptoe, barely able to contain the excitement coursing through her. "By the time you came looking for us in Quincy, we'd already moved on to Independence, Missouri," she told her uncle.

"Is that right? Missouri. Well, no wonder we couldn't find no trace of you."

"Yes, we lived in Missouri for nearly six years. Then we moved to Nauvoo. My mother, her husband, and the rest of my brothers and sisters left Nauvoo three years ago to settle out west—in the Great Basin."

"Is that a fact? Well, I'd say it was nothing short of a miracle that I even laid eyes on you, what with all that movin' around."

Elizabeth suddenly remembered Marie, standing patiently at her side. She reached out to take Marie's arm. "Uncle Benjamin, this is my friend, Marie Le Sueur."

Benjamin Dawson swept his hat from his head. "Pleased to make your acquaintance, ma'am."

Marie smiled briefly. Elizabeth detected a hint of reserve in her demeanor.

"Uncle Benjamin, you must meet my husband, Alexander. And you must come to supper at our home. Can you come tonight? It would give me great pleasure to entertain you in our home."

"Why, thank ye, I'd like that. I surely would."

"All right. We live on Camden Street. You can recognize the house because it's the only white frame home on the block. It has two pillars beside the door, and—"

"I'll find it. And I'll be awaitin' with pleasure to spend the evenin' with you." Benjamin Dawson replaced his soiled hat and prepared to leave.

"Six o'clock. Will that be satisfactory with you?" Elizabeth asked with a broad smile.

"Satisfactory as a honey bee makin' for its hive. I'll see you at six, darlin'."

Elizabeth watched him turn and walk away. In a matter of seconds, he was swallowed up in the crowd. "Oh, Marie, this is incredible! I never believed I'd see my father's side of the family again. I'm so happy." Elizabeth squeezed Marie's arm.

"I'm happy for you, Elizabeth," Marie replied.

She didn't sound happy, though. Or look particularly happy, Elizabeth thought as she eyed her friend's face. "What is it, Marie? Something's bothering you," Elizabeth said, dropping her hand from Marie's arm.

"I don't want to spoil your happiness, Elizabeth, but should you trust this stranger quite so completely?"

"He's my uncle," Elizabeth replied with a puzzled frown. "Why shouldn't I trust him?"

"I don't know. Something about his manner struck me as insincere. Perhaps I'm wrong," Marie said, a frown rumpling her smooth brow.

"Oh, yes, you have to be wrong about that. You heard him; he was excited to finally find me."

"Yes, he seemed to be. But didn't you think it was odd that he didn't inquire about your brother?"

"My brother?" Elizabeth repeated, blinking at Marie.

"I got the impression he wasn't aware of your brother's existence until you told him."

"Well, he probably didn't remember James. It's been a very long time since he's seen or heard from us." Marie's words stirred up an uneasy feeling in the pit of Elizabeth's stomach.

"Perhaps you shouldn't be so quick to tell him about yourself and your family. At least until you find out what he wants."

Elizabeth forced a smile. "Marie, I'm surprised by your skepticism. My uncle is glad to see me, that's all. And I'm awfully glad to see him. Now, let's hurry and sell these pies so I can get home to start supper."

Elizabeth spent the next hour at the town picnic. She hoped Alexander would come by the table where she stood selling pies because she wanted to tell him about her uncle's visit. But Alexander must have been enjoying himself with his friends, for she didn't see a sign of him. Finally, she left the square and hurried home. She fretted over what to prepare for supper, and decided upon a hearty stew. Her uncle probably hadn't had a good, filling meal while traveling from Green County to Nauvoo.

She hummed as she set about readying supper. She was anxious for Alexander to arrive home so she could tell him about the surprising meeting with her uncle, and she hoped he'd be pleased that her long-lost relative was coming to pay a call. Brushing aside every negative thought, she lost herself in the thrill and pleasure of re-establishing contact with her father's family.

Elizabeth cleared the supper dishes from the table while Alexander started a fire in the hearth. Her uncle leaned back in his chair and wiped his mouth with the sleeve of his shirt.

"That was a mighty fine meal, darlin'," he said to Elizabeth. "I ain't et that good of stew in a long time."

"I'm glad you enjoyed it, Uncle Benjamin," Elizabeth replied, warmed by his complimentary words.

"Pull your chair up by the hearth here, Benjamin," Alexander directed, as he placed another log on the fire. The flames leaped up, snapping and crackling as they ate at the wood. Alexander seated himself in a comfortable chair near the hearth. Although the day had been sunny and warm, the evening had brought with it a shower of rain. The fire burned brightly against the dreary weather outside.

Benjamin Dawson situated his chair across from Alexander's. He rubbed his big, broad hands together, then held them out toward the flames. "This is a comfortable house you've built, Alexander," he observed.

"We like it," Alexander replied, smiling.

Elizabeth glanced at the two men beside the hearth. She watched as her uncle held his big hands out to the fire. The picture triggered a memory in her mind; she saw her father doing the same thing. His were big, strong hands, too. She could see him holding them toward the fire on a cold winter's night. It was strange how vividly she remembered her father's hands. They had symbolized security to her. As a young girl, she had trusted her father's strong hands.

"Did you get your timber for this home from around these parts?" Benjamin asked.

"No, this lumber was rafted from Wisconsin. We get much of our raw lumber for the mill from the forests in Wisconsin," Alexander replied.

Benjamin nodded. "Seems like my brothers and me have to keep goin' further and further away to cut trees. Sometimes bein' a logger ain't no picnic."

This time it was Alexander's turn to nod. "Elizabeth's father logged for a time, too, didn't he?" Alexander asked.

"That's right. Us four brothers worked together with my pa for a lot of years. 'Til Abraham up and got married to that little gal's mother," Benjamin replied, gesturing toward Elizabeth.

Elizabeth put away the last of the supper dishes and went to her uncle's side. She placed her hands on his shoulders. "I remember hearing Papa talk about his lumbering days. He and Mama had some happy times."

Benjamin reached up and patted Elizabeth's hand. "Your pa sure did love your ma, that's a fact."

Tears formed unexpectedly in Elizabeth's eyes. Hearing her uncle speak about her parents in such intimate terms wrenched her emotions. She had never really gotten over the death of her father—she'd felt cheated by his loss. The wound was made deeper with her mother's marriage to Christian. Even now, Elizabeth felt resentment spark inside her. Resentment for that which was taken away from her. Resentment for Christian's intrusion into her life. Why couldn't her father have lived? She had loved him so much; she had needed him so much as she was growing up. Her life would have been different if only her father had lived.

She leaned over and kissed her uncle's cheek. It smelled faintly of sweat and grime, but Elizabeth didn't mind. Her uncle was here with her, sharing her home. If she must be deprived of her father's companionship, then she would relish the company of his brother.

Benjamin patted Elizabeth's hand again. "I could sure use a taste of somethin' tart on my tongue, darlin'," he said.

"Bring your uncle and me a brandy, will you, sweetheart?" Alexander asked, glancing up at Elizabeth.

"All right," Elizabeth replied.

"Hold up there, darlin'. Brandy is a mite too rich for my blood. A shot of whiskey will set with me just fine."

"I'll get it for you, Uncle Benjamin." She went to the highboy standing against the parlor wall and reached for the decanter of brandy and a bottle of rye whiskey. Then she selected two glasses. She poured the alcohol into the glasses and carried them over to the men.

"Thanks, sweetheart," Alexander said as he took the glass of brandy from her hand.

"Ah, thank ye, darlin'," her uncle echoed.

Elizabeth sat down in a chair next to her uncle. She never drank alcohol herself—that would have made her feel like a saloon girl—but she didn't mind Alexander's occasional drinking. At the beginning of their marriage,

Alexander's taste for spirits had upset her because she wasn't accustomed to men drinking in her presence. Christian, certainly, had never imbibed spirits, nor had any of her parents' friends. But over time, Elizabeth had come to accept Alexander's affinity for an after-supper drink. She rarely minded his habit now, except when he came home intoxicated after spending an evening with his friends. On those occasions, she usually managed to swallow her annoyance and help Alexander undress and get into bed.

Benjamin smacked his lips together after taking a long draught from the glass Elizabeth had handed him. "Perhaps you and I could do a little business together, Alexander," he said, taking another swig of whiskey.

"That's a possibility," Alexander returned.

"My brothers and I have an open contract with a few of the lumber mills here abouts. I don't see any reason why we can't strike an agreement, if you've a mind to."

"I'm always looking for new sources of lumber for my mill," Alexander replied. He took a leisurely drink from his glass.

Elizabeth sat forward in her chair. She'd like nothing better than to see Alexander and her uncle work jointly together.

"I can send you enough timber to keep your mill operating smooth as honey," Benjamin drawled.

"Do you have a figure in mind for your cut timber?" Alexander asked with an air of nonchalance.

"I expect we could discuss a figure," Benjamin returned.

Elizabeth listened eagerly to the men's conversation. It seemed to take them forever to get around to discussing the finer points of the partnership. They dawdled over their drinks and their conversation until Elizabeth wished she could interrupt and put the agreement together herself. But she knew that was Alexander's way of conducting business. He never gave the impression of appearing hurried or eager to establish an arrangement. They talked and drank until the evening was nearly spent. Elizabeth was a bit annoyed that the whole night had been devoted to business. She had wanted to ask her uncle a dozen questions about her father's family and their old home in Green County. But the opportunity had not arisen, and when her uncle finally got up to leave, it was with a sense of disappointment that she bid him good night. She closed the door behind him and came back to the hearth to sit beside Alexander.

"What did you think of him?" she asked, holding her breath. She hoped Alexander had liked her uncle.

"He's all right. A little crude, but I like him well enough, I suppose."

Elizabeth leaned her head on Alexander's shoulder. "Oh, I like him immensely, sweetheart. You can't imagine how happy I am to see him. After all these years . . ." Her voice trailed off into silence as she thought about the surprise encounter with her uncle earlier that afternoon.

Alexander lifted the brandy glass to his lips. "Perhaps we can strike a bargain with your uncle and his brothers. From what he told me earlier today at the mill, I think we could take advantage of what he has to offer."

Elizabeth straightened in her chair. "At the mill? You talked to my uncle at the mill today?"

"Yes, of course. I thought you knew that."

"No, I didn't. I didn't think you'd met him until tonight."

"He didn't tell you about our meeting at the mill? He came to the mill to discuss the possibility of finding a new market for his raw timber. In the course of our conversation, I learned he was from Green County, so I asked him about the Dawsons. Imagine my surprise when he turned out to be one of the Dawson brothers himself."

"Indeed," Elizabeth replied, frowning.

Alexander took a sip from his brandy glass.

"Did you tell him about me?" Elizabeth asked after a moment's pause.

"Of course. I told him I was married to his brother's daughter and that if he had a mind to, he could find you at the picnic."

Elizabeth's frown deepened. Her uncle had not made any mention of meeting Alexander at the mill. He had given her the impression that he had come to Nauvoo to seek her out, when in reality he had come for the purpose of furthering his business. Had he deliberately misled her? And if so, why would he do such a thing? Or was it just an oversight on his part that he hadn't mentioned his meeting with Alexander?

"What's wrong?" Alexander asked her. "Your scowl is as black as night."

"Nothing," Elizabeth lied. "I'm just tired. It's been a long day."

Alexander nodded. He put his empty glass aside and rose from the chair. "I have a feeling we might be able to turn a handsome profit with your uncle's help." Alexander smiled with satisfaction.

"Yes, I hope so," Elizabeth replied absently. Her thoughts dwelled on the conversation she'd had with her uncle at the picnic that afternoon. The words they'd exchanged went around and around in her head. And then something Marie had said intruded into her thoughts— something about mistrusting her uncle's motives, or at least not placing her complete trust in him until she found out what he wanted. But that was foolishness. He was her blood kin. And he'd been looking for her. Hadn't he? Elizabeth shook her head. Marie was wrong about her uncle. His motives were completely sincere, she was sure of that. And nothing was going to stop her from fostering a relationship with her father's brother.

CHAPTER ELEVEN

"Good morning, Joseph. How are you today?" Elizabeth asked brightly as she entered the front parlor of the Mansion House. Young Joseph Smith sat behind a small desk, sorting through mail.

"Hello, Elizabeth. What brings you down here?" Joseph asked, starting to rise from his chair.

"Don't get up, Joseph. I've just come to inquire about my uncle, Benjamin Dawson. Is he in his room, do you know?"

No, he isn't. I saw Mr. Dawson leave the hotel about an hour ago. Would you like to leave a message for him?"

Elizabeth glanced up the stairs to the floor above. Her uncle had been staying at the Mansion House since his arrival in Nauvoo a few days earlier. "No, I don't think so,

Joseph. I just stopped by to visit with him. I can see him later."

Joseph nodded.

Elizabeth gazed at the mail Joseph had been sifting through. "I'll bet you have a lot of guests this time of year," she remarked.

"The hotel is full. Mother is always up before sunrise, attending to the business."

"I'm sure," Elizabeth said. "Is there any mail for my uncle today?"

"Let's see," Joseph replied. "Dawson . . . Dawson . . ." He thumbed through the pile of letters and newspapers spread on his desk. "No, it doesn't look like it."

"I wondered if Uncle Benjamin had received any correspondence from his brothers," Elizabeth explained.

"I haven't seen any mail come in for your uncle since he's been staying here," Joseph answered.

"Oh, well. No matter," Elizabeth returned. She was faintly disappointed. She wondered if her uncles in Green County knew Benjamin had found her here in Nauvoo.

"But here's something you might be interested in," Joseph said, handing her a newspaper. "See that picture?" He pointed out an advertisement illustrating five ladies dressed in the newest fashion.

"Look at that!" Elizabeth exclaimed. "The newest dresses have three-quarter-length bell sleeves with false undersleeves. And I just had a new frock made with straight sleeves to the wrist. Wouldn't you just know it."

Joseph chuckled. "I know how you like to keep up with the latest style."

"You do know me, don't you, young Joseph?" she replied, giving him a beguiling smile. She looked again at the advertisement. "Aren't those bonnets clever? Close-fitting with smaller brims, and trimmed with flowers. Oh, I really do have to own one of those bonnets."

"You and Julia," Joseph said, grinning. "You're two of a kind. Julia will want a new frock, too, when she sees this advertisement."

Elizabeth laughed. "Your sister and I must visit the dressmaker together." She handed the newspaper back to Joseph.

Joseph refolded it and set it on the desk. His gaze moved to the front page of the paper. "More gold miners flocking to California," he murmured, his eyes on the page. "Listen to this: 'It's been just over a year since the discovery of gold in California, and already the face of the nation has changed forever. In terms of people alone, it is said that more than 70,000 have headed west to the gold fields.'" Joseph's breath was a low whistle.

"Seventy thousand people?" Elizabeth repeated, raising her brows. "I can't even imagine that. I'll bet those mining towns are wild places."

"Gold fever does strange things to people, that's for sure."

"Would you like to pan for gold in a California creek, Joseph?" Elizabeth asked him.

"I might like to give it a try. I've worked as a farmhand, the proprietor of Father's red brick store, and a guide for visitors to Nauvoo, besides helping Mother manage the Mansion House. Prospecting might be kind of exciting."

Elizabeth gave him a playful punch on the shoulder. "Forget the notion, young Joseph. Your mother would never let you go. She needs you here."

"She'd be afraid that I might stop in the Salt Lake valley to see my cousins. I think Mother would rather see me dead than fraternizing with the Mormon branch of the family." Joseph frowned slightly.

His words brought a frown to Elizabeth's brow, too.

Their former affiliation with the Church was a bond they shared. Both of them had been raised under the umbrella of the gospel. Joseph's father, the Prophet, had been murdered when young Joseph was only eleven years old. Since that time, his mother had become bitter about the Church's new leaders, particularly Brigham Young. Julia Smith once shared with Elizabeth a remark her mother had made: "No child of mine will ever be permitted to go to the Great Basin," Emma had vowed.

Elizabeth and young Joseph Smith rarely discussed their feelings about the Church, or their families' involvement in it. But that tie bound them nonetheless. It was the common thread running through their childhood experiences.

"I wonder if my brother, James, is interested in what's going on in California," Elizabeth pondered aloud. "No, it would be entirely out of character for James," she decided with a smile. She very much would have liked to know

James' thoughts about the discovery of gold, and a myriad of other subjects. She missed having James to talk to.

"James is studying to be a doctor, isn't he?" Joseph asked her.

"That's what I understand from his letters," Elizabeth replied.

"Well, I imagine they need doctors in that wasteland where the Mormons have settled."

"I suppose so."

Both of them were quiet for a moment, lost in their own thoughts.

"I guess I should be getting on my way. It was nice talking to you, Joseph. Tell my uncle that I stopped by if you see him, will you?"

"Certainly."

Elizabeth leaned over the desk and pecked Joseph's cheek. "See you," she said.

Joseph raised a hand in farewell.

Elizabeth left the Mansion House and started for her covered buggy. She'd just lifted her skirts to climb in when she heard her name called.

"Elizabeth, darlin'!"

She turned and saw her uncle coming toward her with an ambling stride. "Uncle Benjamin. Hello, there," she greeted him.

Benjamin Dawson reached her side and gave her a quick, hard hug. "Mornin', girl."

"Good morning. I was just looking for you," Elizabeth replied with a smile.

"You were? Now, that's a pleasant how-do-you-do."

Elizabeth grinned. "I came to ask you if you'd like to drive around and see the town a bit. Maybe have a picnic on the banks of the river. What do you think?"

"Why, I'd be pleased and proud to accompany my favorite niece, that's for darn sure."

"All right. I have a picnic lunch all packed for us; it's sitting right here in the buggy. Shall we go now, or do you want to stop at your room in the hotel first?"

"Naw. I wouldn't want to waste a minute that I could be spendin' with you, darlin'." He helped Elizabeth up into the buggy, then climbed in beside her.

"She handed him the reins. "Let's drive up Main Street, and I'll show you some of the sights. Then we'll circle around to the river."

"Whatever you say, darlin'."

Benjamin jiggled the reins, and the sorrel mare pulling the buggy started forward. Elizabeth looped her arm through her uncle's. As she snuggled close to him, she noticed the strong smell of whiskey on his person. She wondered if he'd been to one of the saloons already that morning. Drinking so early in the day seemed a bit unusual, she thought.

"It's a fine mornin'," her uncle proclaimed loudly. "Just look at that sun shinin' on the Mississippi."

Elizabeth glanced at the river. Although she appreciated the Mississippi's charms, she also was well aware of its liabilities. River travel brought goods and people to Nauvoo, but it also attracted the more lawless elements. Gamblers, thieves, swindlers, and drunkards flourished in this river town.

As they drove along Main Street, Elizabeth pointed out places of interest. She and her uncle chatted as the buggy bumped along the rutted road, pulled by Alexander's fine chestnut-colored horse. Elizabeth directed her uncle to turn onto Young Street and thence to the river. They stopped at the river's edge and climbed out of the buggy. From the floor of the buggy, Elizabeth retrieved the lunch basket she'd packed earlier that morning. She chose a grassy spot beneath a tree, near the river's edge, to spread out the lunch.

Her uncle stood on the bank of the Mississippi, gazing at the water lapping near his feet.

"Lunch is ready, Uncle Benjamin," Elizabeth called to him. She patted the ground next to her. "Come sit down beside me and eat."

"This is truly an enjoyable occasion, Elizabeth," he said as he sat down cross-legged on the grass. "I can't believe my good fortune in findin' you."

"I'm the one with the good fortune. You don't know how I've missed associating with my father's family."

Benjamin patted her hand. "I just bet you have, darlin'."

Elizabeth munched thoughtfully on a bit of cheese she'd packed for the picnic. "Tell me about my father, Uncle Benjamin. Most of my memories of him are growing dim."

Benjamin leaned back on his elbows, chewing on a plump leg of chicken. "What would you like to know?" he asked.

"Oh, any little thing. What do you remember most about Papa?"

"His bull-headedness," Benjamin answered without hesitation. "I remember the day Abraham had a fallin' out with our pa. It was over some small thing about lumber-jackin' that the two of them didn't see eye to eye on. Abraham lost his temper and said some hard things to Pa. After that, he took your ma and moved away. He never spoke to Pa again after that day."

Elizabeth's back straightened. "Oh, that's terrible. I didn't know that had happened."

"It's a true fact. 'Course, my brothers and me kept somewhat in contact with Abraham. But we was never close after that."

Elizabeth was silent, pondering the words her uncle had spoken.

"Wasn't long afterward that Abraham took a notion to go lead minin' up in Galena. That's when he was kilt."

Elizabeth felt a knot in the pit of her stomach. She knew her father had been killed while mining, but she wasn't aware of all the details. She'd been too young to really understand what had occurred. "How did it happen, Uncle Benjamin?" she asked in a quivering voice.

"A cave-in. Abraham was workin' too far back inside the mine. They had a hard time of it gettin' to him afterward."

Elizabeth shivered. "Don't tell me anymore, Uncle Benjamin."

"I didn't mean to upset you, darlin'. I was just answerin' your questions, that's all."

Elizabeth nodded glumly.

"There is somethin' else, however," Benjamin said after a long pause. "Somethin' I been wantin' to discuss with you. And now seems like the proper time to do it, seein' as how we've been talkin' about your pa and all."

Elizabeth looked up into her uncle's face. He wore a sober expression. "What is it, Uncle Benjamin?"

"That mine up in Galena . . ."

"Yes?"

"Well, Abraham and his partner owned the claim. Whatever lead come out of the mine was theirs. His partner died some years back, and his share of the claim went to his wife and young 'uns. Word has it that Abraham and his partner had struck a rich vein of ore. Real rich. Only Abraham was kilt before they could mine it. Word has it that the vein is still sittin' there, underneath the rubble of that old mine."

Elizabeth's eyes widened with interest. "Really?" she breathed.

"Yep. Just waitin' for someone of Abraham's kin to claim it and mine it."

"I didn't know that."

Benjamin was silent for a moment. "Seems a shame that there claim is goin' to waste," he commented, shaking his shaggy head.

"Do you know where the mine is located?" Elizabeth asked, considering her uncle's words.

"No, but it would be as easy as shooin' a badger into a hole to find out. All one would have to do is check with the claims office in Galena. They have the records."

"Why haven't you or your brothers done so?" Elizabeth asked. Her head was reeling with this information.

"We've had no reason to. We knew the claim belonged to Abraham's next of kin." He stared pointedly into Elizabeth's eyes. His intense stare made her feel ill at ease.

"Well, I don't have any interest in resurrecting that old claim. That mine killed my father. I don't want any part of it," Elizabeth said vehemently. She shuddered at the very thought of having anything to do with that deadly mine.

"I don't blame you none, darlin'. I wouldn't want no part of it either, if I was you." Benjamin's expression was sympathetic. "Besides that, it would take some cash to get that old mine operatin' again. Clean it out, shore it up properly, outfit it for minin', and so forth."

Elizabeth remained silent.

"'Course, if anyone wanted to do that, outlay some expense up front, they'd end up with a pretty penny in their pocket."

Elizabeth studied her uncle's face. His eyes were lowered so she couldn't see the expression in them, but his mouth worked as if he were chewing on a wad of tobacco. "Would you be interested in resurrecting my father's mine?" she asked quietly.

"Me? Well, I ain't thought about it, to be right honest with you." His mouth twitched more rapidly.

"How much money would it take to reopen that mine, Uncle Benjamin?" Elizabeth asked.

"Well, I wouldn't rightly know until I saw it for myself. Could be as much as a couple hundred dollars."

"A couple hundred dollars," Elizabeth repeated. Her mind was racing now. If she could finance this venture for her uncle, loan him the money to reopen the mine, it would give her great satisfaction. She'd love to do something important for her uncle.

"I don't know, darlin'. Maybe we ought to let sleeping dogs lie," Benjamin said with a frown creasing his brow.

"But if there's a rich vein of ore in that mine like you said, why shouldn't we take advantage of it? You and your brothers deserve part of what's in that mine. You're father's kin, too."

"I don't know," Benjamin repeated. "Could be we'd have to go to considerable expense. Might not be worth the effort. Anyways, I don't know where we'd get the front money we need." Benjamin rubbed his bearded chin.

"If you think there's a chance we could make money on Father's mining claim, then perhaps my husband might be interested in putting up the money for such a project."

"Alexander? By golly, I hadn't thought of that. Do you think he'd be interested in such a scheme?"

"I don't know for sure. We could ask him."

Benjamin shook his head. "It seems like a lot to ask."

"Oh, it isn't really. I know Alexander can get his hands on some ready cash. He might be very enthusiastic about this."

"You think so? I reckon it wouldn't hurt to ask."

"I'll talk to Alexander tonight about it." Elizabeth felt a swell of excitement. She was quite sure that Alexander would be receptive to her idea. She leaned over and hugged her uncle. "I'm so glad you're here with me, Uncle Benjamin," she said with feeling.

"So am I, darlin'. So am I."

CHAPTER TWELVE

"**W**hat did your husband say when you told him about it?" asked Marie Le Sueur as she and Elizabeth sat in the parlor of the Scotts' home, drinking tea from delicate china cups.

"At first, he wasn't receptive to the idea of loaning Uncle Benjamin money. But then I explained to him about the rich vein of ore my father and his partner had discovered before Father's death."

"Did that change his mind?" Marie asked, taking a sip of her tea.

"Not to begin with. But the more we discussed the project, the more appealing it sounded to him. It seems such a waste to let the mine sit idle when it could be producing. Alexander, of course, wasn't interested in operating the mine himself, but he's considering backing the operation with his money. He feels the mine could make a handsome profit if Uncle Benjamin is right about the vein."

Marie ran a finger around the rim of her tea cup. "*If* your Uncle Benjamin is right," she repeated. "Is it possible he could be exaggerating the strength of the vein?"

Elizabeth leaned forward in her chair and smiled. "Marie, you have a suspicious nature, do you know that? I don't see any reason why Uncle Benjamin would embellish the truth about Father's claim. He would stand to lose as much as we would if the mine turns out to be dry." She patted Marie's hand. "Don't worry. Alexander never risks his money unless he's reasonably sure of a good return on it."

Marie took another sip from her cup, then laid the cup and saucer on the side table.

"Uncle Benjamin is coming to the house this evening for supper. He and Alexander can talk then about the mine. I've been thinking about asking Uncle Benjamin if I might come out to Green County this summer to visit. I should so like to meet my father's other brothers. I've heard Mother speak about them, but I can't recall ever meeting them myself."

"That would be nice for you," Marie agreed, smiling.

"Perhaps I could even see the old log home where we used to live. I only have a few memories of the place; I'd love to see it again. I wonder if I could get Alexander to go with me," Elizabeth added as an afterthought.

"I sometimes miss my home in New Orleans, too," Marie said softly.

"How long did you live in Louisiana, Marie?"

"About ten years. My family left France when I was a child. When Father moved to New Orleans, he opened a bakery in the French Quarter. He and my mother still live there."

"Did you meet Emile in New Orleans?" Elizabeth asked.

"Yes. Believe it or not, Emile came into Father's bakery to buy a loaf of bread. I was behind the counter, helping Mother fill orders. I lost my heart to Emile the moment I laid eyes on him." Marie laughed, and the sound of it was like the tinkling of bells.

"That sounds very romantic," Elizabeth returned with a grin.

"How did you meet Alexander?"

Elizabeth set her tea cup on the table next to Marie's and leaned back comfortably in her chair. "It was here in Nauvoo. Alexander was living in Wisconsin at the time, but he came here to visit his cousin. I met him at a dance held in the Social Hall. Oh, I had a good time in those days," Elizabeth added wistfully.

Marie chuckled. "You make it sound as if it all happened ages ago."

"It wasn't really so long ago, was it?" Elizabeth replied, smiling. "Alexander and I have only been married for three years. Yet in some ways, life is so very different from what it used to be."

Images filtered through Elizabeth's mind as she sat quietly remembering the past. She had spent happy years in the fine brick home on Durphey Street, and before that in the snug old log cabin through the block. She smiled as her thoughts lingered on Millicent and Roxana. Her sisters had seemed like such pests while they were growing up together, but how she would love to be with them now! And her little brother, Zachary . . . she winced at the vision of Zachary lying buried somewhere on the prairie between South Pass and the Salt Lake valley. News of his death had been a tremendous blow to her, and had filled her with grief and anger. If her mother and Christian hadn't been so foolish as to follow Brigham Young to that forsaken place in the West, Zachary would still be alive. She wondered how her mother had ever withstood such a trial. The memory of Lydia tugged at Elizabeth's heart. She would give nearly anything to see her mother's face again, feel her mother's arms around her.

"You look far away," Marie said, touching Elizabeth's hand.

"You're right. My thoughts are far away. With my family."

"You must miss your family, just as I miss mine."

"Yes, I do." Elizabeth brightened as a sudden thought occurred to her. "Would you like to see a portrait of my mother?"

"A portrait? Yes, I would. Do you have one?"

"I'll go and get it," Elizabeth replied, jumping to her feet. She quickly climbed the stairs to her bedroom, went to her bureau, and slid out the bottom drawer. Lifting aside the letters from her family, she withdrew a portraiture mounted in a plain, pine frame.

As she carried the framed picture back downstairs with her, Marie looked up expectantly.

"Here it is," Elizabeth said with excitement in her voice. She held the portrait out for Marie to see.

"My, she's beautiful, Elizabeth. What a lovely drawing."

"Yes, isn't it?" Elizabeth stroked the paper as she and Marie gazed at the portrait together.

"Who did the sketching?" Marie asked.

"Christian. My mother's husband. He drew it when we were living in Missouri." Elizabeth studied the sweeping lines of the pencil drawing. Lydia's hair fell long and loose about her shoulders, and the lines of her face were sketched in careful detail. The portrait was an excellent likeness, capturing Lydia's grace and gentleness.

"Your mother was a very pretty young woman," Marie commented. "You are lucky to have this treasure of hers."

Elizabeth nodded solemnly. "This portrait is precious to me. Mother gave it to me shortly before my family left Nauvoo." Elizabeth felt hot tears spring to her eyes.

Marie slipped an arm around Elizabeth's shoulders. "Perhaps you will see your mother and your family again soon," Marie offered.

"I hope so." Elizabeth stared at the drawing. "They're very far away, though. And Alexander doesn't wish to take time off from the mill to make the trip."

"Perhaps they will come to visit you."

"Perhaps." Even though she spoke the word, Elizabeth knew in her heart that her mother, brother, and sisters would probably never return to Nauvoo. Their life now was in the West with the Saints.

Elizabeth set the portrait on the table beside her. "Perhaps I'll show this drawing to my uncle when he comes to the house tonight. He knew my mother when she was young and newly married to my father."

Marie nodded. "I imagine he would like to see it."

Elizabeth refilled their cups, and she and Marie chatted while leisurely sipping their tea. It was late afternoon when Marie left and Elizabeth began preparations for supper.

Elizabeth closed the door behind her uncle's retreating figure. She heard Alexander, who was standing at her side, give a sigh of satisfaction.

"Well, what do you think?" Elizabeth asked him.

"I think, darlin'," Alexander replied, imitating Benjamin Dawson's backwoods drawl, "that we've made ourselves a fine bargain."

"Oh, good!" Elizabeth squealed, standing on tiptoe to kiss his cheek.

"Not only did your uncle and I conclude a favorable agreement for purchasing timber for the mill, but I think we have the makings of a lucrative mining operation."

"You won't be sorry, Alexander," Elizabeth said, taking his arm. "I just know Uncle Benjamin will make a significant profit on your money."

"He'd better, or I'll have you to thank for it. It was you who talked me into the proposition in the first place, don't forget." Alexander leaned over and kissed Elizabeth on the mouth.

Elizabeth giggled. "And if we make a large return on your money, will you thank me for that, too?"

"Of course, darlin'," Alexander drawled. "I'll be as thankful as a coyote in a chicken coop." Alexander drew Elizabeth into his arms.

She snuggled against him. "I'm happy about this arrangement, Alexander, because it gives me a chance to do something for my family. Thank you for making that possible." Elizabeth looked up into his eyes and smiled.

"Four hundred dollars' worth of doing something for your family," Alexander replied. "That's pretty generous of you." He frowned slightly.

"I was as surprised as you were when Uncle Benjamin said he required four hundred dollars to get started instead of two hundred. But I guess he was right about needing money to buy supplies and equipment to reopen the mine. And like he told us, he might need some sort of cash advance to put up at the claims office."

"Four hundred dollars is a big investment, Elizabeth. I hope we haven't made a mistake." Alexander's frown deepened as he released Elizabeth from his embrace.

"Do you have that much money set aside, Alexander?"

"I did have, but I just purchased a bay stallion with impeccable bloodlines from a fellow in Warsaw. I might have to put a mortgage on the mill in order to get the cash for your uncle."

"You bought another horse?" Elizabeth asked. Her displeasure over this piece of news registered in her voice.

"Yes, just a few days ago. He's a beauty. Sleek and swift. I'm anxious for you to see him."

"Alexander, you have several blooded horses already. They've cost you a fortune," Elizabeth said, moving a step away from him.

"Do you have a problem with that, Elizabeth?" His tone grew suddenly cold and accusing.

"It's your money, Alexander. I just thought we were going to start putting some by for a rainy day—perhaps use it to take a trip out west."

"Out west? Forget that notion, Elizabeth. I have no intention of wasting weeks in a covered wagon just so you can visit your parents." Alexander gave her a withering stare, then walked over to the liquor cabinet, poured himself a glass of brandy, and swallowed a big mouthful.

The elation Elizabeth had felt began to evaporate. Alexander's curtness hurt her. Suddenly she felt uneasy about persuading Alexander to lend his money to her uncle. What if something went wrong? What if the ore was not as plentiful in the mine as her uncle anticipated? Then, too, there could be difficulties getting to the vein. The mine had suffered a cave-in once before. What if the whole venture turned out to be a fiasco?

Elizabeth shook herself. That wasn't going to happen. Everything would proceed as smoothly as Uncle Benjamin had said it would. Alexander would get his money back, plus a nice return on his capital. And Uncle Benjamin would be pleased with Elizabeth for giving him the opportunity to reopen the mine. Both Alexander and Benjamin should end up having plenty of money to line their pockets.

Elizabeth put a hand on her husband's shoulder. She felt Alexander stiffen under her touch. "I'm sorry I was disagreeable about the new horse, Alexander. I really am looking forward to seeing it."

Alexander took another draught from his glass. "I don't want you to question my decisions again. Do you understand, Elizabeth?"

"I won't, sweetheart. I'm sorry," Elizabeth answered meekly.

"Good." Alexander finished his drink in one last gulp, then set the glass aside. "Let's go up to bed now."

Elizabeth nodded.

Alexander took her by the arm and led her upstairs to their bedroom.

CHAPTER THIRTEEN

Elizabeth sat on the parlor couch, reading a recently published book entitled *Wuthering Heights.* The brooding tale of love and mystery intrigued her, and its characters fired her imagination. She'd failed to notice the quick passage of time because she'd been so immersed in the novel. When she looked up at the tall clock standing against the parlor wall, she was surprised to see that it was well after midnight. Alexander should have been home hours ago.

She wondered what was keeping him. His lodge meeting with the Masons would have ended before now. Elizabeth set the book on the couch beside her and glanced at the clock again. The late hour and the stillness of the house induced in her a melancholy mood, which was compounded by the gloomy tale she'd been reading. She fell into dismal contemplation. Weeks had passed without any correspondence from her uncle, and with each passing day she grew more uneasy. Alexander had taken out a mortgage from the bank, to be payable in three months. A month and a half of that time had already elapsed. She'd made regular trips to the post office hoping to receive some word from Galena, but so far nothing had come. Her uncle's silence unnerved her. She ached to know the status of their project at the mine.

Then, too, she hadn't been feeling well of late. She tired easily, which was uncommon for her, and often felt sick to her stomach. She guessed this condition was due to concern over her uncle's lack of communication. If something had gone wrong at the mine, or if some misfortune had befallen Alexander's money, then a truly disastrous state of affairs would ensue—and Alexander would be furious with her. That thought set her stomach churning.

She left the book on the couch and stood up. A sudden attack of dizziness assailed her; she closed her eyes for a moment to steady herself. It was then she heard the sound of horses' hooves coming toward the house.

Elizabeth went to the window and pulled aside a corner of the lace curtain. In the darkness, she couldn't be sure if one of the pair of riders she saw dismounting their horses in front of the house was Alexander or not. She let the curtain fall back into place and went to the door, where she stood with her ear against it, listening for Alexander's familiar voice. Footsteps and low murmuring voices approached the door, then a quick, hard rap.

"Open up," a deep voice commanded.

Elizabeth didn't recognize the voice, but she responded to its gruff command. She slid back the bolt and drew open the door. Alexander stood unsteadily in the doorway next to a man Elizabeth had never seen before.

Alexander muttered something incomprehensible as he stumbled into the room. The stranger followed him inside.

"Alexander? Are you all right?" Elizabeth asked as she reached for him.

He pushed her away. "This is no affair of yours," he said in a slurred voice. He staggered to the couch and sat down heavily on it.

Elizabeth looked from Alexander to the stranger standing beside the door.

"He's drunk," the stranger stated without emotion. "I brought him home."

Elizabeth stared at the man. His face was nearly hidden by a low-fitting hat, but she noticed the expensive cut of the clothes he wore, and the glimmer of a sapphire ring on his finger.

Alexander flung off his frock coat and stretched out on the couch. "Take your winnings and get out of here," he said.

"That suits me just fine," the stranger replied. He glanced at Elizabeth as he turned to leave.

"Thank you for bringing him home," Elizabeth said quietly.

The man tipped his hat.

"Can you tell me where he was tonight?" she asked on impulse.

"The riverboat, playing cards. I'll collect my winnings and go now."

"Yes, get outta here," Alexander muttered.

Elizabeth bit her lip. The queasiness in her stomach had returned, leaving her weak and perspiring. "My husband has apparently spent his evening drinking and gambling," she said to the stranger. "Does he owe you money from his card playing?"

"No," the man answered.

"I'm glad to hear that."

"It's the bay stallion waiting outside the door that belongs to me."

Elizabeth's jaw dropped open. "Not Alexander's expensive new horse," she cried in disbelief.

The man shrugged his shoulders. "I'll be going now."

Elizabeth watched him mount his own horse and lead the stallion after him. "Oh, Alexander. How *could* you?" she whispered, turning to look at her husband. Alexander lay motionless on the couch, his eyes closed, his breathing heavy. His starched ruffled shirt was rumpled, and marred by a brown stain just below the collar. Whiskey. Alexander reeked of it. The smell sent a wave of nausea washing over her. She gripped the top of the couch, drawing in deep gulping breaths of air.

The following morning, Elizabeth was ill and kept to her bed. Alexander had spent the night sleeping on the couch, and when he awoke he was in a foul temper. He went to the mill shortly before noon, and after he left Elizabeth struggled to get up from bed and dress. She hadn't dared raise the subject of last night's losses with Alexander. She knew he was angry about losing the horse. *He should have known better,* Elizabeth thought grimly as she put away the few breakfast dishes. The riverboat gamblers who plied the Mississippi were notorious for their skill at cards and for their trickery. Their reputations were no better than common thieves. She had little doubt the man she had met the night before, dressed in fancy clothing and sporting expensive jewelry, was a professional gambler.

Elizabeth rested most of the afternoon. She didn't feel well enough to even read from her novel. When Alexander came home from work, he was still upset. He went out again after supper, and didn't return until after Elizabeth was asleep for the night.

The next afternoon, Marie called at the house.

"Oh, my. You look like you're not feeling well at all," she said when Elizabeth answered her knock.

"I've been ill, but just having you stop to visit makes me feel better already. Come in, Marie."

She followed Elizabeth to a seat in the parlor. "How long have you been unwell?"

Elizabeth brushed a lock of hair out of her eyes. "Off and on for a week or two. I should be feeling better right away."

"If you don't, I'm going to send Emile's friend over to see you. He's a physician."

"Please don't bother, Marie. I'm sure I'll recover soon. Tell me, how are you and Emile doing?"

"We're fine. We're having a dinner party at our home this Friday evening, and that's the reason I came to see you. We want you and Alexander to come for dinner."

"Thank you for the invitation. We'd love to be there."

"We're having just a few friends over. Nothing too big or fancy."

"It should be very nice." Elizabeth tried to sound enthusiastic, but the thought of food made her nausea worse.

Marie stayed for about thirty minutes more, reiterating her promise to send for the doctor if Elizabeth didn't feel better shortly.

Elizabeth wasn't any better over the course of the next few days. She made herself do a few household chores and took the buggy out once to visit Julia Smith. But most of the time she occupied herself with nothing more arduous than needlework, playing the square piano Alexander had given her, and reading.

On Friday, even though she still felt ill, Elizabeth was determined to attend the Le Sueurs' dinner party. Alexander had promised to come home early from the mill so they could arrive at the party on time. Elizabeth was lying on the couch in the parlor when she heard him enter the house. He slammed the door behind him.

"Elizabeth!" he shouted.

"Here, Alexander. I'm in the parlor."

Alexander stormed into the room. His face was flushed, and his gray eyes threw off sparks like flint striking stone.

"What is it, Alexander? What's wrong?" Elizabeth scrambled to her feet.

Alexander stood with his hands clenched into tight fists at his sides. "What's wrong?" he parroted. "I'll tell you what's wrong. Your misguided desire to do something charitable for your family has just cost me nine hundred dollars. And it could very possibly mean losing the mill, as well."

"What are you talking about?" Elizabeth asked, consternation flooding through her.

"I sent one of my men up to Galena to see why we hadn't heard from your uncle. Benjamin never visited the claims office there. And, in fact, the claim to the mine your father had was transferred into someone else's hands years ago. Neither you nor your thieving uncle can get your hands on the ore in that mine."

Elizabeth felt suddenly dizzy. The room spun around her. She abruptly sat back down on the couch.

"I don't believe it," she said, stunned.

Alexander stalked to the liquor cabinet and threw open the cabinet doors. "You'd better believe it, Elizabeth. You've been duped. We've both been duped. Your uncle has taken my money and dropped out of sight." Alexander poured himself a shot of whiskey. The liquid splashed from the rim of the glass onto the polished wood of the cabinet. He downed the drink in one gulp, then poured himself another.

"I'm sorry, Alexander. I didn't have an inkling Uncle Benjamin wasn't being honest with us. I can't believe he'd do such a thing . . ." Elizabeth's voice trailed off into a whisper.

"Nine hundred dollars, Elizabeth. Nine hundred dollars just washed down the creek." Alexander dumped the contents of the second glass of whiskey into his throat. "And it was money put up by the bank as a mortgage against the mill."

Elizabeth stared at him, her eyes swimming.

"Where am I going to get that kind of money in six weeks to pay off the loan?" he shouted. "Where?"

"I don't know." Elizabeth cowered under his rage.

Alexander slammed the empty glass onto the cabinet and strode back to Elizabeth's side. "I warned you if anything happened to that money . . ." he said menacingly.

His furious face was only inches from hers. She backed away from him.

"We could lose everything—everything I've worked so hard for," he bellowed. "Do you understand that?"

"Yes," Elizabeth replied, tears beginning to trickle down her cheeks. "I'm sorry, Alexander. I don't know what else to say."

Alexander bent closer to her face. "When I get my hands on Benjamin Dawson, I'll murder him. I promise you that."

Elizabeth's breath stopped in her throat. She could hardly summon breath enough to speak. "Please, Alexander, don't say that. You don't mean it."

Alexander grabbed her by the arm, his fingers digging into her flesh. "You'll pay dearly for this, Elizabeth. I'll make sure of it." His eyes burned in fury. He glared at Elizabeth a moment longer, then roughly pushed her away. Without another word, he left the room. She watched him climb the stairs to the floor above.

Elizabeth burst into tears. She covered her face with her hands, sobbing uncontrollably. Her thin frame shook with each sob, and her honey blonde curls matted against her wet cheeks.

Elizabeth sat on the edge of the bed, a dazed expression on her face. The doctor Marie had summoned to see her had just let himself out the door. His examination of her had been quick and perfunctory. "There's nothing wrong with you that nine months won't cure," he'd pronounced briskly. The words rattled in her ears. She was pregnant. She was going to have a baby. That possibility hadn't even occurred to her. Of course she was happy about it. But it was the wrong time for a baby—a bad time. Alexander would not be pleased with her, she knew that. He hadn't forgiven her yet for her uncle's treachery. He'd placed the blame for the loss of his money on her shoulders. It was a heavy burden to bear.

Alexander had scarcely spoken a word to her in two weeks, ever since the night he'd come home with the news of her uncle's disappearance. He'd been working day and night at the mill since then, trying desperately to scrape together enough cash to pay the mortgage. He'd also sent one of his employees to search for Benjamin Dawson, but it seemed that Benjamin had disappeared. Alexander's man hadn't been able to find a trace of him. Even a trip to Green County to talk with Benjamin's brothers hadn't turned up anything. The Dawson brothers were away cutting trees, the man was told by everyone he spoke with.

Alexander swore he would never stop looking until he found Benjamin Dawson. Not only had Alexander lost the four hundred dollars he'd invested to reopen the mine, but he had also given Benjamin five hundred dollars more as advance payment on several loads of cut timber. The timber had never arrived at the mill, and Alexander was in dire financial straits.

The shock and stress of the news, along with Alexander's stony silence, had sent Elizabeth to bed. She'd hired an errand boy to take a note to Marie, telling her she didn't feel well enough to attend the dinner party, and the next morning Marie had come to see her. She insisted on sending for the doctor, but Elizabeth had put her off until this morning.

Elizabeth had never met the doctor before he came to the house to examine her. He was a brisk, blunt man with thinning gray hair and breath that smelled of garlic. He told her to expect the baby in about seven months, and advised her to get plenty of bed rest and eat well. She was to send for him if she didn't start feeling better soon.

This pregnancy was a shock to her, and it would be to Alexander as well. She dreaded telling him about the baby, fearing that this news would distance him from her further. Elizabeth crawled back into bed. She stared forlornly at the ceiling, thinking about how she was going to break the news to her husband.

*"There is no sacrifice required
at the hands of the people of God
but shall be rewarded to them an hundred fold,
in time or eternity."*

Parley P. Pratt,
member of the Quorum of Twelve Apostles

CHAPTER FOURTEEN

"More apple pie, James?" Inger held the serving knife poised in the air, ready to slice him a second piece.

"No, thank you. It was delicious, but I can't eat another bite." James patted his stomach.

"How about you, Lars?" asked Inger, turning to her brother.

"Sure. I'll have another piece."

She cut a generous slice of pie and served it onto her brother's plate. Then she returned to her seat at the table between the two young men.

The log cabin was just as Inger had envisioned it four months earlier, when Lars and James began construction. It consisted of a single room with a curtain for privacy, and a stone hearth. The floor was made of split logs, and a multi-colored rag rug lay before the hearth. Inger had embroidered a Scandinavian forest scene, and it now hung by the door. The single window was embellished with cheerful yellow curtains. Beside the porch grew wildflowers and hollyhocks, basking in the July sunshine. Inger rested her chin in her hand as she listened to the conversation taking place at the table.

"So, anyway," Lars was saying, "Captain Stansbury said he could use someone who knew the plant and animal life of the valley, and could make some sketches for him."

"You'll be perfect for the job," Inger said, patting her brother's hand.

"She's right, Lars," James agreed. "Who knows better than you the kind and variety of plant life? You've been studying and sketching it ever since we arrived in the Basin."

Lars' voice betrayed his enthusiasm. "I'm excited about the prospect of accompanying Captain Stansbury and his Army Corps of Engineers on their government survey. They'll be mapping and recording scientific information in this valley and in the Provo valley. We should be gone about a month or two, I imagine."

"Promise me you'll be careful, Lars," Inger said with a solemn face. "You might come into contact with Indians."

"We probably will—Utes, most likely. They're more concentrated in the Provo valley than they are here. It should be interesting. I've never seen any Utes, except for a few stragglers who've come to the fort to barter."

"You stay away from them, Lars. They frighten me," Inger said sternly.

"Now, sis, you haven't forgotten that these Indians are descendants of the Book of Mormon people, have you? Do you want me to turn my back on them? I was thinking of doing a little proselyting."

James hid a grin behind his hand. It was true what Lars said about the Indians being ancestors of Book of Mormon people, and as such were part of the house of Israel, but no proselyting was being conducted among them at present. Brigham Young's policy was to treat the Indians kindly and with fairness; any trade with them was to be carried out only at their encampments.

"When the Indians are converted and living peacefully among us, that's when I'll feel comfortable about your rubbing shoulders with them," Inger said.

Lars chuckled, then forked a piece of pie into his mouth.

"The truth is, it's their land," James pointed out. *"We're* the intruders."

"I thought we'd settled in Mexican territory," Lars mumbled with his mouth full of apple pie.

"President Polk did a nice bit of bargaining when he arranged the treaty which gave this piece of property to the United States," James observed, referring to the huge tract of land ceded to the United States the year before, in 1848, by the Treaty of Guadalupe Hidalgo.

"Now, if President Taylor will decide the question of slavery within the Mexican Cession, perhaps Deseret can be annexed as a state," remarked Lars.

James pondered his friend's comment. He knew a petition for statehood was being carried to Washington, D.C. by Brother Almon Babbitt. And he was also aware of the controversy over slavery currently being waged in Congress. "President Taylor has made it pretty clear that he wants California admitted directly as a state. I think he'll divide the rest of the Mexican Cession into territories," James said thoughtfully.

Inger leaned her elbows on the table. "Do you think California will be admitted as a slave state, or free?" she asked, looking at James.

"If President Taylor lets the Californians themselves decide the question of slavery, it only makes sense that they'll opt to enter the Union as a free state. It will be purely a matter of economics—there's not much call for slavery in the gold fields," James replied.

"Ah, yes, the glitter of gold," Lars remarked, pushing his empty pie plate aside. "The discovery of gold hasn't been a complete curse, though. Gold seekers coming through here from the East are paying high prices for foodstuffs and fresh pack animals. I know of a fellow who sold his horse to a gold miner for $200.00. And he'd only paid $30.00 for the animal."

"Even so, Lars, gold fever can be a dangerous snare for the Saints," Inger argued. "I heard one of the brethren say that quite a few of the tares had gone to the gold mines, and some of the wheat had probably gone with them."

Inger's comment caused James a moment of solemn reflection. A few of the Saints had, indeed, become infected with gold fever and left the valley for the gold fields of California. James couldn't think of any gold seeker, Mormon or Gentile, without having Franklin Metcalf's face bob up in his mind. Metcalf and Etta had married during the winter. But in the early spring, when the trail to California was clear of snow, Metcalf had slipped out of their cabin one dark night and ridden off for the gold fields, leaving Etta abandoned and alone. James had agonized over her plight. He'd considered going to see her, for he knew she was embarrassed and hurt, but he didn't know what to say to comfort her. So he had just let matters slide, and shortly afterward Etta moved away without James having spoken to her.

He had been sorry ever since. He should have worked up the courage to go see her, console her, offer some warmth and understanding. Perhaps things would have worked out for the two of them in time. But he hadn't done it, and now it was too late. Etta was living somewhere in the Provo valley with her family, who had been among the first group of settlers called by Brigham Young to colonize the smaller valley to the south. James passed a hand across his forehead and uttered a frustrated sigh.

"Why the sigh, James?" Inger put a hand lightly on his shoulder. "Did you change your mind about having that second piece of pie?"

James' furrowed brow smoothed as he smiled at her. Inger seemed to have a way of making him forget his troubles. Her good humor was infectious. He would enjoy carrying out the favor Lars had asked of him—to watch over Inger while he was away with Captain Stansbury conducting the government survey.

"I was only thinking about how much I'm going to enjoy eating my share of your cooking—and Lars' share too—while he's gone with Captain Stansbury."

"I wish you hadn't asked James to look after me while you're away," she said, turning to her brother. "And don't say I should stay with Kirstine or Johanna. I want to be in my own house. I'm perfectly able to take care of myself."

"I couldn't rest if I thought you were all alone, Inger," Lars replied. "We've already been over this."

She gave James an apologetic smile. "I hate to inconvenience you, James. You have enough to do with your work at Dr. McCaffrey's and your responsibilities at home."

"It's not an inconvenience. I'm glad Lars asked me. But I would have come here often to check on you anyway, even if he hadn't asked. You know that." James reached over to pat her cheek as he spoke. The softness and warmth of her skin took him by surprise.

Inger's face flushed at the touch of his hand. She stared at him a moment before dropping her gaze. For an instant, James thought he read more than simple gratitude in the expression in her eyes and the blush on her cheeks. The notion unnerved him.

"Then that's settled," Lars announced. "When I get back from the expedition, I'll have some extra money in pay. We can buy a milk cow, Inger, and a new plow and hoe."

Inger smiled at her brother.

James pushed his chair away from the table. "Well, I'd better be getting along. I have a long day at Dr. McCaffrey's office tomorrow. Thanks for supper, Inger."

James stood and reached for his hat. Inger and Lars walked with him to the door of the cabin. A moment ago he had felt flustered by Inger's gaze, but now her eyes reflected nothing more than geniality. Perhaps he had misread her expression. He felt a trace of disappointment.

Lars clapped him on the back. "Thanks for everything, James."

James nodded. "You leave the day after tomorrow?"

"Yes. At sunrise."

"Have a safe trip. And don't worry about anything here at home." James and Lars exchanged a handshake, then James bid Inger good night and left the cabin.

He began the walk back to his own place with his hands in his pockets, reflecting on the evening he had just spent with Inger and Lars. He'd enjoyed the meal Inger had prepared, the pleasant conversation, and the entertainment afterward. Inger had sung for him, with Lars accompanying her on his harmonica. The sweet tones of her voice still lingered in his ears as he walked along the dirt street. On either side of the road stretched large fields of ripening wheat. The smell of grain hung in the still air, and the sight of the golden wheat with its clean, husky odor pleased his senses. Mud and straw adobe brick homes, the color of sunflowers, and red painted barns marked his passage along the route toward home. The properties were bounded by split-rail fences weaving a pattern across the acres of fertile fields. Towering above the valley that nestled fields, fences, and homes, the mountains reigned, purple in the fading light. The peaceful, pastoral scene filled James with contentment.

The following afternoon, Dr. McCaffrey went to pay a call on a patient who was confined to bed. James felt fairly confident about being left alone to handle the routine complaints of those who came to the office. Over the last six months in which he had been apprenticing with Dr. McCaffrey, he had gained a good deal of experience. He had set broken bones, lanced boils, performed minor surgeries, and treated a variety of ailments and illnesses. He had seen patients suffering from dyspepsia, ague and fever, whooping cough, black canker, typhus fever, consumption, and gout. He had prescribed, mixed, and dispensed scores of medicines. He had rejoiced at the births of babies, and felt anguish over the patients he could not rescue from death. He felt deep satisfaction with his work, and was gaining confidence in his abilities. The Saints in the valley were beginning to call him "young Dr. Kade," the sound of which fell sweetly on his ears. Technically, however, he was not yet a qualified physician. He felt keenly the need to expand his knowledge by attending medical college, but the expense of schooling and the cost of traveling to Chicago, where the nearest college was located, were prohibitive. In order to further his education, he occupied his free time with study and reading. Dr. McCaffrey subscribed to a number of medical journals, all of which James read voraciously. He'd also digested every one of the books on medicine McCaffrey had sitting on his office shelf. The more he learned, the hungrier he became to know more, experience more, and increase his fund of information. He continued to keep accurate records on every patient he saw, although Dr. McCaffrey considered it a waste of time.

The afternoon passed quietly; only two patients came to the office, each with minor complaints which James easily treated. Between patients, he wrote a long letter to Elizabeth. He told her about his medical practice, and described for her the log cabin the Kades had built outside the fort on a choice city lot. He reported on the construction of public buildings, the digging of irrigation ditches, and the successful cultivation of hundreds of acres of fields. He rehearsed news of the Church, including the recent division of the city into nineteen wards, each presided over by a bishop, and related incidents and anecdotes about the Church's leader and prophet, Brigham Young. Roxana and Millicent were growing into fine, beautiful young women, he explained, with personalities as different as summer and winter. Roxie was thirteen now, and being courted by her first beau. Millicent was eleven and full of fire and mischief.

When he finished with the letter, he sealed it in an envelope. Salt Lake City boasted a post office, but mail delivery was slow and irregular; it could be months before Elizabeth received his letter. He leaned back in his chair and clasped his hands behind his head, his thoughts focusing on

Inger Johanssen and the company he had shared with her and Lars the evening before. He couldn't get the earnest look in Inger's eyes out of his mind, or the soft feel of her cheek against his fingers. He found himself wanting to be with her.

James stood and looked outside the window of the adobe house that served as McCaffrey's office. The July sun was hot on his face where it came in through the window. Inger and Elizabeth . . . they were as different as two women could possibly be. Where Elizabeth was proud, stubborn, and fiercely independent, Inger possessed humility, grace, gentleness, and charm. And her life was rooted in the gospel of Jesus Christ. Although the two of them had been childhood friends, it didn't take much imagination to guess what Elizabeth's attitude would be toward Inger now. That was part of the reason he didn't mention Inger or Lars in his letter; Elizabeth would be scornful of his friendship with them. But something else stopped him from sharing his feelings for Inger on paper. It was almost as if Inger occupied a secret corner of his heart. Not even he, himself, had fully explored the scope of his feelings for her. And until such time as he did, her place in his heart would remain concealed.

James moved away from the window, releasing a pent-up sigh. He decided to visit Inger tomorrow, after Lars left with the expedition. His heart quickened a beat at the thought.

CHAPTER FIFTEEN

James bent over the row of ripening corn, churning up the soil with his hoe and discarding the weeds. The afternoon was hot, and perspiration dripped from his forehead. He intended to finish this row of corn, change out of his work clothes, and then pay a visit to Inger Johanssen as he'd promised himself the night before. He put his back into the work, anxious to be finished.

"James, would you come inside for a moment, please?"

James straightened and looked over his shoulder. His mother was standing in the doorway of the cabin, motioning for him to join her. He set down the hoe he'd been using to weed the vegetable garden and strode to the house. His mother waited for him at the back door.

"Brother Babcock is here and wants to speak to you," she said as he approached the doorway.

"Brother Babcock?" James repeated. He knocked some of the loose dirt off his trousers and tucked in his shirttail. Then he followed his mother through the back portion of the cabin and into the parlor.

The large room wasn't strictly a parlor, although his mother referred to it as such. It was where the family ate their meals and gathered together in the evenings, as well as a place to entertain guests. The room was separate from the area where his mother prepared the meals and did the family's laundry. Another smaller room on the ground floor served as his parents' bedroom. A wooden ladder led to a half-story floor above, where Millicent and Roxana had their beds. James occupied the small attic loft.

Although the one-and-one-half story log house was rough-looking on the outside, it was comfortable inside. Windows with glass panes let in the sunlight, a stone fireplace kept the cabin warm, and the interior walls were brightened with a coat of whitewash. A split-rail fence surrounded the property, enclosing a garden area, a small orchard of apple trees, a barn, and a smokehouse.

Brother Babcock rose from his chair when James entered the parlor. "Hello, Brother Babcock. It's nice to see you," James said, extending a hand.

The older man grasped James' hand and pumped it up and down. "Nice to see you, too, boy."

"What can I do for you?" James asked, wondering why Brother Babcock was paying him a call. "I hope no one at your house requires the services of a physician."

The portly man shook his head. "No. That's not why I came by."

Lydia stood at James' side. "Your wife and family are well?" she inquired.

Brother Babcock nodded. "Well and happy, thank you, Sister Kade. In fact, that's part of the reason I've come to see your boy." He turned back to James. "Brother Brigham has just issued a call to me and my family to help settle the country north of here, near the northern tip of the Great Salt Lake."

"Oh. When will you be leaving?" James asked.

"In a few weeks. Before I go, however, I have something I want to give you, James. I haven't thanked you properly for saving my life last winter. I can never repay you for that. This gift is just a token of my gratitude."

"No need to thank me, Brother Babcock. Besides, McCaffrey was the one who did the doctoring."

"No, son. Credit is given where credit is due. It was you who saved my life on that mountain by your quick action. You and the goodness of the Lord. Come outside with me, boy."

James exchanged a quizzical look with his mother, then he followed the older man outside. Brother Babcock walked ahead of him with a pronounced limp, an impairment left from his accident in the canyon. James was curious to see what Brother Babcock had in mind to give him. The older man walked over to his horse, whose reins were tied to a bush growing beside the cabin. The horse was a dark chestnut color, with black legs and tail, and a finely-shaped head.

Brother Babcock stood beside the horse, patting the animal's neck. "This fellow is yours, son. He's a sturdy, dependable Morgan. I brought this gelding all the way from Illinois, and he has served me well. I want you to have him."

"What?" James exclaimed. "I can't take your horse! That animal must be worth a good sum of money. I appreciate the offer, Brother Babcock, but I can't possibly accept." James was stunned by the man's proposal.

"You listen to me, boy. This is only a fraction of what I owe you. Not only have you doctored me, but you've also seen to my children when they've been down with the fever. I have two strong oxen to help me pioneer a new area for the Lord, and this is a small sacrifice to make for all the good Lord has given me and my family. You have more use for this animal than I have. You're a doctor, boy. You need a strong, fast horse to carry you quickly to your patients. This horse will take you wherever you need to go."

"Brother Babcock, I can't possibly . . ."

The older man put up a hand to stop James in the middle of his sentence. "I won't hear any more about it. This Morgan is yours. Do with him as you like. You can keep him or you can sell him. You do as you see fit, boy."

James clamped shut his jaw. He could see from the intractable expression on Brother Babcock's face that his mind was firmly set. James watched in silence as the heavy-set man untied the reins from the bush and handed them to him.

Brother Babcock patted the horse's rump. "You'll find this horse is strong enough for farm work, and fast enough for pleasure riding. The Morgan is an all-around fine breed."

"I don't know what to say, Brother Babcock. This takes me completely by surprise. Thank you. I appreciate the gift." James' words ran together in one jumbled heap.

"My pleasure, boy. You keep up your good work. This valley needs a fine doctor like you."

"Thank you." James gazed at the horse standing patiently beside him. His eyes roved over the animal's shiny coat, his sturdy, muscular legs, and his lean body. The horse snorted and tossed his head. His black mane rippled against his sinewy neck.

"You tell your pa hello for me," Brother Babcock said as he gave the horse a final pat on the nose.

"I will."

"Take care, boy." Babcock turned and started down the road on foot. James thought his step seemed more sprightly as he walked away.

James' eyes came back to the gelding at his side. He felt suddenly giddy with excitement. This beautiful animal belonged to him! He had never owned his own horse before; in fact, the family had only one horse to help with the work on the farm, a big sorrel draft horse. He was anxious for his father to return from hunting so he could show him this prize.

He stroked the Morgan's sleek back. His hand traveled the horse's withers and down along his foreleg. He noticed the animal's distinctive markings—white socks on his hind legs only, a narrow white strip on his forehead. He was the most handsome creature James had ever seen.

"Mother!" James shouted exultantly. "Come out here and see what I have."

"He's beautiful, James," Inger said, stroking the horse's neck. "How kind of Brother Babcock to offer you his horse."

James stood at the horse's head, the reins gathered in his hand. "I told him I couldn't accept such a gift, but Brother Babcock was adamant about giving me the gelding. And I have to admit, Inger, I'm thrilled with him. He's a pleasure to ride. His trot is quick and vigorous, and his canter is smooth. He seems to have a calm temperament. Look at the shape of his head, and his arched neck. Isn't he magnificent?"

"He truly is a magnificent animal, James." Inger rubbed the horse's forehead. "What are you going to call him?"

"I don't know. I haven't even thought about a name." James ran a hand through the gelding's dark mane.

"He should have a fitting name," Inger declared.

"Well, he has a stripe on his forehead. And he can run like the wind. How about 'Streak'?" James suggested.

"Oh, a noble animal like this one deserves a noble name," Inger replied. Her blue eyes danced. "Maybe you should name him after an ancient Greek or Roman hero."

"You mean like 'Aristotle' or 'Sophocles'?" James grinned at the lithesome girl standing beside him.

"Yes. Or what about 'Odysseus'?"

"Odysseus?"

Inger flashed him a smile.

"Odysseus, huh? How do you like that name, boy?" He tugged on the reins so the horse's head was forced downward, then he released the pressure on the reins and the gelding's head bobbed up again. "Well, look at that. He likes it."

Inger burst into laughter.

James led the horse to a hitching post near Inger's cabin door, and tied the reins to a metal ring fastened to the post. "In all truth, I didn't come here just to show off my new horse. I came to see how you're getting along without Lars. Did he leave this morning like he'd planned?"

Inger nodded. "He saddled up at first light. He was excited and could hardly wait to get going."

"And you've been all right today?" James asked.

"Of course."

James' eye lingered on the curving lines of the pale blue muslin Inger wore. The dress was embellished with lace cuffs and a square lace collar. At the base of the collar, Inger had pinned a blue cameo brooch. James reluctantly withdrew his gaze and focused on the grounds around the Johanssens' snug cabin. Inger had set stones in the ground to serve as a border for her flower and vegetable gardens. A small corn patch grew behind the house, and wild sunflowers and hollyhocks turned their broad faces to the sun. A pussy willow tree was sprouting beside the cabin door. "You really have things fixed up nice around here, Inger," he commented.

"Lars and I are perfectly content with our little plot of ground." She reached for James' hand. "Come inside and sit for a few minutes, can you?"

James liked the feel of Inger's fingers curling around his. He let her lead him inside the cabin. It took a moment for his eyes to adjust to the dimmer light inside the cabin after being out in the bright sunshine. He noticed the cabin was tidy and clean. A vase filled with fuzzy pussy willow branches sat on the table. Inger pulled a chair away from the table for him to sit on, then she took a seat for herself.

"I'm going to be fine here, James. I've plenty to keep me busy. And when I get lonesome, I can always go visit Kirstine or Johanna."

James nodded. Inger's two older sisters lived in the valley with their husbands and children. James remembered Johanna as being plain-faced and stout. She always wore her hair arranged into a braid ringing her head. He thought Kirstine was prettier. She had pale skin, wide blue eyes, and yellow hair that fell to her waist. She reminded James of a delicate flower. Inger was the sister nearest Elizabeth's age; they were young girls during the years the two families lived in Green County. The Johanssens and the Kades didn't have much opportunity to rub shoulders after moving to Missouri because of the persecution raging against the Saints. Both families were driven out of Missouri in 1839 with the rest of the Saints. The Kades settled in Nauvoo, Illinois, and the Johanssens made their home across the river in the town of Montrose. James recalled seeing the Johanssen children a couple of times while in Illinois, but his friendship with them, and particularly with Lars, developed after both families came west to the valley.

"What do you hear from Elizabeth?" Inger asked. "Have you received a letter from her lately?" Inger gazed at James as she waited for the answer. In the muted light of the cabin, her eyes were the color of violets. James blushed when he realized he was staring at her.

"Uh, no. We haven't heard from Elizabeth in several months. The last time she wrote, though, she said everything was going well."

"Elizabeth was always such a pretty girl. I remember being so envious of her beautiful long ringlets. I could never get my own hair to curl like that." Inger laughed, and the airy sound of it was like a feather tickling James' ear.

"Elizabeth would thank you for that compliment, I'm sure," James smiled.

"I wonder what's happening in Nauvoo," mused Inger. "Does Elizabeth ever say much about the town?"

"Once in awhile. Mostly she writes about how successful Alexander's business is."

Inger's smile was tolerant. As James looked at her, he couldn't help noticing the narrow line where her dress hugged her waist. Her flaxen hair trailed down her back in one long braid, a splash of sunshine against the sky-blue cloth of her cotton dress.

"Do you ever think about the old times in Nauvoo, James? About how beautiful the city was, and how flourishing and prosperous."

"Sure I do. A lot. But sometimes it makes me sad to think about it."

"Me, too—though it shouldn't, for I always loved visiting Nauvoo, and in Montrose we had a happy life." Inger sat forward in her chair, her eyes fastened on James' face. "When I was a girl, I'd often slip down to the river when I was supposed to be doing chores in the house. I'd sit on the bank, watching the riverboats go by, and wonder where they were going when they rounded the bend of the river and I couldn't see them anymore. I often thought they were on their way to China or India, or some other exotic place I had read about." Inger laughed softly. "I thought the Mississippi flowed all the way to China."

James smiled as he listened to her, recalling memories of his own, as a young boy sitting beside the river, watching the steamers chug up and downstream with their cargoes of people and goods.

"When we left Illinois," Inger continued, "I believed with all my heart we would return there to live some day. I guess I still believe that to a certain extent."

"Would you want to go back?" James asked. "I wouldn't. I'm happy here in the Great Basin."

"So am I. But I'm not so sure I wouldn't go back to Montrose if I had the chance—even if it was just to retrieve my mother's dishes." Inger smiled slyly, as if she were enjoying a private joke.

"Your mother's dishes?" James questioned. "Is there some meaning in that statement I'm not catching?" James folded his arms across his chest. "Well, are you going to explain or not?"

"You'd laugh if I told you," Inger replied.

"Not if you don't want me to."

Inger knit her fingers together. "You know my mother passed away while we were living in Montrose . . ."

James nodded. He remembered how upset his mother had been to learn of Gerda Johanssen's death. Inger's mother had taken ill and died, leaving Inger's father to care for his five children.

". . . My sisters and I saved a few of her things as keepsakes, but we had to leave most of it behind when we came west. Mother owned a set of lovely porcelain plates and saucers she brought with her from Denmark. She carried them with her to Green County, then to Independence, and finally to Montrose. She treasured those few pieces of china because they had belonged to her mother."

"Uh-huh," James said, listening closely.

"The morning before we left Montrose to head west, I buried those dishes in the cellar of our house."

"You buried them?" James repeated, his brows hooking up in surprise.

"Yes. I planned to come back some day and get them. And while I was away, I didn't want anyone to steal them. So I hid them."

"In the cellar under the house?"

"It was rather clever, don't you think?" Inger said with a grin.

"Yes, I suppose so."

"I loved those dishes of Mother's." Inger bit her lip in thought. "I promised myself I'd get them back. And I will, too."

"I just bet you will," James agreed. He leaned back in his chair and crossed one leg over his knee. "Tell me about this house of yours in Montrose. What was it like?"

"Oh, it was a nice house. Papa and Jens built nearly all of it themselves. It had three big rooms, and a separate cooking and eating area. The distinctive thing about the house was that Father built a double door in the floor of the pantry with a ladder leading down to the cellar. Rather than going outside to a separate cellar to get our milk, cheese, eggs, and other foods that needed to stay cool, all he had to do was open the doors in the floor and get what we needed from the cellar of the house."

"That's an ingenious idea. Where in Montrose was your house located?" James asked. He was curious to know more about Inger's life before she and her family had come to the Great Basin.

"You couldn't miss seeing it. It sits right along the river bank, a stone's throw from the ferry landing. The house is built of timber, and the roof is faced along the edges with blue tiles that Father had specially made in one of the brethren's kilns. It's a Scandinavian custom; many roofs in Denmark are made of red or blue tiles."

"It sounds nice, Inger. You must have hated leaving your home in Montrose as much as I disliked leaving my red brick home in Nauvoo."

"I remember visiting in your home. It was a lovely place, James. Was your father able to sell it before leaving Nauvoo, or did he have to leave it unsold like my father did with our home?"

"No, Father was able to sell the house and farm, but at a fraction of its value. Like you, we left most of our possessions behind. Father had collected a sizable library of books, ranging from the classics to current writers like Hawthorne, Cooper, and Dickens. He also had histories, biographies, books of poetry, and political and economic essays. It was a real sacrifice for him to leave all of them in the hands of our enemies."

Inger nodded. "I imagine your father had a lot of books. He was in the newspaper business, wasn't he?"

"Yes. He wrote for *The Evening and the Morning Star* in Independence, Missouri, and then for the *Nauvoo Neighbor* in Illinois. He hopes to help get a paper going here in the valley. He's farming right now, like everyone else. But writing is his passion."

"And doctoring is *your* passion." Inger settled back in her chair. "Have you always wanted to become a doctor, James?"

"For about as long as I can remember. Mother said I used to bandage my sisters from head to toe whenever they'd scrape a knee or bruise an elbow."

Inger chuckled.

"I'm going to need to know more than how to bandage cuts and bruises, however, before I can hope to become an effective doctor." James frowned, thinking about his need for additional training. "I had hoped to attend medical school."

"Medical school." Inger nodded thoughtfully. "Yes, that would be important for you to do."

"Important, but impossible. I'd planned to go to medical college when we were living back east. But now I can't just pick up and go riding off to Chicago." James gave her an indulgent smile.

"Why not?"

"Why not? Well, because I, uh . . ." Her directness caught him off guard. "I have responsibilities here, for one thing."

Inger regarded him with a steady eye. "You have a responsibility to yourself, James, and to your patients, to become the very best physician you can be."

James stared wordlessly at her. Her intuitiveness sent shivers along his spine. "It's not that simple, Inger," he said at last. "There are lots of reasons why I can't go right now."

Inger folded her hands in her lap. "When you are a renowned physician—a *certified* renowned physician, that is," she amended, "I'll take pride in knowing I was among the patients to be treated under your knowledgeable hand."

James rolled his eyes, grinning.

"I'm entirely serious, James," Inger insisted. "I haven't forgotten about the medicine you prescribed for me last winter when I was ill."

"I know. That's the humorous part. The medicine didn't help you at all, did it, Inger?"

Inger's eyes took on a mischievous gleam. "Well, it tasted bad enough for me to believe it was helping."

"There, you see. That's the exact reason why I need to go to medical school. If the prescription didn't help you, I want to know why."

"When you return from medical school, I shall obligingly come down with another case of 'winter fever' so you can try out your new medicines on me," Inger stated.

"Now, that's not funny. Don't even joke about getting sick."

"I'm only trying to make you see how important it is for you to go to school." She sat forward in her chair, her eyes bright with passion. "You must find a way of accomplishing it, James."

James smiled at her. He was surprised that he hadn't taken closer notice of her wisdom, wit, and beauty. He wouldn't make that mistake again. Inger was an intriguing girl, and he intended to spend as much time as possible getting to know her better.

CHAPTER SIXTEEN

James had spent the afternoon at Inger's place, helping her whitewash the walls inside her cabin. A couple of stones had come loose on the chimney, and he'd repaired those as well. Inger had been in a playful mood, dabbing his cheek and nose with whitewash and teasing him about the supposedly sloppy job he was doing with the paint. They had passed the evening hours laughing and talking, until the moon climbed above the mountain's peak. And now it was time to bid her good night. James reluctantly put on his hat.

Inger walked with him to the hitching post outside her door. "I'm disappointed that you wouldn't sing even one song for me, Inger. I've never known you to be shy about singing," James teased as he untethered his horse.

"That's because I usually have Lars to accompany me on his harmonica. His mistakes drown out my sour notes." She laughed at her own words.

"How about just one verse of 'Shenandoah' before I go? That's my favorite."

"I will if you join me."

"Me? You're joking. I can't carry a note."

"Perhaps next time," she answered. Her tone was inviting. She stood next to James, her slim figure a silhouette in the darkness. Overhead, the moon and stars were concealed behind silvery clouds.

"Can I take that to mean a yes?" asked James. He stepped a pace closer to her, holding the reins in his hands. Her calico dress looked gray in the night shadows, and the flaxen braid she usually wore was wound around the crest of her head.

Moonlight suddenly streamed through a patch of wispy clouds. The light played on her circlet of braided hair, transforming it into a shimmering halo. James experienced a fluttering in the pit of his stomach as he gazed at her, as if a dozen butterflies had taken up residence there.

Inger seemed oblivious to the effect she had on him. "Thank you for your help with the cabin, James," she said. "And for your company. I didn't realize how much I was going to miss my younger brother. Your visits have brightened my days considerably."

"I'm glad to be of service." A breeze stirred the air, carrying the sweet scent of Inger's hair on its wings. James breathed in the heady fragrance.

Inger nuzzled her hand between the horse's ears. "I didn't mean to imply I enjoy your company just because Lars is away. I always enjoy your company, James."

"And I very much enjoy yours," he returned in a breathless voice. He wanted to say more—how he'd relished being with her over these last few weeks while Lars was away with the expedition. How he disliked having to leave her tonight. He wanted to take her in his arms, feel her soft breath on his lips.

The intensity of his feeling surprised him. He glanced up at the golden ball of light in the night sky, and decided the moonlight was to blame for causing this reeling in his head and the perspiring of his hands. He wondered if there was a medical term for when one is struck senseless from the effects of moonlight.

Inger's gaze followed his upward. "Look, James. The sky is clearing. Make a wish on the first star you see."

James stared at the sky. His wish was for the courage to tell Inger how much he cared for her. When he lowered his eyes, he found Inger watching him. She quickly averted her gaze.

"Inger, I . . ." James began.

"Yes?" She looked up at him and her eyes were luminous, like twin moons.

"I . . . uh . . . I'd better be going," he stammered.

"Yes, it's getting late."

He swung into the saddle. "I had a nice time this evening. Thank you," he said with his heart pounding.

"So did I."

He sat astride his horse, hating to rein him onto the dirt road and lose sight of her. "You won't forget about the buggy ride you promised me for tomorrow evening?"

"I won't forget. Come early and I'll fix you supper."

"Will you make apple pie?"

She laughed. It was like a melody floating on the breeze. "Yes, James. I'll bake you an apple pie."

"Then I'll be here. Six o'clock?"

"Six is fine."

"All right. See you then." He nudged Odysseus with his heels, and the gelding sprang forward. As the horse trotted away from Inger's cabin, James twisted in the saddle to glance back at her. She looked like an angel as she stood in the shower of moonlight.

James drew a deep breath to clear his head. He whistled as he rode the distance to his cabin. When he reached the wooden barn behind the house, he led Odysseus inside and removed the horse's bridle and saddle. He stood for a moment in quiet reflection, rubbing the animal's neck. A thought had been forming in his mind over the last few days, although he hadn't mentioned it to anyone yet—not even Inger.

His hand moved along the Morgan's sturdy back. Odysseus was a strong, hardy animal, capable of carrying James over the 1,200 miles of open country between the Salt Lake valley and Chicago. It would take James perhaps six weeks to make the trip on horseback. If he left in mid-August, a few weeks from now, he could be in Chicago in time for the fall term of medical school. He stroked the gelding's back. The horse's coat was sleek and smooth beneath James' fingertips. Brother Babcock's gift to him had been a godsend. Odysseus was exactly the animal he needed to make the trip to Chicago.

Even so, there remained obstacles blocking his way. For one thing, Lars probably wouldn't be back from his expedition with Captain Stansbury by the middle of August. Inger had received several letters from him detailing his activities, but he hadn't yet mentioned when he'd be returning home. James had promised to look after Inger while her brother was away. He couldn't leave, not after giving his word to Lars.

He didn't want to leave Inger, anyway. Spending his free time with her had become a habit—one he didn't wish to break. Of late, she had been in his thoughts almost continually. Even when he was busy with other tasks, her image floated into his mind. He found himself constantly wanting to be with her.

James wasn't sure how Inger felt about him, however. Sometimes she gave him the impression that she cared for him. More than once he had caught her at an unguarded moment, gazing at him. He had seen the color rush to her cheeks when he touched her hand or stood close to her. Yet at other times, she seemed aloof—almost deliberately so. James shook his head. It was impossible to guess her feelings.

But Inger wasn't the only reason keeping him from going. Late August and early September was harvest time, and his father would need his help harvesting the crops. It took every ounce of manpower to wrest food enough from the desert soil to feed the settlers. No, he couldn't possibly go during harvest season.

And, ultimately, there was the issue of money. A term at the medical college would cost a good deal of money. Tuition and books. Lodging and food. He'd have to wait until the following term before he could even think about going—give himself time to save up enough money for his expenses. But then it would be winter, and impossible to get through the mountains. Perhaps in the spring? He frowned at the difficulties facing him.

Giving Odysseus a final pat on the haunch, James left the barn and headed for the house. When he stepped inside, he found his sisters in bed and his parents away for the evening. He moved quietly in the dimness of the cabin so as not to wake the girls. He wasn't ready for sleep himself; he was too keyed up from the evening's visit with Inger.

"James?"

He glanced up to the half floor above, where his younger sisters shared a bed. "What are you doing awake?" he whispered to Roxana.

"I can't sleep. It's too hot."

James climbed the wooden ladder and pulled a chair to the bedside. Millicent lay curled up next to the wall, snoring softly in her sleep. "Mother said you were a big help to her in the garden today," James said, smoothing the dark hair from Roxana's perspiring brow.

"We weeded and hoed rows and rows of vegetables. We should have a plentiful harvest this year," Roxana replied.

"That's good, because I got awfully tired of eating thistles, pig weeds, and sego lily roots last spring."

James could see Roxana's smile in the stream of moonlight flooding the cabin window. "Me, too. I hope I never have to eat another thistle root." She took James' hand and laid her cheek against it. "James?"

"Umm?"

"Do you ever think about getting married?"

James chuckled. "Getting married? How did we get on that topic?"

"I was lying here thinking what it will be like to leave Mama and Papa, and you and Milly, and move away to a different house. What if I don't like it? Leaving all of you, I mean."

"Well, it won't be exactly like leaving us. You'll still be part of the family, and you can come home any time you want. And it won't just be a 'different' house; it'll be *your* house—yours and your husband's house."

"What if I can't come home as often as I want? What if I have to move far away from all of you, like Elizabeth and Alexander?" She gripped his hand tighter.

"Believe me, Roxie, when the time comes, you'll be excited to set up housekeeping with your husband, wherever it may be. There's no need to worry about that," James told her.

Roxie released his hand and leaned up on one elbow. "Do you ever worry about such things, James?"

"Sure I do. I worry about finding the right girl to be my wife. What if no girl wants to marry me?"

Roxie giggled. "Oh, James, any girl would want to marry you. You're so kind and good. And handsome."

"You think I'm handsome?" James asked, nudging her shoulder.

"I'd say you're probably the most handsome brother I have."

"Now that's a real compliment, considering I'm the *only* brother you have."

Roxie didn't say anything for some seconds. Then she spoke in a quiet voice. "If Zachary had lived, he'd be eight years old now. He would have liked it here in the valley, wouldn't he? He could have chased butterflies in the meadows, and caught frogs in the streams."

"Yes, he would have liked it here," James answered solemnly. Zachary's image played in his mind.

"Sometimes, when I'm alone in the dark, I get afraid of dying."

A knot formed in James' throat. "You don't have to be afraid of that, Roxie. Nothing's going to happen to you."

"I know. Sometimes I just worry about it." Roxana sighed.

"You worry about too many things. And worrying late at night only makes things seem bigger than they really are. Now go to sleep; Ma will be upset if she finds you still awake when she comes home." James bent down and kissed the top of her dark head. "Go to sleep," he ordered.

"All right."

James stood up and pulled the chair back to its place against the wall.

"James?"

"Now what?"

"I love you."

"I love you, too, Roxie."

It was half-past nine the next evening when James knocked at the cabin door. Inger opened it and saw immediately the look of dismay on his face. "What's happened, James? You're white as a sheet."

James stumbled inside and slumped down onto a chair. He tried to keep his voice from trembling. "I'm sorry I didn't get here in time for supper, Inger. I've been with a patient all evening. A little girl. We lost her." His voice faltered.

"Oh, no. I'm so sorry, James." Inger sat down on the edge of a chair opposite him. "Do you want to tell me about it?"

James drew a ragged breath. "Diphtheria. The child had been suffering with it for the past several days, and her mother had been treating it with patent medicines and home remedies. When I arrived at the house, the child had a plaster of hot salt and tobacco applied to her neck in an effort to draw off the infection."

The vision of the dying girl, with the medicine-filled cloth across her swollen throat, and her parent's frantic pleas for help, swam before his eyes. His initial examination revealed the child had all the classic symptoms of the disease—the yellowish-gray false membrane growing over the throat and nasal passages, swollen glands under the jaws, discharge from the nose, difficulty in breathing, hoarseness, and a hard cough.

"The girl could barely draw a breath by the time I was called to her bedside. I tell you, Inger, watching that child struggle for each breath was heartbreaking. Her little face was pallid and covered with sweat. She kept clutching at her throat, but her attempts were so feeble, and so hopeless." James shivered, even though his body was clammy with perspiration.

Inger's eyes filled with tears. "There was nothing you could do to save her, James. It was out of your hands."

James abruptly got to his feet. "If her mother had only called me earlier—as soon as the patch appeared in the child's throat—we might have been able to help her. Such a waste, Inger. Such a dreadful waste." He began pacing the room.

Inger watched him stride back and forth.

"Poultices, plasters, and patent medicines. Those are like gnats battling big black beetles in dealing with this disease." James was talking under his breath, almost forgetting Inger's presence. "She should have been treated with a third dilution of Belladonna; sixth dilution of 'Lachesis; Mercurius . . ." He ticked off the trove of homeopathic medicines used to combat diphtheria. "I don't know. Perhaps it wouldn't have helped anyway," he concluded in despair.

"Come sit down, James. Rest yourself," Inger begged him.

He took his seat again, and put his head in his hands. "She died right before my eyes, Inger. While I stood there, helpless to do anything to save her. Her parents are devastated."

Inger covered his hands with hers. "Perhaps God had his own purposes for that little girl."

James looked up. Inger's face was bent close to his, her eyes brimming with sympathetic tears. "I need to believe that, don't I?" he asked solemnly.

"I know you already believe it, James. After all you can do, the outcome rests with God. We can be grateful that we know His eternal plan for us."

James stared at Inger's face. She knew what he was feeling, and that was a great comfort and strength. He grasped Inger's hands in his. "Thank you," he whispered. "Thank you for sharing your abiding faith. It buoys me up."

She didn't reply, but only looked at him with a steady gaze.

James pressed her hands in his for a long moment. Then he gently let them go and leaned back in his chair, relaxing the taut muscles in his body. "I need to learn more, Inger. Know more. If I'm to become a capable physician, I must take every advantage to study medicine and the treatment of disease."

"You're talking about attending medical college, aren't you?"

"Yes. I feel I've reached the point where I can progress no further without formal schooling. It's so frustrating not to be able to tap the knowledge I know is available at medical school."

"Then you must go to medical school," Inger said with conviction.

"How can I? I haven't the financial means to go to school. Besides, I'm needed at home."

"You'll have to find a way, James. Have you asked for Heavenly Father's help? Have you prayed and fasted about the matter?"

"Endlessly. But I see no possibilities opening up for me."

"You must have patience, then, and faith. No prayer goes unanswered. Some just take a little longer to answer than others."

"I hope you're right, Inger."

"I know I am. Surely God will not deny you the righteous desires of your heart, James."

She smiled and put a hand on his knee. He felt a sudden impulse to hold her in his arms, feel the soft touch of her cheek against his, inhale the sweet fragrance of her hair. He resisted the urge, and instead got to his feet and stood beside the window, staring out.

Inger stood, too. "Will you eat something, James? I can warm supper for you."

He shook his head. "Thank you, but I'm not hungry."

"No, I suppose you wouldn't be," she murmured. She moved away from him and paused at the table, her hands resting on the back of a chair.

"I'm sorry you prepared supper for me, and then I wasn't here to eat it," he said, feeling awkward about the apology.

"Don't concern yourself about that at all, James. We'll do it another time."

"Yes, another time. That would be fine."

"Go home now, and get some rest. You've had a trying day," she told him in a gentle voice.

"You won't mind if I don't stay?"

"Of course not," she replied, smiling. "I know you'll be back."

"You have the understanding heart of a woman, Inger, and the soul of an angel," James told her with a smile.

"Go home, James. And sleep."

He walked to the table where she stood, leaned across it, and kissed her cheek. "The soul of an angel," he whispered in her ear.

CHAPTER SEVENTEEN

"What did you think of Mr. Thornlie's demonstration, Milly?" asked James as he and his sister crossed the plowed fields toward their home.

"I liked it a lot. I wish you had volunteered to have your head read by the phren . . . phrento . . ." She searched for the correct pronunciation of the word.

"The word is 'phrenologist.' Mr. Thornlie is a phrenologist," James said with a grin.

"Yes. I liked the way he ran his fingers over that man's head to read his bumps."

"That's one way of describing it," James laughed. "He was feeling the shape and irregularities of the skull, which phrenologists say are projections of the underlying brain. They claim to be able to analyze a person's mental characteristics and personality, as indicated by the projections of the skull. Fascinating stuff, huh?"

Milly glanced up into her brother's face. "It sounds like you don't believe in the science of phrenology," she said, mimicking the term she had heard earlier that day at the public demonstration by Mr. Thornlie, whose travels had brought him to the valley.

"I don't know if I do or if I don't. But it was interesting, nonetheless." James picked up a smooth, round stone from his path and tossed it aside.

Milly walked beside him, the ends of her red braids poking from beneath her bonnet. "Thank you for taking me to see the demonstration, James. I really liked it."

"I figured you would."

"I'll race you to the house," she challenged, charging ahead of him.

"Oh, yeah? You'll lose, you little scamp," James replied. He loped easily alongside his younger sister, staying just enough ahead of her to fuel the contest.

Millicent hitched up her skirts and ran as fast as her legs would carry her. Her ankle-high shoes left prints in the deep, rich soil of the field.

When they neared the cabin, James slowed his pace, allowing Millicent to burst through the cabin door before him.

"I win!" she shouted. She collapsed onto a chair, clapping her hands together and giggling.

"So you did. Well, you're a faster runner than I suspected." James squatted down in the open doorway, his hands resting on his knees. He wanted to watch the afternoon shadows stretch themselves out over the fields. It was mid-September, and much of the harvest had been gathered in. James thought the furrowed ground looked tired, as if worn out from the effort of the growing season.

Millicent hummed a tune as she sat on the chair, swinging her stockinged legs in time to the rhythm. James studied the patterns of light and shadow the sun was painting on the empty fields.

"When I grow up, I think I'm going to become a phrenologist," Millicent mused.

"An excellent occupation, Milly."

"Girls can be phrenologists, can't they?" she asked, leaning forward with a sudden worried expression.

"Of course they can. Girls can be anything they want to be."

"Then I'll become a phrenologist and read people's bumps. And if I find something wrong with them, I'll send them to you for doctoring."

"That sounds like a very good plan. And I'll send my patients to you to have their heads read. We can work as a team."

Millicent heaved a huge sigh of contentment.

James sat in silence for a few moments more, then he got to his feet. "I'm going to run over to Inger's place. Tell Mother where I've gone, will you Milly, and that I'll be home in time for supper." He tugged one of Millicent's long red braids.

"Okay." She jumped out of her chair and dashed past James into the yard. In another moment, she was engrossed in picking wildflowers growing along the ditch that ran near the cabin.

James shoved his hands into his pockets and walked to the barn to saddle Odysseus. The sun felt warm on his face, and the soil beneath his feet was loose and dry. In a few minute's time he was astride his horse, approaching Inger's cabin.

He found Inger sitting on the porch with a bowl of snap beans in her lap. She waved when she saw him coming up the dusty road. James noticed the slimness of her waist where the strings of her apron tied around her.

"Hello," he smiled, pausing at the foot of the porch.

"Hello yourself," she responded with a grin. "Won't you sit down?"

"Thank you." He planted himself on the porch, his back against the post. "How are you today?"

"Satisfied."

"Satisfied? About what?" he grinned.

"As you can see, I have a whole bowl full of snap beans here, fresh from my garden. And they're about the biggest and prettiest beans I've ever had the pleasure to lay eyes on." Her slim hand caressed the beans heaped inside the bowl.

"You find pleasure and beauty in whatever you happen to be doing, Inger. It's one of the things I like about you."

She favored him with another broad smile.

"Have you heard from Lars?" he asked.

"Not since receiving the last note he scribbled off to me. I read that one to you."

"Yes—the one about catching a fish with whiskers like a cat in the Utah Lake. I remember that letter. Lars tends to spin poetry out of the most ordinary experiences," James observed.

Inger laughed. Her laughter seemed to infuse itself into the beans resting in the bowl in her lap. When she snapped off the ends of them, they gave way with a crisp, merry sound. "And how is the young doctor today?" she asked, her eyes on her task.

"Satisfied."

Inger glanced up at him and grinned.

"Dr. McCaffrey is turning more and more of his patients over to me. He rarely goes with me now on house calls."

"He must trust your skill and judgment."

"I'm by no means able to deal with every emergency yet. We had to do an amputation of the leg yesterday. That is to say, Dr. McCaffrey did the surgery and I watched."

"Oh, dear. That sounds unpleasant." She was snapping the ends off the beans more quickly now.

"Unpleasant, yes. But it saved the man's life."

Inger pushed a straying strand of yellow hair from her cheek. Her hair was loosely braided into one long, golden streak down her back. The dress she wore was a yellow and pink plaid. James thought she looked like morning sunshine.

"Yesterday I visited a friend of mine, Sister Whittier, who is ill. Do you know Sister Whittier?"

James shook his head.

"Well, she's been ill with the grippe for several days. She's been taking 'Swain's Panacea' in the hope it will cure her."

James rolled his eyes skyward. "'Swain's Panacea' won't do her a bit of good. It's like every other patent medicine. People waste their money on such concoctions; but more importantly, those kinds of remedies dissuade people from seeking medical help."

"That's just what I told Sister Whittier."

"Also tell her that 'Swain's Panacea' is nothing more than a mixture containing sarsaparilla, oil of wintergreen, and corrosive sublimate—a dangerous mercury compound that has undoubtedly killed some who have ingested it."

Inger's hands paused in their work. "Oh. I will most certainly relay what you've told me."

"Good."

"Are all patent medicines so dangerous, James?"

"No, not all of them. Some are merely powerful purgatives. Others do no harm, but certainly no good. Collectively, patent medicines are a bane to the medical profession." James' brows came together in a fierce scowl.

Inger resumed plucking the ends off her bowlful of beans. "What about herbal medicines? Mother was quite knowledgeable about medicinal plants and herbs. She taught all of us girls something about it."

"Herbal medicine has its place. I think it can be very effective at times," James replied, shifting his position on the porch. "How much do you know about it?"

"Mother taught us how to dig the roots of various plants, and how to store them properly. She knew all their uses. She showed us how to make powders from barks and dried herbs. I learned how to make a variety of medicinal teas."

James gazed out across the vacant fields as Inger talked. In the distance, he caught sight of a lone traveler making his way down the rutted road. "I think a knowledge of herbal medicine is a very good thing to have," he commented absently. His attention was divided between what Inger was telling him and the traveler on the road.

"Well, I'm finished with these beans. I'm going to cook them up for supper. Will you stay for supper, James?"

"Uhh . . . " James muttered, squinting across the field at the oncoming stranger.

"Supper, James. Will you stay for supper?"

"Inger, look over there," he said, pointing to the figure on the road. "I think it's Lars."

"Lars? I don't expect Lars home for another few weeks," Inger murmured. She laid the bowl of snap beans aside and stood up, gazing intently at the person who was drawing nearer.

James rose to his feet also. "It is Lars, isn't it?" The figure was close enough now for the two of them to see that the man was dressed in brown trousers and a plaid shirt, and was carrying his hat in his hand.

"Why, that's Jens!" Inger gasped. "My brother, Jens." A stunned look flashed across her face. She started toward the approaching man, and after a moment of hesitation, greeted him with an embrace.

James stood watching them. He was curious to see this brother he had heard so little about. He knew only that Jens had left the bosom of the family years before after having some sort of disagreement with his parents. The family had lost contact with him since, and Lars had once made the comment that he thought his brother was dead.

"Jens, this is James Kade," Inger said. Her voice was breathless with emotion. "His family and ours were neighbors when we lived in Green County."

James approached the pair and put out a hand to Jens. The man took it, and the two of them exchanged a brief handshake. Upon closer inspection, James saw this man was an older, grimmer version of Lars. Though his features resembled those of his younger brother, Jens' eyes lacked the warmth and good humor which so characterized Lars. And the mouth had a cruel turn to it. He was taller than Lars, and heavier, but he possessed the same shock of unruly yellow hair, intense blue eyes, and ruddy complexion.

"It's nice to make your acquaintance, Jens."

"Likewise," the other man answered. His voice was deep and gruff.

"Come inside the house, Jens," Inger invited, taking his arm. "You, too, James."

Inger and her brother started toward the cabin. They'd taken only a few steps when Jens flung a glance over his shoulder. Although the look was brief, James sensed hostility in it, as if Jens viewed him as a potential menace.

"Thanks, Inger, but I think I'll be going. You visit with your brother, and I'll see you in a day or two."

"You're welcome to stay, James." Her eyes shone, and she kept a tight hold on her brother's arm.

"I'll come back another time. Soon, I promise. Jens." James nodded at the older man, whose expression was guarded. Then he quickly turned and walked away.

The exchange with Inger's brother sent a chill down his spine. He shuddered as he mounted his horse and started toward home. Something about Jens' manner repelled him and frightened him at the same time. He almost hated to leave Inger alone with him. But that was a ridiculous thought. This man was Inger's brother, and she seemed happy to see him. Even so, he wished Lars were home. He would have felt better about leaving Inger with her brother if Lars had been there, too.

James spent that evening at home in the company of his father. His mother and two sisters had gone to a ladies' meeting at Brother Orson Pratt's house. He and Christian sat in their chairs, reading. After a time, James put his book face down on the floor because he couldn't keep his mind on the words. He kept seeing Jens Johanssen's face staring up at him from the page—staring with eyes as cold and hard as ice. He wondered what Jens was doing here in the valley, and why he had come. He felt uneasy about leaving

Inger alone with him, and he couldn't get out of his mind the malevolent glance Jens had given him.

"Is something the matter, James? You've been awfully quiet this evening."

His father's voice startled him, and he looked up at Christian with wide eyes. "No, Father, everything's fine. I was just mulling some things over, that's all."

"If you need someone to talk to, I have a good listening ear," Christian said.

"I know, Pa. Thanks."

James felt a twinge of guilt over keeping his troubled thoughts to himself. He generally discussed his concerns with Christian, and together they came up with solutions. But this time, James preferred to keep his feelings private. He wanted to work out his own conclusions.

Christian went back to his reading while James slouched in his chair, his thoughts dark. He wished he knew more about Jens' character than only what could be read in the man's face. He pondered that point for some moments.

"Pa?"

"Yes, son."

"Do you believe a person's character shows in his countenance?"

Christian put down the book he'd been reading. "That's an interesting question, James. Yes, I believe I do. If you're talking about the Saints, those who are righteous and have the Spirit with them, I know their countenances carry a special glow."

"And what about those people who aren't Saints—who are disobeying the laws of the land and the laws of God. Does it show on their faces, too?"

"I think it eventually does. Dishonesty, debauchery, and violence eventually reveal themselves outwardly as well as inwardly."

"I think so, too," James replied.

Neither of them spoke for a moment. Then James asked, "What is it that makes one man hold fast to the gospel and another turn away, when both had opportunity to receive it?"

"That answer is simple. It hinges on what is in a man's heart."

James spent a moment digesting that pearl of wisdom. "I'm glad you and Mother remained faithful. I don't know where I'd be if you hadn't."

Christian smiled at his son. "Your mother and I were introduced to the gospel and embraced it. We were like tender new plants, cultivated by the gospel's message. But you've had the influence of the gospel most of your life. You've benefitted from sun, rain, and careful pruning, which has strengthened your testimony and caused you to grow, like a stalk of wheat, tall and straight."

Christian leaned forward in his chair. "Then, when harvest is nigh, the winnowing comes. All good gardeners know they must separate the wheat from the chaff in order for the grain to be useful. The grain is threshed—beaten, flailed, subjected to hardship. Then the worth of the grain is exposed. The chaff falls away, and the wheat is strong and hardy because of its experiences."

James listened, spellbound, to his father's parable.

"You are like the wheat, James—strong, straight, and hardy. You remind me of Nephi in the Book of Mormon. He was a strong young man too, valiant in his testimony of Christ and unerringly committed to obeying the commandments of God, no matter what the cost was to himself. Nephi was always an example of righteousness— to his brothers, to his enemies, to those who followed his leadership."

"Nephi has always been a great example to me, Pa. I wish I were more like him. But I think the only thing Nephi and I have in common is the fact that we were both blessed with goodly parents."

Christian smiled. "The Lord expects much from you, James. When the winnowing is completed, then a bountiful harvest will come forth."

James got up from his chair and went to his father's side. He put his arms around Christian's neck and hugged him. "Thanks, Pa."

CHAPTER EIGHTEEN

"Place that cloth on one more time, James. The patient is starting to awaken," Dr. McCaffrey directed.

James held the ether-soaked cloth over the woman's nose and mouth. She slipped deeper into unconsciousness.

"I'm almost through here. Just another moment or two," McCaffrey said as he stitched the incision closed.

James held the cloth in place while he watched McCaffrey work. The woman lay limp and unmoving on the table, blood seeping from the incision in her belly. The thirty-year-old woman had come to the office complaining of pain in her stomach; she supposed she might be with child because of the swelling and soreness in the area of her abdomen. James' examination revealed she was not pregnant, but suffering from a tumor. When he explained to her that surgery would be required to remove the tumor, she had adamantly refused his help. People *died* from surgery, she'd told him. And she was right. Even if the operation was successful, too often the patient expired afterward from infection and gangrene. The problem was a frustrating one for any physician.

When the woman's tumor grew larger and she became more seriously ill, she agreed to the surgery. This kind of operation was only made feasible through the recent discovery of ether vapor. It was a boon for physicians and patients alike, for with the application of ether the patient was rendered unconscious, allowing the physician to perform surgery without haste or pain to the patient. Dr. McCaffrey had been using ether in his surgeries for only about a year; its properties were new to the medical establishment. The use of ether had been publicly demonstrated at the Massachusetts General Hospital in 1846 by a dentist named William Morton, who accomplished surgery without pain on his patient using ether vapor. James was fascinated and delighted by the opportunities presented to physicians for more complex types of surgeries made possible with the use of ether. It presented the biggest advancement in the field of medicine since antiquity.

"There, I'm finished," Dr. McCaffrey said, wiping his bloodied hands on a towel lying on the table.

James lifted the ether-laden cloth from the patient's face. "You did a fine job with that surgery, Dr. McCaffrey," he said.

"Thank you, James. You could have carried out the surgery yourself. You have the skills and knowledge for it."

"But not the experience. You were the proper one to perform that operation."

"The only way to gain experience, my boy, is by doing." McCaffrey covered the woman with a blanket and began putting away his surgical instruments. "And I think you're ready to do exactly that."

James paused in the midst of stoppering the bottle of ether. "What are you saying, sir?"

McCaffrey pulled at his drooping gray mustache. "I'm thinking of retiring very soon, James. That should come as no surprise to you. I told you at the beginning of our venture together that I planned to go back to Vermont. I think the time has arrived."

"But, sir, I'm not qualified yet to take over your medical practice. I haven't sufficient experience or skills."

"Hogwash, my boy. You know more than I did when I began practicing. You'll learn as you go along." McCaffrey walked over to the small table that held a pitcher and basin. He dipped his hands into the basin of water prepared earlier; James watched the water turn pink from the blood on McCaffrey's hands.

"I don't feel competent, Dr. McCaffrey. I need more training. Perhaps a term at the medical college . . ."

McCaffrey cut him off. "A waste of time, in my opinion. Everything you need to know about medicine can be learned right here in this office." McCaffrey dried his hands on a clean towel. "Especially now, with that confounded new organization, the American Medical Association, trying to impose its rules on the medical colleges. Those schools spend more time haggling with each other over college requirements and lengths of term than they do in educating their students."

James made no response to McCaffrey's comments, because he fervently disagreed with them. The American Medical Association, formed two years earlier in 1847, was struggling to develop regulations for the dozens of private medical colleges that had sprung up around the country. It advocated improved medical education, promoted stricter medical ethics, and supported public health measures. Most medical colleges bestowed degrees after completing one academic term, which lasted anywhere from eight to fourteen weeks. In addition, they generally required students to serve an apprenticeship of one or two years prior to admission. At the first meeting of the American Medical Association, it was proposed that colleges lengthen the academic year to six months. Some colleges were adopting the recommendation; others continued with their current regimens.

"Wipe that look of consternation off your face, boy. I'm not ready to leave the practice tomorrow, but you ought to be preparing yourself for it. In the future, I plan to assume more of an advisory role, allowing you to take over the work that goes on here at the office," McCaffrey said.

James swallowed hard. The prospect of personally handling every medical case that came into the office was staggering. He felt the weight of it press down on his shoulders. "I hope I'll be equal to the task, Dr. McCaffrey," he murmured.

"Of course you will, James. You're going to make a fine physician. Now see to the comfort of our patient while I attend to a few errands. I'll tell the woman's husband that he may come in now."

McCaffrey put on his hat and left the office without further conversation. James bent over the woman lying on the table and watched the rhythmic rise and fall of her chest. She was still unconscious from the effects of the ether. He tucked the blanket around her.

A moment later, the patient's husband entered the room. He'd been anxiously waiting outside while his wife underwent surgery. "Dr. McCaffrey said my wife came through the surgery fine." His eyes darted to the still figure lying on the table. "Is she going to be all right?"

"I hope so. The operation went very well. If we can prevent infection from setting in at the site of the incision, she should heal without incident," James told him. "You may sit with her if you like. She should be waking up shortly."

James watched the man slide a chair to his wife's bedside and reach under the blanket to take her hand. He turned away to allow the couple their privacy. Sitting down at the desk, he withdrew a clean sheet of paper, and a pen and ink. He dipped the quill pen into the ink bottle and began rehearsing on paper the details of the surgery just completed. He was still writing when a knock sounded at the door. He laid his pen aside and went to open it.

"Inger! This is a nice surprise. Come in."

"Are you engaged with a patient, James? I can come back later if you're busy," Inger said.

"No. Your timing is perfect. Dr. McCaffrey and I just finished up with a surgery. I was only recording a few remarks. Come in."

Inger glanced inside the office. She saw the man sitting by his wife, who was by this time beginning to regain consciousness. "Can you step outside for a moment, James, where we might have a private word?"

"Of course." James followed her to two chairs sitting on the porch outside the door of the doctor's office. He frowned in concern. Something was wrong; Inger didn't ordinarily pay him a visit during office hours. He guessed it had to do with Jens.

"I'll only take a moment so you can get back to your work," Inger said in a subdued voice.

"I have as much time as you need, Inger. What is it? Has something happened with Jens?"

Inger sat down stiffly on her chair. "Oh, James. He's so changed. He frightens me."

"I don't think you should stay in the cabin alone with him, Inger. Come home with me. You can stay at our place until he leaves."

Inger shook her head. "You misunderstand me, James. I'm not afraid for myself. I'm afraid for Jens."

"What do you mean?"

Inger slid forward in her chair. "He's like a wild man. Not in the outward sense, but here." She pointed to her heart.

James' frown cut deep furrows in his brow.

"Let me explain so that you can understand." She drew a deep breath. "I was only eleven when Jens left home, but I remember well his disobedience and disrespect for my parents. My mother was a strong-willed woman, and in her own way tried to shape Jens into an honorable son. Although she was stern with him, she loved him. He was her eldest child."

James nodded.

"My father was gentler. Jens was a great trial to him." She sighed softly. "When my parents became acquainted with the Mormon Church and were baptized, they were especially anxious for Jens to embrace the gospel, too. Although Jens was baptized, he never accepted the gospel. And as he grew older, he grew more rebellious. He left home when he was seventeen. He never had any contact with the family after that, although occasionally we would hear word about him through others."

"Which wasn't often good news, am I right?"

Inger nodded. "Yes. We heard he'd gotten into a drunken brawl and spent the night in jail. Or that he'd stolen someone's property. Apparently he drifted from place to place. We heard rumors that he was in Far West, Missouri." Inger's lip trembled. "And that he'd allied himself with the mob who drove the Saints out of Missouri."

James clenched his fist. "I don't want him setting foot back in your cabin. What's he doing here, anyway? It's certainly not family ties that have brought him."

Inger shook her head. "No, he's not interested in reestablishing ties with us. He's here to sell goods to the gold miners. Knowing we're of the Mormon faith, I suppose he assumed we were in the valley, but I think he sought us out simply for a place to stay while he's conducting his business."

"Well, he can just stay somewhere else," James said. He was seething with anger.

"In spite of everything he's done, he's still my brother. I want to help him if I can."

"He's a dangerous man, Inger, and he could bring danger to you. I don't think you should have anything to do with him."

"I want to let Johanna and Kirstine know he's here. Together, we might have some influence for good on him."

James wanted to protest, but he pressed his lips together and remained silent. He wished Jens had never come.

"I've borrowed a horse and buggy from a friend, and I'm going to ride out to Johanna's place now and speak to her. I wanted to let you know where I am, so you wouldn't worry about me if you came by the cabin and found me gone."

"Would you like me to go with you? I know Johanna's homestead is across the Jordan River, some distance away." James formed a mental picture of Inger's oldest sister. From what Inger had just told him about their mother, Johanna apparently was of similar temperament. Johanna had married later than most women, and when she did it was as a plural wife. Her husband was a bishop serving the people west of the Jordan River. He and his first wife already had five children when Johanna was sealed to him, and Johanna had given birth to two more children.

"No, I think I should go by myself," Inger replied. "I'll have more success with Johanna if I speak to her alone. She's very bitter toward Jens."

"All right. But promise me you'll let me know immediately if there's the slightest hint of trouble from Jens. I mean it."

"Yes, James. I promise."

James took Inger's hand into his. It was cool, and light as a feather. "I promised Lars I'd look after you. I intend to keep that promise."

She smiled. "And all this time I thought it was because you enjoyed my company so much."

"Of course I enjoy your company. You know that's not what I meant, and that —"

Inger interrupted him with a soft laugh. "I was only teasing you, James."

James' tight expression eased. He kept hold of Inger's hand as he walked with her to her buggy and helped her up into it. He handed her the reins. "Be careful driving out to Johanna's."

"I will."

"I'll see you tomorrow. You can tell me how your visit went."

She nodded. "Thank you, James, for listening to me. It means a great deal to me just to know you're there when I need you."

"I'm glad you find me indispensable," he grinned.

"I do—much more than you know."

She shook the reins, and the gray mare hitched to the buggy tossed her head and started forward in a trot.

James stood in the road, watching the buggy until it was out of sight. He shoved his hands into his pockets and walked back to the office porch, his heart hammering. He realized Inger had just told him that she cared for him.

James knocked at the cabin door with a feeling of trepidation, hoping Jens would be away for the evening so he and Inger could talk privately. He was anxious to hear about her visit with Johanna. And he couldn't deny the fact that he just wanted to be near her.

Inger answered his knock. His smile faded when he saw her moist and red-rimmed eyes. "I'm not able to talk right now, James. Can you come back later?" she asked in a quivering voice.

"What's wrong? What's happened, Inger? Has Jens done something to harm you?" His words rushed out in a single breath.

Suddenly a hand darted out and grasped Inger's arm, jerking her away from the door. "Is that your young doctor friend? Tell him to come inside," a deep voice growled.

Jens appeared in the open doorway, his hand still clenched around Inger's arm. James' breath caught in his throat. He looked from Jens' pale and perspiring face to Inger's frightened one. "What's going on here?" James snapped, stepping into the cabin.

Jens loosened his grip on Inger's arm. With a start, James realized the man was injured. His shoulder was soaked with blood, and as he took a step backward he swayed on his feet. James thought Inger's brother was going to collapse on the spot where he stood. Jens' eyes were bright as with fever, and his lips a white gash in his wan face.

Inger hurried to James' side. "I'm sorry," she rasped in his ear. "Jens ordered me not to let anyone inside."

"Are you all right?" James asked her. "You're not hurt?"

"No, I'm not hurt," she answered, her voice shaking.

"Of course she's all right," Jens snarled. "You've got eyes, ain't you? It's me who needs your attention. You're a doc, right?"

Inger's eyes welled up with fresh tears. "He's been shot, James. He came to the house just before you arrived, bleeding and pale as death."

"Yes, I'm a physician," James replied, focusing on Jens. "Who did this to you?"

"What difference does it make who did it? I've been shot. I got a slug in my shoulder that's wrenching the life out of me." Without warning, Jens pulled a revolver from under his shirt and pointed it at James.

Inger's startled gasp filled the room. James immediately stepped in front of her to shield her with his body.

"And you're going to remove it for me, my young friend." Jens waved the gun at him. "Get over here."

James started toward the injured man, with Inger following behind him.

"You stay where you are, sis," Jens ordered menacingly.

"Do as he says, Inger," James said in a low voice. "I'll take care of this."

"You ain't taking care of nothing but this shoulder of mine. I said get over here!" Jens brandished the gun wildly.

"Put down the gun, Jens. I can't do anything for you until you lay down that revolver."

Jens' white face was shiny with perspiration. The hand holding the gun trembled.

"Come on, Jens. Every minute you stand there is one minute less you've got to live if you don't let me remove that bullet. And I can't do it with a gun pointed at my head."

James could see him hesitate. A moment later, Jens stuffed the weapon back in the waistband of his trousers, under his shirt. He sank down onto Lars' bed, which rested against the wall of the room.

James strode quickly to the bed and bent over Inger's brother to inspect the wound. He was immediately assaulted by the stench of whiskey clinging to the man. James pressed his lips together, trying to ignore the revulsion he felt for Inger's older brother. "Get me some hot water, Inger, and some cloths. Do you have any bandages in the house?"

"No, but I can tear some strips of cloth for you," she answered, her eyes darting to her brother's face. She quickly went to get the things James requested.

Jens moaned and closed his eyes. His breathing was labored. James watched him for an instant, then walked to the cupboard where Inger kept her cutlery and selected a small, sharp knife. When he turned back to Jens, he could see the man was on the edge of consciousness. The whiskey had served a useful purpose after all, James thought ruefully. Removing the bullet would be painful, and Jens was better off unconscious. James wished he had his surgical knife, but there was no time to go to McCaffrey's office and get it. Jens was losing a dangerous amount of blood; the crimson stain on the shoulder of his shirt was spreading.

For a split second, it occurred to James to withhold treatment. Jens, no doubt, had been embroiled in mischief when he'd taken that bullet in the shoulder, and James was thoroughly repulsed by the man's character. But the thought left him as quickly as it had come. He had no right to choose whom or whom not to help. That was God's province. Didn't the scriptures say the Lord God sends the rain on the just and the unjust alike? It was James' responsibility as a physician to help anyone in need, whether or not he felt they deserved his assistance.

James quickly tore the bloodied shirt away from Jens' shoulder. The wound oozed blood. Jens groaned and rolled his head to one side, but he didn't open his eyes.

"Here are the cloths and hot water, James. I'm tearing you some strips for bandages right now." Inger set a small stack of cloths and a pan filled with water on the bedside table.

"Thank you," James murmured as he examined the bleeding wound in Jens' shoulder. He dipped one of the cloths in water and sponged the area around the wound. The ball did not appear to be lodged too deeply beneath the skin; James could see a glimmer of its shiny, slick surface. He took the knife in hand and carefully began to probe the wound. Jens cried out in pain, and his body jerked.

"Try to hold still," James said, his eyes on the wound. The directive was unnecessary, for Jens lapsed into unconsciousness when James again inserted the tip of the knife into his shoulder.

Inger brought the strips of bandages and sat silently near James' side as he worked to remove the lead ball. The operation took only a few minutes. James located the slug, extracted it, and set it on a cloth on the table. Then he sponged the area again and bandaged it. Inger covered her brother with a blanket.

"Will be recover, James?" Inger inquired anxiously.

James nodded. "I think he's more inebriated than seriously hurt." He looked up into Inger's face. She was hovering over his shoulder, her eyes riveted on her brother's still figure. Her look of concern melted James' heart. He took her hand in his. "He'll be all right," he said softly.

As Inger glanced at him, a tear rolled down her cheek. James fumbled in his pocket for a handkerchief and gently dried the tear from her face. Then he put the handkerchief into her hands. "Did Jens tell you exactly what happened?"

Inger dabbed the handkerchief to her eyes. "No. He was nearly incoherent when he arrived here, ranting about someone trying to cheat him out of a case of whiskey."

James frowned. "Probably some trouble over the sale of his goods."

"Yes." Inger continued to gaze on her brother's face.

James stood up from the chair, took the pan of bloodied water, and went outside with it. He dumped the water into the dirt beside the cabin, then came back indoors. He eyed Jens' bandaged wound; the cloth bandage was already blotched with scarlet. He sat back down on his chair next to Inger. "Did you see Johanna yesterday?" he asked, hoping to take her mind off Jens' unconscious condition.

"Yes. When I arrived at Johanna's place, Kirstine was there visiting. I told them both about Jens being here in the valley. Kirstine began crying when she heard the news . . . you know how tender-hearted she is." Inger's lip quivered, and tears started in her eyes.

"Go on. What did Johanna say?"

"She was adamant about not wanting anything to do with Jens. She refused to see him—didn't even want to talk about him." Inger wiped her eyes with the handkerchief. "Johanna is terribly bitter and unrelenting in her feelings for him."

James covered Inger's hand with his own. He hated seeing her in such distress and being incapable of doing anything to relieve it. "All of you are probably better off not having anything to do with Jens. I know that sounds harsh, but it's the advice Lars would probably have for you if he were here." He put his arm around Inger's shoulders and drew her close to him. He wished he could do something to take away her pain. She looked so fragile, so helpless and forlorn, sitting next to him with the handkerchief pressed to her eyes. His heart was filled with tenderness for her.

"After Jens recovers, I'm worried about what he might do to the man who shot him," Inger said in a whisper.

"So am I. If some dishonesty was involved over the sale of his goods, there might be repercussions. The constable may even need to be brought into it."

Inger twisted the handkerchief she clutched in her hands.

"I think it might be best to relieve Jens of his gun before he wakes up," James remarked quietly.

"Yes. Do it, James."

James withdrew his arm from around her shoulders and carefully started to reach for Jens' revolver. The gun lay exposed at the man's waist, tucked in the waistband of his trousers. Just as James closed his fingers over the cold steel, Jens grabbed him by the wrist. Jens cried out in pain with the motion, and he fell back, profanity bubbling from his lips.

James lost his hold on the gun. He frowned, concerned more for the moment with Jens' condition than with gaining possession of the weapon. "Lie still, Jens, or you'll start that wound bleeding uncontrollably," James cautioned. He started to replace the blanket across Jens' arm, but Jens flung it aside.

The injured man struggled to sit up. "Get out of my way," he barked.

Inger leaned toward her brother. "Please, Jens, lie still. You're weak, and you've lost a lot of blood."

Jens was sitting up straight now. He blinked his eyes, trying to focus on his sister's face. His own face was ashen. "I have to get out of here," he muttered. He started to get to his feet, but James stopped him.

"You're not going anywhere, Jens. You've just regained consciousness. You need to rest and recuperate from that bullet wound."

James' answer was the gun pointed in his face.

"Jens, what are you doing?" Inger gasped.

"Tell your doctor friend to back off. Don't either one of you try to stop me," Jens threatened, holding the revolver pointed toward James' head. He rose unsteadily to his feet, grimacing with pain.

James' heart began beating in double-time. He kept one eye on the gun, and the other on Jens' pallid face. He believed Jens capable of using the weapon.

"Jens, put the gun down," Inger pleaded. "You don't know what you're doing."

"Shut up!" Jens cried. He shifted the direction of the gun barrel from James' head to Inger's, and then back again to James. "Where's your horse, Inger?" he asked in a rasping voice.

"I don't have one. Lars has it with him," Inger whispered.

Jens cursed in frustration.

James was raging inside. A current of hatred like he'd never experienced before was coursing through him. If Jens hurt Inger in any way . . ."

Jens took a menacing step toward him. "I'll have to borrow your horse, my friend."

"No, don't take Odysseus!" Inger cried out. "We'll find you another horse."

Jens' glare rested on his sister's face. "I don't have time for that. But thank you for the offer," he answered sarcastically. "Your doctor friend will be happy to loan me his horse, won't you?" He turned to James. James saw malice smouldering in his eyes.

"Go ahead and take it, Jens. But you won't get far. I removed the bullet from your shoulder, but the wound will continue to bleed if you don't lie quietly."

"I'll have to take my chances on that, now, won't I? You see, I can't afford to wait around. I've made an enemy or two in your town. Gold miners are a nasty breed." He turned to Inger. "Go get my saddlebag. It's lying on the floor over there." He gestured with his gun to a place beside the door where the saddlebag lay in a heap.

Inger gave James a frightened glance as she walked to the saddlebag and picked it up. She handed it to Jens without speaking.

"That's the girl. You mind real well, sis." Jens placed the saddlebag over his good shoulder, wincing in pain with the movement. "Now, both of you get over against that wall." He nodded to the far wall opposite the door.

James took Inger's hand and led her to the spot Jens directed.

"I'm sorry I can't stay for supper," Jens said in a sardonic tone. "I have to be on my way."

A squeaking noise came from Inger's throat.

"You plan to leave behind your wagon and goods?" James spat out the question. It was all he could do to restrain himself from physically attacking Jens.

"Why would I do that? Just because I have a little gold dust in my saddlebag doesn't mean I'm gonna forget about my rig." He glanced at the saddlebag slung across his shoulder, and greediness gleamed in his eyes. "But I need a horse to get to it. So I appreciate the loan, my young friend."

Jens began to back out of the room toward the door of the cabin.

"Jens, please don't do this. We can work something out . . ."

"It was nice seeing you, sis," Jens sneered. "Don't try to follow me, or send the law after me. Believe me, you'll be sorry if you do."

With that threat on his lips, Jens opened the door of the cabin and slipped out. Through the open doorway, James watched him throw his saddlebag across Odysseus' rump and haul himself up into the saddle. He dug his heels into the horse's flanks and lashed the ends of the reins against his neck. Odysseus sped off at a gallop.

"Oh, I'm so sorry, James," Inger sobbed. "How could my own brother behave like this?"

As she dissolved into tears, James enfolded her in a tight embrace. She let him hold her, comfort her. He closed his eyes, grateful to have the grim encounter with Jens over and Inger safely in his arms. He gently kissed the top of her head. The nearness of her, the feel and smell of her, set his blood racing. He forgot his keen anger with Jens, and the sting of losing his horse. He stood silently with Inger in his arms, her cheek against his face.

CHAPTER NINETEEN

"And here's a sketch of Utah Lake. It's quite barren of timber around the lake, but the plant and animal life are bountiful," Lars explained as he showed the sketch he'd drawn to James and Inger. James looked at it carefully. He was fascinated by the drawings and the experiences Lars had been relating concerning his nine-week sojourn with Captain Stansbury's expedition.

Lars had returned home from the expedition two days before. James was glad to see his friend again; Lars looked healthy and robust from his labors in the out-of-doors. His flaxen hair was bleached even whiter by the sun, and had grown well past his ears. His face was tanned a deep brown, and his eyes were bright with enthusiasm.

"And this drawing is of a Timpanogos Ute. This fellow came to camp one morning, hoping to trade a pony for guns and alcohol. Captain Stansbury wouldn't allow any bartering with the Indians, however, because he knew dealing with them could easily lead to misunderstandings and problems."

James and Inger sat close together, their heads almost touching, as they inspected Lars' drawing of the scantily-clad Indian.

"Did you see a lot of Indians?" Inger wanted to know.

"Quite a few. The Timpanogos Utes occupy the lands around Utah Lake. They're a hunting and seed-gathering people who move from place to place in search of food. During the summer months they live in the mountain valleys, and in the winter they follow the buffalo, deer, and antelope into the warmer regions of the south. Other bands of Utes, such as the Pavantes, San Pitch, and Uintahs occupy different areas. But the Timpanogos were the ones we sighted the most."

"Are they causing any problem for the settlers in the Utah valley?" asked James. He was thinking of Etta Stanton and her family, who were homesteading there.

"The settlers are building a compound called Fort Utah. I think this past summer has been fairly calm as far as Mormon and Indian relations are concerned, but when I left the area I heard there had been some trouble. Something about corn being stolen, and a couple of animals killed by the Indians."

"I hope it doesn't turn into anything worse," Inger commented, frowning.

James hoped so, too. Even though his feelings for Etta were no longer romantic, he was still concerned about her welfare.

Lars pulled out another drawing from the two dozen or so sketches he had brought home with him. "Here's another sketch of the Utes. This is a squaw and her papoose."

James studied the features, clothing, and hair styles of the Indian woman and her child. She wasn't an attractive woman in the conventional sense, but she had a certain dignity about her. Lars had managed to portray not only her appearance, but an inner quality of strength and self-reliance.

"These are really excellent drawings, Lars. I'll bet Stansbury was pleased with your work," James said.

"He seemed to be happy with the sketches I did for him, and I enjoyed doing them. He and his men will be continuing their survey for a few more months yet, but my part is finished." Lars sounded a trifle disappointed.

"Would you have liked to stay longer with the expedition?" his sister queried.

"In some ways, I guess. I enjoyed the exploration and the variety of scenery. But sleeping in a bedroll on the ground every night can get pretty tiresome." Lars grinned. "Besides, I missed my sis."

Inger kissed his cheek. "I missed you, too. And I needed you," she added softly.

"I'm sorry I wasn't here when Jens showed up," said Lars in response to her inference. "I know the whole incident was painful for you."

"I couldn't have handled it without James beside me." Inger's gaze fastened on James. She gave him a small smile and leaned against his shoulder. Her touch started his heart pounding.

"So after Jens left our cabin and escaped on James' horse, he apparently passed out. Is that right?" Lars asked.

"Yes. Someone found him lying on the roadside, bleeding, and carried him to the constable's office. James' horse was located later, with Jens' saddlebag still across the saddle," Inger explained. James slipped an arm around her waist, and she moved closer to him.

"And the pouch of gold dust was still in his saddlebag." Lars shook his head in amazement.

James took up the narrative from that point. "When Jens came to and found himself in the constable's office, he slipped away at the first opportunity. He didn't even wait to collect his gun and his gold dust from the constable. I guess he figured the constable was the last person he wanted to see. It wasn't until after he disappeared that the constable discovered there was an outstanding warrant for his arrest."

"So now he's gone, and none of us knows where he is. That's typical of Jens, isn't it? He's never cared about anyone but himself." Lars began gathering up his sketches and stacking them together in a neat pile.

"At least you're home safe and sound, Lars. I worried about you while you were away," said Inger. As she spoke, she laid her head on James' shoulder. The thumping of his heart was so loud that James thought she surely must be able to hear it.

Lars straightened his pile of sketches and set them beside him on the floor. When he looked up, his eyes widened at the sight of Inger and James cuddled so closely together. "Okay. What's going on here that I'm missing?" he asked with a lopsided grin.

"Nothing. What do you mean?" Inger bit her lip to keep from smiling.

"I know something is happening here. Out with it, you two. What's the secret?" Lars looked from Inger to James, and then back to his sister again. "Well?"

"It's no secret, Lars. In fact, now seems the perfect time to declare my feelings." James looked at Inger as he spoke.

"Declare your feelings?" Lars repeated, his brows hitching up in surprise.

James took Inger's hand into his. "I've been waiting for Lars to get home before speaking outright, Inger. I didn't want either you or Lars to think I was taking advantage of a situation where you were here alone and unchaperoned."

He felt Inger's hand tremble in his, but her gaze on his face remained steady. James clasped her hand more tightly. "I know we're not the same age, and I've worried about that—worried you might view it as a stumbling block." He paused, trying to frame his words into what his heart was feeling. Inger's gaze didn't waiver.

"You've come to mean more to me than I can express. Even though I may be young, I am serious-minded and dedicated to hard work. I have a profession started, and will have the ability to support you and care for you —"

"Shhh." Inger cut him off by placing a gentle finger to his lips. "You don't need to make excuses or explanations, James. Don't you know I love you, too?" Inger's eyes held his. Her words stole his breath away so that he couldn't utter a sound.

"Good golly, James. *Say* something!" exclaimed Lars.

James glanced at his friend. Lars' grin ran from ear to ear. His eyes returned to Inger's face. "I love you, Inger. I love you with all my heart." He leaned forward to kiss her. The feel of her soft lips on his sent his head reeling, and he felt as dizzy as a spinning top.

"I love you so, James," she whispered.

James kissed her again, then drew back in wonder. "You're sure? You have the same feelings for me as I hold for you? That doesn't seem possible."

She laughed softly. "I've been in love with you ever since I was a girl and living in Montrose."

"But you never said anything, or gave any indication of your feelings."

"Oh, I wanted to," she smiled. "Most of the time I dash headlong into a situation and end up making a fool of myself. I didn't want that to happen with you. Besides," she added, dropping her gaze, "I knew you were in love with Etta."

"You are an angel, Inger Johanssen." He stroked her hair. "An angel straight from heaven."

"Hey, you two. Have you forgotten I'm still here?" Lars grinned. "I can step outside if you like."

Inger laughed and reached for his hand. "You're not going anywhere, Lars. You're staying right here to celebrate this moment with us."

"Absolutely," James confirmed. "Who means more to Inger and me than you do?"

Lars chuckled. "Yes, I see. It's clear that the two of you are a fitting pair."

"Thank you for a delicious supper, Sister Kade," said Inger as she helped Millicent and Roxana clear the dishes from the table.

Lydia took the dishes from the girls and placed them in a metal tub filled with soap and water. "You're welcome, Inger. It's a great pleasure having you and Lars here to spend the evening with us."

James watched the exchange between his mother and Inger with a smile on his lips. When he told his parents that he had proposed marriage to Inger, and she'd accepted, they had been delighted. Especially his mother. She had always harbored a special spot in her heart for the Johanssen girls. This union would bring her great joy.

"I'll have to get your recipes for James' favorite meals. I'm afraid I'm not much of a cook."

Lydia smiled at her. "That's not what James tells me."

"James is very kind," Inger returned.

"I can come and help you cook," Millicent volunteered.

"How nice of you, Milly. I accept your offer," Inger replied, giving the younger girl a hug. "I'll be counting on you to come to our home often to visit after James and I are married. You, too, Roxie."

Roxana smiled shyly at her.

"I will. I can even help you with chores if you want me to," Millicent answered eagerly.

"Well, of course I do. That would be a great load off my mind." Inger hummed a tune as she carried the dishes from the table to the metal tub for washing.

"Do you hear that?" James asked. He poked Lars in the ribs with his elbow. The two of them had been talking with Christian while the women put away the food and cleared the table.

"Hear what?" Lars asked.

James nodded toward Inger.

"Do you mean Inger's humming? She always hums or sings while she's working around the house. You'll get used to it, James," he grinned.

"No, Lars. That's not just humming. Look at her. That's an entire symphony playing."

Lars chuckled. "The music of the heart. Now I know you're truly in love, my friend."

James didn't reply; he was too intrigued with watching Inger.

After the dishes were put away, Lydia and the girls sat down. James pulled his chair next to Inger's, and clasped her hand in his.

"Inger, your mother would be happy with this match, I expect," said Lydia.

"I know she would," Inger replied. "She spoke so often of her dear friend, and of James and Elizabeth."

"Well, I suspect she's looking down from heaven right now, and nodding her head," Christian put in.

"I hope so." Inger laid her head against James' shoulder. "And Papa, too."

Lars smiled at the mental picture being drawn.

James saw Millicent lean over and whisper in Christian's ear. "Are they looking down from heaven, really, Papa?" he heard her ask.

Christian put an arm around her and whispered back. James couldn't hear his reply, but whatever it was seemed to satisfy Millicent. She smiled and sat back contentedly in her chair.

"I think now is a good time to give James the parcel we brought for him, don't you, Lars?" Inger gave her brother a meaningful look.

"What parcel?" asked James. He hadn't any idea what the two of them meant; he hadn't seen them carry a package into the house.

Lars stood up and went to the peg beside the door where his frock coat hung. From the coat pocket he withdrew a small package tied in brown paper and string. He handed it to James. "Inger and I talked about this, and both of us want you to have it."

"What is it?" James' face held a puzzled look as he took the package.

"Just open it, darling," said Inger.

James smiled to himself as he untied the string and began unwrapping the paper. This was so like Inger; she loved orchestrating surprises. As the paper peeled away, he was startled to see a thick roll of currency fall into his lap. "What's this?" he asked. He looked up at Inger for an explanation.

"It's money we got from exchanging the gold dust Jens left behind. We want you to have it," Lars told him.

"It's so you can go to medical college," Inger added softly.

"I can't take this," James sputtered. "This is *your* money. The constable gave it to you when Jens fled town. It's a very nice thought, but I can't accept it." James picked up the money from his lap and held it out to Lars.

"That's right, James, it is our money. Therefore, we can do as we please with it." Lars' tone was uncharacteristically stern. "And what we want to do with it is to assist you in becoming the very best physician you can possibly be. And that means medical college."

Inger cupped her hand over James' fist full of money. "Neither Lars nor I want the money, James. We just would have given it to the bishop to distribute among the needy Saints. We want you to have it for your schooling."

"That's kind of you both, but this money also belongs to Johanna and Kirstine," James answered with a frown. He was shocked and dismayed over this unexpected gift. "Surely they can use the money, or at least have a say in what you choose to do with it."

"We've already talked with Johanna and Kirstine. Johanna won't touch it; she wouldn't take the money if she were starving and living in the streets, simply because it came from Jens. Kirstine didn't want it, either. In fact, she's the one who suggested we give it to the bishop. She and Peder have what they need," Lars explained.

James turned the cash over and over in his hands. The impact of what they were telling him was beginning to sink in. His throat felt dry, and his chest hurt.

"The Lord moves in mysterious ways, James. I believe your prayers have finally been answered," Inger whispered, slipping an arm around his shoulder.

James looked into her eyes. They were the bluest, clearest eyes he had ever encountered. They seemed capable of seeing into his mind and his soul, and knowing just what his heart was feeling.

"Perhaps a simple 'thank you' would be in order, son."

James glanced at his father. A grin was spreading across his face. When he looked at his mother, he saw tears in her eyes.

"Papa's right, James. You should take the money and be grateful," said Roxana quietly.

James stared at the money in his hands. An overwhelming feeling of elation welled up inside him. It burst forth in a swell of laughter. Inger began laughing, too, and then Lars. James laughed until his eyes ran with tears.

When he was finally able to catch his breath, he said with feeling, "Thank you. I don't know how to express my gratitude for this. To have the opportunity to go to medical school sitting right here in my hands . . ." He shook his head, at a loss for words. "Thank you, Lars. And thank you, my sweet angel." He kissed Inger tenderly.

"But, James," Millicent demanded, tugging on his sleeve. "Nobody has said how *much* money is there."

Everyone laughed at her remark. Millicent looked around the room, a perplexed frown on her face.

"There's enough for travel and schooling, Milly. And then some to spare." James put his arm around her shoulder and hugged her.

"I think this calls for a celebration," Christian announced. "Lars, did you bring your harmonica?"

"I did. I always carry it with me."

"Then play us a lively tune, Lars, and we'll sing."

Lars pulled his harmonica out of his trouser pocket, wet it with his lips, and launched into the jaunty melody of Stephen Foster's new tune, "Oh, Susannah." Inger raised her voice in song, as did Christian, Lydia, Roxie, and Millicent.

James gazed at the currency clutched in his fist. With this money, he would be able to start the spring term at college. At last he was to have the opportunity to complete his training as a physician. His dream was actually coming true! He would go to school in Chicago, earn his certificate, and then come home and marry Inger Johanssen. He couldn't stop grinning long enough to join in the singing.

"When this city was in its glory,
every dwelling was surrounded with a garden . . .
but now all the fences are in ruin, and lately
crowded streets actually rank with vegetation.
Of the houses left standing, not more than one out of ten
was occupied, except by the spider and the toad."

CHARLES LANMAN,
AN ENGLISH JOURNALIST WHO VISITED NAUVOO
AFTER THE SAINTS' EXODUS

CHAPTER TWENTY

Elizabeth fitted the small bonnet over Emmaline's head and tied the ribbons under her dimpled chin. She nuzzled the baby's cheek. "Mama loves you, Emmy," she cooed. The baby smiled and gurgled as she looked into Elizabeth's face.

Elizabeth wrapped her in a light blanket and carried her downstairs. "Does my baby want to go bye-bye?" she said to the child as she walked.

She let herself out the door of the white frame house and locked it behind her, stepping gingerly over the dead mayflies scattered on the porch beneath the lamp. The insects were especially irksome this spring; Elizabeth couldn't remember an April when they'd been so numerous.

She covered the baby's face with a corner of the blanket as she carried her to the waiting buggy. "Good morning, Marie," she greeted her friend when she reached the carriage.

"Morning, Elizabeth. Here, let me take Emmaline for you while you climb in the buggy."

Elizabeth placed the baby in Marie's outstretched arms. When she'd arranged herself in the seat, she took Emmaline into her lap. The baby wiggled in her arms and kicked her tiny feet. Elizabeth lifted the blanket away from her face and smiled at her. The child grinned back happily.

"How is that little cherub this morning?" asked Marie as she gave the reins a shake. The single horse pulling the buggy started forward at a fast clip.

"She kept me awake most of the night because she didn't want to sleep. She wanted to play," Elizabeth replied. "Didn't you?" Elizabeth smiled, stroking the baby's cheek.

Marie glanced at the child with a smile. "She's certainly growing fast. You must be doing all the right things."

"She's nearly four months old now. Alexander thinks she's still too young for me to be taking her about, but she seems to enjoy the outings."

Elizabeth cuddled the child, and Emmaline stared at her with big, round eyes. She had inherited her mother's blue eyes, but the rest of her features were Alexander's. She had his nose and mouth, and the fuzz on her head was the same dark color as Alexander's hair. Elizabeth thought she was the most beautiful baby she'd ever seen.

"I'm glad you decided to come with me to the temperance meeting, Marie; I think you'll enjoy it. I understand Miss Susan Anthony is a wonderful speaker. I was thoroughly impressed with her opinions when I read about the address she gave last week in Springfield. I'm really looking forward to this."

"So am I, although I don't know too much about Miss Anthony."

"I've only recently learned of her myself. I'm more familiar with Mrs. Amelia Bloomer's voice. She puts out an excellent temperance paper called the *Lily*. Have you ever read anything from it?"

Marie shook her head. "No, I haven't. What kinds of things does Mrs. Bloomer have to say?"

"She advocates all sorts of reforms, from temperance to the abolition of slavery. But she's primarily concerned with women's rights."

"Isn't she the one who encourages women to wear those curious Turkish pantaloons? I'm not quite sure I like the look of the short skirt over pantaloons. I know Emile wouldn't like it."

"It's a bit bizarre, I agree," Elizabeth rejoined. "But the costume does call attention to the plight of women, who are treated with much less equality than men."

"Well, the meeting this morning should be an interesting one." Marie jiggled the reins and the horse quickened his pace. "Does Alexander mind you going?"

"To the temperance meeting? I didn't tell him." A frown crossed Elizabeth's brow. Alexander would be truly upset if he knew she planned to attend the meeting. The two of them had already experienced several disagreements over her involvement in the women's movement. Alexander believed women should stay at home and concern themselves solely with domestic duties, but Elizabeth was caught up in the popular reform movements of the day, especially in the crusade for women's rights. She also had keen interest in the question of slavery. She was adamantly opposed to the practice, believing slavery to be a great evil and offense to the country and to humankind. Her views on a variety of other issues needing reform were equally passionate.

The baby began to squirm in Elizabeth's arms. She sat Emmaline upright and bounced her on her knee. "Women should have the same rights and privileges as men," Elizabeth declared with feeling. "If men protest against the institution of slavery, for example, their opinions are received as valid arguments. But if a lady wishes to express her opinion, it's quite another story. Men feel that women have no business speaking in public or participating in political affairs."

Marie gave Elizabeth a sidelong glance. "I had no idea you felt so strongly about this."

"Since I've been confined at home with my pregnancy and Emmaline's birth, I've done quite a bit of reading. My stepfather is a newspaper man, and he instilled in me an appetite for reading the papers, magazines, and journals. I read about a meeting held by Elizabeth Cady Stanton and Lucretia Mott in Seneca Falls, New York, where a Declaration of Principles was drawn up, patterned after the Declaration of Independence. What was set forth in that document really started me thinking. It pointed out that married women don't even have the right to own property or to make a valid will. Women have always been subordinate to men, but now it's time for some of these age-old ideas to change."

By this time, the two women had reached the Masonic Hall where the lecture was to be delivered. The Hall was a handsome structure built in the Federalist style and was one of the few three-story buildings in Nauvoo. The women secured the horse and buggy under a shade tree and went inside. The room where the meeting was to be held was filled to capacity. Most in attendance were women, some like Elizabeth with small children in their arms, but a few gentlemen were also present. Elizabeth watched with anticipation as Miss Susan B. Anthony took the podium. The woman appeared to be around thirty years of age and was rather plain-looking, but when she began to speak it was with eloquence and conviction.

Elizabeth listened with rapt attention to every word spoken. Miss Anthony began her remarks with reference to the vices of alcohol, attacking drinking on moral and religious grounds, and describing the blight it caused on families and at the workplace. She touched on the establishment of the American Temperance Union, founded in 1826, and the strides it had made over the last two decades. She also quoted statistics from sociological studies done on the effects of drunkenness, noting the correlation between alcohol consumption and crime.

One man in the audience jeered when Miss Anthony explained how several states had obtained strict licensing laws and liquor taxes, calling for Illinois to join them. His outburst was met with cold stares from the women seated around him.

Miss Anthony moved from the topic of temperance to the controversial subject of abolition, and she vividly portrayed the condition of slaves in the South. Elizabeth clutched her baby closer to her breast as she listened to pitiful descriptions of slaves being beaten by their masters, and families being torn apart as children and parents were put on the auction block for sale. Miss Anthony referred to the institution of slavery as "human bondage," and suggested gradual emancipation for the slaves.

Elizabeth found Miss Anthony's comments on women's rights to be most enlightening. She discussed women's traditional place in society, and quoted the words of renown suffragette Abby Kelley, who said: "We have good cause to be grateful to the slave. In striving to strike his irons off, we found most surely, that we were manacled ourselves." Elizabeth nodded in agreement with Miss Anthony's depiction of women as legally, socially, and economically inferior to men. She even dared express the opinion that women should be allowed the right to vote!

Elizabeth was impressed by the things she heard. When the hour was spent, she and Marie drove home in the buggy, eagerly exchanging their thoughts on the lecture. When they reached Elizabeth's door, she thanked Marie for accompanying her to the meeting, and the two of them made plans to get together the next afternoon.

Elizabeth put the baby in her cradle for a morning nap, then changed out of her best dress. The gray-striped silk she had worn to the temperance meeting was one of only two new dresses Alexander had allowed her since Emmaline's birth. She slipped into one of her older frocks which was uncomfortable to wear. She had gained a few extra pounds during her pregnancy, and now most of her old clothes were tight-fitting.

She pulled the soft quilt up around Emmaline's shoulders and tiptoed out of the nursery. The bottle-green cotton frock she wore was tight around the waist. She frowned, wishing she could pay a visit to the dressmaker. Although Elizabeth had enjoyed sewing for herself before she was married, she never made her own clothing now. She employed the services of a young woman in town who was an excellent seamstress. But she knew it would be a long time before she would be able to order another dress. Alexander's business at the sawmill was in a slump; new railroads, canals, and bridges had come to Illinois, but they'd bypassed Nauvoo. The city was no longer the thriving, growing town it had been when the Saints occupied it. After their departure, new settlers such as the Icarians and immigrants from Germany, Switzerland, and France had moved in; but now the steady stream of colonization had ended and Nauvoo was turning into a sleepy riverside village. Grass and weeds grew in the streets on the flats, the fences were falling into disrepair, and many of the Saints' homes sat unoccupied and neglected. River boats continued to dock at the Nauvoo landing, discharging passengers and goods, but the city was only a shadow of its old self.

In addition to the losses imposed on his business by the economic decline, Alexander had not yet recovered from the financial debacle caused by the treachery of Benjamin Dawson. Elizabeth's stomach knotted just thinking about the fraudulent affair with her uncle. She had placed implicit trust in his words because she so desperately wanted some connection with her father's family. She now knew Benjamin had lied about trying to find her after Abraham's death, and about wanting to reestablish family ties. In truth, he had come to Nauvoo looking for new markets for his cut timber and had become acquainted with Alexander at the mill. When he saw how prosperous Alexander's business was, and then discovered he was married to Abraham's daughter, he recognized a perfect opportunity to take advantage of the situation. The truth wrenching Elizabeth's heart was that he had used her to get to Alexander's money. Alexander had hired two ruffians to search for him, and although Elizabeth knew her husband desperately needed the money he had advanced to Benjamin, she hoped the men wouldn't find him. She was crushed by what her uncle had done, but she didn't wish him any harm.

Alexander had managed to borrow enough money from his acquaintances in town to repay the loan he'd taken out at the bank, but he was having a difficult time paying back his creditors. His business at the mill was floundering in spite of all his efforts. Elizabeth rarely enjoyed any time with him;

he usually stayed at the mill through the supper hour and spent most evenings away from home. His attitude toward her had turned cold and distant, for he still blamed her in part for the loss of his money. Not even Emmaline's birth had warmed his feelings for her. He had been displeased with the news of her pregnancy, and had shown her little affection during the months of her confinement.

Alexander, however, had grown quite attached to Emmaline, and whenever he was at home he spent some time in the nursery with her. He was quick to criticize Elizabeth if he thought she was not taking adequate care of the child; among other things, he didn't think Emmaline should be taken outside the house where she might be exposed to illness or accident. That was part of the reason Elizabeth hadn't told him about her decision to attend the temperance meeting.

Elizabeth hurried downstairs and took her broom from its place near the side door. She went outside and began sweeping away the dead mayflies littering the porch. Alexander didn't like seeing the insects there when he came home from work. Elizabeth briskly brushed them off the porch, their crumpled wings and dry, lifeless bodies rustling against the broom as she swept them into a dustbin. She knew the adult insects lived only a few hours, or a few days at the most, and they had no mouths or stomachs so they did not eat during their short lives. Elizabeth couldn't help wondering what purpose there was to their brief and joyless existence.

When she'd finished her task, Elizabeth went back inside the house. She replaced the broom and then stood pensively for a moment, gazing out the parlor window. She missed Alexander's companionship. As she stood staring out the window onto the street, watching people pass by, she felt suddenly very lonely. She had no family of her own nearby, and no close friends except Marie. She felt as if she were all alone in the world. Immersing herself in causes and reform measures helped to dull her feelings of isolation, but such activities could not fill the void of being separated from those she loved the most. She felt as if her life had become pointless and without purpose. A picture of the dead mayflies scattered on the porch flickered across her mind. The image disturbed her, so she swept it from her consciousness. At least she had Emmy to love . . . thank goodness she had Emmy to love.

That afternoon Elizabeth visited the post office, where she found two letters waiting for her—one from her mother and the other from Millicent. She tucked the letters inside Emmaline's blanket and hurried home to read them. Laying Emmy on the couch beside her, she eagerly opened the letter from her mother. It was dated five weeks earlier, and had come by way of the newly-established overland mail service. Stagecoaches carrying the mail now took about thirty days to travel from the Great Salt Lake City to Independence, Missouri—a tremendous savings in time from the undependable, intermittent delivery system of the past.

Her mother wrote about the activities of each member in the family. Roxana and Millicent were busy with their schooling, and Christian was involved with readying the first issue of a newspaper, to be called the *Deseret News*, for publication in June. James was away at medical college in Chicago. He and Inger Johanssen intended to be married as soon as he returned, and then James would step into Dr. McCaffrey's practice. Lydia expressed her delight over James' engagement and described Inger's many sterling qualities.

Elizabeth frowned as she read through her mother's words of praise for Inger. James had written her earlier from Chicago to tell her about their relationship, and she had been surprised by the news. She couldn't imagine what James found attractive in the girl; she thought her brother should have chosen a more refined, cultivated young woman. Inger was not at all the person she had visualized as a wife for James and sister-in-law for herself.

Her mother then inquired about Elizabeth's health, urging her to rest during the period of her confinement. Elizabeth felt a swell of disappointment; her mother had apparently not yet received the letter she'd written announcing Emmaline's birth. The fact that Lydia did not know about the baby upset her.

Lydia closed by sending her love and expressing her longing to see Elizabeth. When she'd finished reading the letter, Elizabeth carefully refolded it and slipped it back into the envelope. Then she opened Millicent's note. Her younger sister's correspondence was much shorter and written in Milly's bold, hurried hand. Milly declared her impatience with having to sit in the classroom all day when she preferred being outdoors. She described the beauty of mountain flowers and clear, canyon streams. She explained about Roxana's new beau, and her sister's diligence and excellence in school. Roxana had won the spelling bee, she reported, and was preparing for a spelling competition with another school in the valley. Both she and Roxie were learning how to crochet lace. Elizabeth smiled as she read her sister's eager account of what was taking place at home.

She reread both letters, then carefully placed them with the others she kept in the bottom drawer of her bureau. Emmaline began to fuss and cry; Elizabeth laid her in the cradle, and in a moment the baby drifted off to sleep. She went downstairs to start supper for Alexander. She had no idea whether or not he'd be home to eat with her, but she wanted a hot supper ready in case he did. She made a loaf of cinnamon bread and put it in the bustle oven to bake, then prepared chicken and potatoes in the big black kettle in the hearth.

When Emmaline awoke from her afternoon nap, Elizabeth nursed her and changed her soiled diaper. She played pat-a-cake with Emmy and sang to her. Finally, she sat at the table to eat supper alone. The evening dragged by with only Emmaline to enliven it, and after a time she put the baby to bed for the night. Then she slipped into bed herself and lay awake for a long time, unable to sleep. Just as she was finally drifting into unconsciousness, she heard the front door open and Alexander's footstep on the stairs.

CHAPTER TWENTY-ONE

The following day was Sunday. Alexander went to the mill to work, while Elizabeth took Emmaline to Sunday meeting with her. During the first two years of her marriage, Elizabeth hadn't attended any meetings or allied herself with any of the denominations in town. But over the last few months, and especially since Emmaline's birth, she had felt the need for some sort of religion in her life. The Catholic church was a strong presence in Nauvoo, as were the Methodist and Presbyterian faiths. Elizabeth no longer believed in many of the doctrines and principles of the Church of Jesus Christ of Latter-day Saints, and those she still privately agreed with she did not practice. Doing so would attract scorn and ridicule from many of her acquaintances in Nauvoo, and particularly from Alexander.

And so she chose to attend the Presbyterian church—not because she believed it to be the correct church or to embody Christ's pure gospel, but because its principles and practices were easy to incorporate into her life. The practice of Presbyterianism did not ask much from her, and it required no sacrifices.

The Presbyterians met in the old Seventies Hall on the flats. A merchant from Quincy, along with some other new citizens in town, had purchased the building in 1846. The Reverend Matthew Waldermeyer was pastor. During the period when the Saints were in Nauvoo, the Seventies Hall had been used for worship, lectures, and classes. The second floor of the building had housed the town library.

Emmaline was fretful during the last half of the meeting, and Elizabeth had to stand in the back of the room and rock her. When the meeting concluded she went home, nursed Emmaline, and put her to bed for a nap. Alexander arrived shortly afterward.

"I just came home to get something to eat, then I have to go back to the mill. I'm meeting with some men this afternoon who might be interested in buying into the business," he said.

Elizabeth hurriedly warmed him some chicken, and potatoes and gravy, left over from supper the night before. "You're thinking about taking in partners?" she asked.

Alexander seated himself at the table and picked up his fork. Elizabeth set the plate of food in front of him. "That's right. I don't see that I have any other choice if I want to save what's left of the business," he said coldly.

Elizabeth sat down across the table from him. "But if you establish a partnership, Alexander, you'll lose sole control of the mill. I don't think you'll be happy with that situation."

"Of course I'm not happy about it," he snapped. "Do you have another solution? Perhaps you'd like to introduce me to one of your other uncles," he added contemptuously.

"Please, Alexander, let's not fight over that again. I'm sorry about what happened with Uncle Benjamin. I had no idea he was planning to steal your money."

Alexander gave her a withering stare.

Elizabeth sighed. "Have you been able to locate Uncle Benjamin?"

"Not yet, but I will. And when I do, believe me, he'll pay for what he's done."

A shiver ran down Elizabeth's back. "Perhaps Uncle Nathaniel and Uncle Jeremiah are more honest in their dealings. They may yet ship you the cut timber you paid for in advance."

Alexander regarded her with a sarcastic expression.

Elizabeth tried changing the subject. "Emmaline has learned a new trick. She can blow bubbles, and she knows it makes me laugh."

His look held a glimmer of interest.

"She made raspberry noises with her lips today at meeting. She thought it was great fun."

Alexander forked a piece of chicken into his mouth.

"But then she became cross, and I had to stand and rock her."

"How did she like the temperance meeting yesterday?" Alexander asked. His eyes narrowed.

"The temperance meeting?"

"Yes. I understand you were there."

Elizabeth swallowed. "Yes, I was at the meeting."

"I dislike you participating in that kind of thing, as I've told you before. Those suffragettes have crazy ideas, and they're the laughingstocks of reasonable and responsible people."

"You mean reasonable and responsible *men*, don't you, Alexander?" Elizabeth was surprised by her own boldness. She seldom spoke disrespectfully to her husband.

Alexander's gray eyes turned as cold and hard as slate. "I won't have you becoming an embarrassment to me, Elizabeth. I'm telling you to stay away from those women's organizations."

Elizabeth felt a hot fury flare inside her. "And if I choose not to?"

Alexander slowly and deliberately set down his fork. He leaned across the table until his face was only inches away from hers. "I wouldn't recommend that course, Elizabeth. You're my wife, and I can make things very uncomfortable for you if I choose to do so."

Elizabeth glared at him a moment, then reluctantly lowered her eyes.

Alexander picked up the fork again and resumed eating. He glanced once at Elizabeth, and his face seemed cut from stone.

Neither of them spoke after that. Alexander finished his meal, then left to return to the mill. Elizabeth washed his plate and put it away in the cupboard. She went to the parlor and sat down in her favorite upholstered chair, gazing at the painting that hung over the fireplace opposite her. Alexander had purchased the expensive Thomas Cole painting for the occasion of her twenty-first birthday. Cole was one of the leading artists of the so-called Hudson River school of American art. He specialized in romantic pictures of grandiose landscapes. This painting, entitled *The Oxbow*, was a special favorite of Elizabeth's. She sat staring at the painting, but not seeing it. Her thoughts centered on Alexander, and the disintegrating state of their marriage.

Elizabeth stepped into the front hall of the Mansion House hotel. She nodded at an older gentleman who passed her in the hallway on his way out the door—one of Emma Bidamon's boarders, she supposed. She glanced down the hallway and then into the front parlor, looking for Julia Smith. Inside the parlor, tidying the room, were Julia's brothers, thirteen-year-old Frederick and eleven-year-old Alexander. Their younger brother, David Hyrum, was cleaning the furniture with a feather duster. Emma had been five months pregnant with David when the Prophet Joseph was killed; the child was nearly six now. He was a handsome boy, and of all the children he looked most like his father.

"Hello, boys," Elizabeth said to them from the doorway of the parlor.

Frederick and Alexander both looked up. "Hello, Mrs. Scott," Frederick answered. "Can I help you with something?"

"Yes, thank you, Frederick. I wanted to see Julia. Is she at home?"

Frederick shook his head. He was a good-looking lad with dark hair and dark eyes like his mother. "No. She and Elisha have gone out. I don't know when they'll be back."

Elizabeth nodded. Julia Smith and Elisha Dixon had married a short time earlier, and were currently living at the Mansion House. They had plans to move to Texas, however, and Elizabeth wanted to see Julia before they left.

Tell Julia I stopped by, will you, Frederick?"

"Yes, I will."

"I'll come back another time to see her. Goodbye, boys."

Both of the older boys waved, and young David went back to his dusting.

Elizabeth left the hotel and started for her carriage. She and Alexander had attended the party held at the Mansion House following Julia's marriage. It had been a nice affair. Julia was the adopted daughter of Joseph and Emma Smith, taken in as a baby with her twin brother, Joseph, when Emma's own twins had died in Kirtland, Ohio, in 1831. Her brother, Joseph, had passed away the next year. Elizabeth had only recently learned these facts; she'd never realized the Smiths were not Julia's natural parents. When the two of them were girls and close friends, Elizabeth had not known Julia was adopted. Discovering that circumstance had curiously affected the way she felt about her own stepfather, and had made it easier to accept her relationship with him. She wished she had known about Julia's family situation much earlier, for it might have made a difference in the way she connected with Christian.

As she was stepping into her carriage, young Joseph Smith came riding up on his horse.

"Hello, there, Elizabeth," he hailed her as he pulled his horse to a stop.

"Afternoon, young Joseph. Where have you been off to on this beautiful spring day?"

"Doing a few errands for Mother. What brings you down here?" he asked.

"I came to visit Julia."

"I don't believe she's at home," he replied, dismounting from his horse.

"I know. Your brothers told me."

Joseph stroked his horse's neck as he held the reins in one hand. "How is Alexander?"

"He's fine. Working a lot of hours at the mill, as usual."

"I saw him the other day. He said business is real slow. I guess many businesses in town are suffering." Joseph shook his head. His dark, unruly hair fell across his broad forehead. He was rather short and stout, with a round, barrel-shaped body.

"You saw Alexander at the mill?" Elizabeth asked. She wondered what business Joseph would have at the mill yard. She knew he had been working with the Warsaw and Rockford Railroad Company as a contractor and foreman to build roadbed for the laying of tracks.

"No, not at the mill. I spoke to him here at the hotel. He was just leaving the hotel with a young lady." Joseph colored suddenly. He began to make a pretense of straightening the reins on the horse's neck.

"Oh." Elizabeth felt a rush of blood to her face. What was Alexander doing at the hotel with a young lady, she wondered. She wanted to question Joseph about what he'd seen, but she was reluctant to ask.

"Alexander's isn't the only business in town that's having difficulty," said Joseph in a hurried tone. "The railroad company I've been working for has just gone into receivership and scrapped their whole construction project."

"I'm sorry to hear that," replied Elizabeth. Her mind was still focused on Joseph's earlier words concerning her husband.

"Yes, I was disappointed about it. We'd already completed a few miles of roadbed. But I think I have a good prospect on the horizon. I may be able to acquire several acres of choice residential property in the center of town for an excellent price."

"That sounds like a good opportunity for you."

"Yes. Land development might be something I'd be interested in pursuing. There's fifteen acres of farm land outside the city for sale. If I can pick up the acreage for a low price, I could easily turn around and resell it at a profit."

"I hope it works out for you, Joseph." Elizabeth shrugged her shoulders, abandoning her thoughts of Alexander and the young woman. She was probably just the wife of an acquaintance of his whom he had bumped into and was saying hello.

Joseph patted his horse's nose. "What have you been up to lately? How's that little baby of yours?"

"Emmy is growing like a vine. I left her at home in the care of a young girl who lives next door so I could visit Julia and run a few errands. She is a delight."

"I'll bet she is."

"Are you still keeping a hand in the tourist business?" Elizabeth asked.

"Yes, we still get a few requests for tours around the city. Since Captain Bidamon has left for a stint in the gold fields, however, I haven't had the time myself to devote to it. Frederick will soon be old enough to take over my job."

Elizabeth knew that Captain Bidamon was the force behind the lucrative guide service he and Joseph had developed. Many visitors who came to Nauvoo were curious to see the city Joseph Smith had established, and Bidamon maintained a team and buggy at the Mansion House for the purpose of showing visitors around town. Joseph generally acted as driver and guide. He'd earned a considerable amount of money in fares and tips from this venture.

"I did meet an interesting person through the guide service, however," Joseph remarked.

"Oh? Who is that?"

"His name is James Chadsey. He's just recently moved here to Nauvoo from the East. He chatted with me about the city before purchasing some farm land."

"He's a farmer, then?" Elizabeth asked.

"Yes, but he also claims to be a medium."

"A medium? You mean he's one of those people who can communicate with the dead?" Elizabeth's attention was immediate.

"Yes. He's held a number of seances already. I've attended two of them. They're amazing meetings, Elizabeth. I'm convinced Chadsey is not a fraud."

"Really, Joseph?"

"You should come to one of his meetings. I know you'd like it."

Elizabeth would, indeed, like to attend a seance circle. She'd been intrigued by the occult ever since first hearing about it. She knew something of the theory and practice of Spiritualism from reading about it in newspapers. Spiritualism was gaining immense popularity throughout the country, along with the trance-like state called Mesmerism. Some ministers were even drawing parallels between spiritualist techniques and religion.

"Have you experienced any manifestations for yourself, Joseph?"

Joseph changed the reins from one hand to the other and leaned closer to her. "I've seen the table around which we were sitting move and shake. I've heard rappings on the wall spell out a message which Chadsey can interpret."

"Honestly? That's fascinating."

"Yes. And I'll tell you something more." He leaned closer to her ear. "When Chadsey places a pencil in my hand, I can write out messages coming from my father."

Elizabeth's heart skipped a beat. "Joseph, you're not serious!"

"Entirely serious. I wouldn't joke about a thing like that, Elizabeth. You know I revere my father's memory."

Elizabeth fell silent, thinking about what Joseph had told her. She wondered if it would be possible to receive some sort of spiritual manifestation from her own deceased father. She wished she had the courage to attend one of Chadsey's meetings.

"I'm glad you told me about Mr. Chadsey, Joseph. Perhaps I'll have a chance to talk with him one day."

"You should seize an opportunity to do so. I firmly believe supernatural events are taking place, and that Mr. Chadsey has the power to receive communications from the dead."

A chill passed through Elizabeth. Joseph's words were eerily reminiscent of something she had heard his father, the Prophet, once say in a sermon at the grove. He had talked about power from beyond, too, but he was referring to the power of the priesthood invoked to perform such ordinances as baptism for the dead. She received a fleeting impression that Spiritualism was a corruption, or counterfeit, of gospel doctrines she had known. She discarded the thought almost as quickly as it occurred to her. Spiritualism was, after all, more appealing and dramatic, and definitely more popular with the people. Mormonism had never been popular except among those who practiced it. She shrugged off the remaining wisp of conscience she'd felt and prepared to climb into her carriage.

"Do you want me to tell Julia you stopped by?" Joseph asked as he helped her up into the buggy.

"Yes, thank you. Tell her I'll come to see her again in a few days. I know she and Elisha are leaving for Texas soon."

"I'll tell her."

"Goodbye, Joseph. I enjoyed our conversation."

"So did I. See you later, Elizabeth."

She waved to him as the sorrel mare pulling the buggy started forward. Joseph lifted his hand in farewell, too, then he started toward the stable with his horse.

Elizabeth reined the mare up Main Street. She hadn't gone far when she turned in her seat to glance back at the Mansion House. The large frame building sat quietly beneath the leaves of several shade trees in the yard. Elizabeth remembered when the place was alive with activity—the voices of young children romping in the yard, the constant flow of people coming to converse with the Prophet, the bustling about the house as Emma gave instructions for the comfort of her guests. But all seemed silent now, and doleful.

Elizabeth's gaze moved to the partially-built structure situated across the block from the Mansion House.

Construction on the stone and brick building, referred to as the Nauvoo House, had begun shortly before the Prophet's death and had never been completed. It was on the scaffolding of this structure that Elizabeth had heard Elder Willard Richards give an account of Joseph and Hyrum's murder in Carthage. Recalling that June day clearly, she remembered standing beside the road in the hot sun, straining for her first glimpse of the wagons carrying the bodies of the dead brothers, and hearing the moans and cries of the people around her. The scene was seared in her memory.

She remembered, too, the aftermath of the tragedy. Brigham Young and Sidney Rigdon had each shared their views pertaining to the succession of the presidency of the Church following the Prophet's death. Brigham Young convinced the people that leadership of the Church rested with the Quorum of Twelve Apostles, and nearly all of the Saints had followed him west to the valley of the Great Salt Lake. But Rigdon and a few other dissatisfied members remained behind. Sidney Rigdon returned to Pittsburgh, where he had been living prior to the Prophet's death, and there organized his own church.

Elizabeth had heard of others who became disaffected and drew followers away from the main body of the Church. William Smith, the Prophet's brother, had associated himself for a time with a dissident member named James J. Strang, who had established a church in Michigan. But just this spring, Smith had called a conference in Covington, Kentucky, where he proclaimed himself "president pro tem" of the Church. He argued that the office of President of the Church should be passed from father to son as a right of lineage in the Smith family and, hence, the rightful heir was Joseph's eldest son, Joseph Smith III. But since young Joseph was not yet old enough to take up the office of President, it fell upon William Smith, as the only surviving brother of the Prophet, to act as President for the time being. Elizabeth was curious to see what would become of this claim. She knew Joseph was a serious-minded young man, but she also knew that he was not interested in taking over the reins of the Church in his father's place.

A few other factions had sprung up since the Prophet's death, led by such prominent men as Lyman Wight, William E. McLellin, Martin Harris, John C. Bennett, and David Whitmer. Elizabeth found this splintering of the Church to be a mass of confusion, and she preferred to have nothing to do with any of the groups. As she urged the horse up Main Street, she turned her back on the unfinished Nauvoo House, and on the Mansion House where Joseph Smith had resided in life and where his body had reposed in death.

CHAPTER TWENTY-TWO

Elizabeth dipped her pen in the bottle of India ink. She held it poised above the page of clean, white paper, uncertain of quite how to begin her reply to Christian. She had received a letter from him two weeks before, and its contents had unsettled her mind.

She dated the letter at the top of the page—"May 27, 1850"—then wrote the salutation. She paused, a frown wrinkling her brow. She set the pen down beside the paper and picked up Christian's letter to read again. He had expressed his usual wish for her good health and happiness, and he had inquired about Alexander. What followed was the part that disturbed her.

The family had just received her letter telling them about Emmaline's birth, Christian wrote. Lydia longed to see both her and the baby, and Roxie and Milly were missing her sorely. He went on to express his own feelings for her. He mentioned some of the misunderstandings they'd had in the past, but assured her that he had always loved her and only wanted what was best for her. He asked Elizabeth to forgive him for any mistakes he might have made in his role as parent. He understood her feelings concerning the fact that he was not her natural father, he said, and wished he could have been more sensitive to her needs as she was growing up under his care.

Elizabeth's throat was dry as she read the words on the page. She gripped the letter tighter in her hand. All of the family wanted desperately to see her and the baby, Christian continued. He understood Alexander's reluctance to leave his lumber business in order to take a long journey out west; therefore, he had a proposal for her consideration. He would like to travel back to Illinois to get her, and then the four of them—he and James, who would be finished with his term of medical school in Chicago, Elizabeth and the baby—could make the trip together to the Salt Lake valley. She could stay in Deseret as long as she wished, and when she was ready he would accompany her back to Illinois.

Elizabeth swallowed the hard, dry lump rising in her throat. Her first reaction, upon reading the letter through, was one of delight. She yearned to see her family and to present Emmy to them. She imagined the entire sequence of events in her mind's eye—the exciting trip over the plains and mountains, the joyous reunion with her mother, sisters, and brother. She could actually feel their arms around her and hear their mingled exclamations upon spying Emmaline for the first time. She saw the cozy cabin her mother had written so much about, and felt the warmth of the rag rugs beneath her bare feet. She smelled the sweet aroma of her mother's freshly-baked bread. All of it had passed before her mind in an instant.

But then her heart had grown cold inside her, as if a layer of ice had formed around it. No, accepting Christian's offer would mean humbling herself in front of him, acknowledging her share of the blame for the disharmony between them. The more she thought about it, the more rigid her heart became. Christian's offer was sincere, she knew, but she couldn't bring herself to accept it.

She laid Christian's letter down on the desk and stared at it. She studied his name at the bottom of the sheet, written in a clear, legible hand. The precise lettering of his signature made her scowl even blacker. It reflected Christian's exactness, his desire to always be found doing the right thing, taking the correct course, like an unerring compass. She had always thought that Christian was too easily led by high-sounding ideals, and too quick to press his ideals on others. Part of her yearned to accept Christian as her parent without reservation, just as James did. But another part of her couldn't—wouldn't—forget that Christian was not really her father. Her father lay buried in the ground of Green County, Illinois.

Memories filled Elizabeth's head. In her mind she formed a picture of her natural father, Abraham Dawson. She recalled his dark, brooding eyes, his black hair and curly beard. His big hands had always symbolized security for her. Even though the family—her father and mother, she and James—had lived in a small, crude cabin in the backwoods of Green County, she had known a happy childhood. Happy until that day when she was six years old—the day their neighbor, Mr. Slater, brought the news of her father's death.

Elizabeth shivered with the memory of it. She closed her eyes, experiencing again the pain she had felt as a child. She had been devastated by the loss of her father. James had seemed to accept it, but of course he had been too young to really grasp the significance of their father's passing. Her mother had mourned in her own quiet way. She had tried to comfort Elizabeth, but Elizabeth had shut everyone out. She wanted to insulate herself in the pain, wrap herself in her own private misery. No one, not even her mother, could penetrate the cocoon of suffering Elizabeth had spun for herself.

Things might have gotten better, Elizabeth had reasoned, if her mother had not made the mistake of selling their farm in Green County and moving to Independence, Missouri. The move proved to be the beginning of a long nightmare for Elizabeth. In Missouri, her mother joined the Mormon Church. The Mormons in Missouri were hated and persecuted for their religious beliefs, and Elizabeth's family was driven from place to place by lawless mobs bent on destroying the Saints. The memory of all they had suffered burned in her mind with blazing clarity. All of the security Elizabeth had felt in Green County was snatched away with her father's death—snatched away and replaced by uncertainty, fear, resentment, and hurt.

Elizabeth groaned aloud. She got to her feet and began pacing the room. These memories tortured her. She knew she shouldn't dwell on them, nurse them, but she felt powerless to control them. She forced herself to sit back down at the writing table. The feel of the sturdy desk beneath her hand helped to quiet her emotions. She rubbed her fingers across the smooth, polished wood; it lent her a measure of reassurance. She was safe now—safe here in Nauvoo.

Her thoughts returned to the letter before her. Christian wanted to reestablish a bond with her, fortify the family ties. She recalled meeting Christian for the first time; it was at the Whitmer home in Independence, where she and her family were staying temporarily. Christian had come there to recuperate after being injured in a fight with a member of the Missouri mob. At first she had thought him to be pleasant and kind, but when her mother decided to marry him, she had taken a dislike to him. It hurt her to see how easily her mother could forget her father and marry another man. She had never voiced her feelings, of course; her mother was free to marry whomever she chose. But Elizabeth thought her mother had made a big mistake in choosing Christian. The marriage had also solidified Lydia's involvement in the Church. Both she and Christian were strict about keeping gospel principles and seeing that their young children did likewise. Elizabeth hadn't always agreed with her parents' ideas. Most of the time she had done what they wanted her to do, but after meeting Alexander she began feeling more adamant about making her own decisions. She had married Alexander against her parents' wishes, and made the decision to stay in Nauvoo while the rest of her family moved west.

Elizabeth drew a shaky breath. Perhaps all along Christian had loved her and understood her better than she'd thought he had. She knew within her heart that the ill feelings she had borne for her stepfather all these years had been foolish and prideful. With maturity, she had gained some insight into the reasons for her behavior. And with Emmy's birth, she had begun to understand the depth of a parent's love for his child.

But all that couldn't change the past or alter the course of the present. As much as she desired to accept Christian's offer to take her to the valley of the Great Salt Lake, she could not humble herself enough to do it. She picked up her pen again and began to write. She thanked him for his gracious offer, but regretted to say that she could not accept it. Emmaline was too young to make such a long and arduous trip, she wrote, and she preferred not to leave Alexander and Nauvoo. But she would appreciate his extending her love to Lydia and the others.

She knew Christian would read between the lines she had written. He would think she still carried ill feelings for him, and he would assume the real reason why she couldn't accept his invitation was because she didn't wish to be with him or have anything to do with him. And she would allow Christian to believe that. Let him go on believing it.

She dipped her pen into the ink a second time and wrote out the words quickly. She described Emmaline's newest accomplishments, praised Alexander's hard work at the mill, and briefly described her own activities. Then she signed her name. She held the pen a moment longer, reading over what she'd written. Then she folded the letter and slipped it inside an envelope.

She still had several hours until it was time to start preparations for supper, so she decided to take the letter to the post office. She went upstairs to rearrange her hair and change into a prettier frock, choosing the blue velvet day dress she'd had made before Emmy's birth. The dress was fashioned with a Basque bodice and a round neckline edged with lace frill. The straight sleeves ended in a ruffle of lace at the wrists, and the full skirt was flounced and ornamented with a fancy border.

Elizabeth took a last look at herself in the mirror, then put on her fringed shawl and blue velvet bonnet. She took Emmaline from the cradle, wrapped her in a light-weight blanket, and went downstairs and out the front door of the white frame house. She asked the young boy living next door to hitch the horse to the buggy, and she gave him a coin for his trouble. Then she and Emmaline set off for the mercantile which housed the city post office.

A female acquaintance of Elizabeth's was in the mercantile making a few purchases. Elizabeth delivered her letter to the clerk behind the counter for posting, then spent several minutes in conversation with the woman. Afterward she did a bit of browsing herself, purchasing a small sack of white sugar and a bit of pink ribbon to fashion a bow for Emmaline's frock.

When she stepped outside the mercantile into the street, she was surprised to see the sky to the north had turned dark and lowering. A strong wind had come up, too; it lashed against her bonnet and sent her skirts billowing. She covered Emmy's face with a corner of the blanket, holding the baby close to her breast as she made her way to the carriage. The mare whinnied and restlessly stamped her feet, her tail swishing in agitation as Elizabeth approached.

Elizabeth climbed into the carriage, holding Emmaline securely in her lap. She touched the whip to the horse's back, and the mare started forward with a jerk. The wind was more intense now, whipping the shawl around her shoulders. She eyed the sky nervously; it was growing blacker and more threatening with each passing moment. Thunder rumbled in the distance.

The chestnut-colored horse snorted and tossed her head, then broke into a fast trot as Elizabeth urged the mare to quicken her pace. A sprinkling of rain began to fall, and Elizabeth cuddled Emmaline closer to her. A sudden fear gripped her as she looked overhead to see dark, scudding clouds. Occasionally, spring weather spawned deadly tornadoes; Nauvoo had experienced some of these in the past. She prayed the black clouds moving across the sky above her didn't carry within them the seeds of a violent, twisting windstorm.

As Elizabeth pressed the horse on to a faster pace, she noticed people in the street scrambling for shelter.

Her heart began beating so hard that it hurt her chest. She clutched Emmaline to her and brandished the reins across the horse's back with a brusque hand.

By the time Elizabeth reached her door, the rain was pelting down and the wind was whipping. Lightning flashed across the sky. Elizabeth could feel an ominous tingle in the air. She stabled the horse, taking no time to unharness it from the carriage, and dashed to the house with Emmaline in her arms. She slammed the door behind her and bolted it. The wind howled outside, and the sound of it sent shivers down her spine. She ran to the parlor windows and quickly shuttered them, then did the same with the rest of the windows in the house. As she closed the shutter on the upstairs bedroom window, she glanced out at the angry sky. A dark, heavy mass of clouds boiled overhead just north of the city. As she watched, a snakelike streak of whirling air suddenly stretched from the cloud. Elizabeth screamed and slammed the shutter closed. Emmaline, frightened by her mother's cry, burst into a loud squall. Elizabeth clasped the child to her and dashed to the far corner of the room. She huddled in the corner, her back to the window and her body shielding Emmaline. The shrieking, roaring wind outside hammered the windows and shook the house. Lightning lit up the room. Elizabeth buried her face in Emmaline's blanket, hugging the wailing child.

The following morning, Alexander did not go immediately to the mill. Instead, he took Elizabeth and Emmaline with him in the carriage for a drive around town to survey the harm done by the whirlwind. The tornado had set down northeast of the city limits, but its ferocious winds had uprooted trees and damaged a few buildings in the city.

As Alexander drove the carriage along Mulholland Street, Elizabeth held Emmaline tightly in her arms. The baby wriggled and cooed. Elizabeth caressed the child's small, dimpled hand.

"I was so frightened yesterday by the tornado," she said to Alexander. "I was afraid Emmy would be snatched right out of my arms by the wind." She hugged Emmaline closer.

Alexander glanced at the child cradled in his wife's arms. "You should have gone downstairs to the cellar with Emmaline. You were foolish to stay upstairs unprotected. Those winds could easily have torn the roof off the house."

"I know. But the storm came upon us so suddenly that I didn't have time to even think what to do." Elizabeth shivered. When Alexander had arrived home the day before, after the fury of the storm had passed, he had become angry with Elizabeth for taking what he thought were inadequate precautions to protect herself and Emmaline against the swirling winds. His anger and harsh words had reduced Elizabeth to tears. She was already upset by the experience of being all alone, with Emmaline to safeguard, against the wrath of the storm. Alexander had offered her neither comfort nor solace—only cold disapproval. His disaffection stood between them like a towering stone wall.

Alexander shot her a dark look. "You'd *better* be thinking, Elizabeth. You have a child for whom you are responsible."

"I know that, Alexander," she answered tersely.

He jostled the reins. The handsome gray thoroughbred pulling the carriage arched his neck and picked up his feet in a smart clip. "I hadn't intended to say anything about this, but you might as well know," Alexander began in an icy tone. "The men I sent to Green County to search for your thieving uncle have finally located him. He and his worthless brothers have been lumbering up in Wisconsin."

Elizabeth held her breath. Her heart felt as if it had stopped beating. Every nerve was strained. She was fearful of what Alexander was going to say next.

"My men and your uncle had a slight altercation."

Elizabeth froze.

"Don't worry, Elizabeth. He's not dead—though if I'd gotten my hands on him, he would be. He was only roughed up a bit. My men plan to convince Benjamin to come back here to settle the debt he owes me. But I highly doubt that your beloved uncle, or any of his brothers, will want to try seeing you again."

Elizabeth's breath rushed from her throat in an audible hiss. Alexander had made sure she would never see her uncle again. Never see any of her father's family again. Her heart seemed to constrict inside her until it felt like a tight, hard knot in her chest. She turned away from Alexander and watched with stony silence the vista passing outside the carriage.

As they drew closer to Wells Street, she caught her first clear view of the temple building. When she saw it, a tremor passed through her body. The north wall of the temple lay in ruins. She couldn't take her eyes off the startling scene as Alexander approached on the rutted dirt road. He halted the carriage directly in front of the temple.

"Well, look at that," he said in smug tone of voice.

Elizabeth climbed down from the carriage without uttering a word, carrying Emmaline in the crook of one arm. She took a few steps toward the ruined building. The gray blocks of stone from the north wall of the temple lay strewn upon the ground, and shards of shattered glass were scattered over a wide area. She gazed at the temple without speaking. The air was completely still, and the street around her was empty and deserted. The silence fell profoundly on her ears.

In her mind's eye she saw the tall, gleaming temple as it looked when it was first completed. It had stood majestically on the hill, a monument to the Saints' industry and sacrifice. She recalled the terrible days after the exodus of the main body of the Church, when a force of mob-militia had set siege to the city, demanding that the few remaining ill and destitute Saints leave Nauvoo immediately. The leaders of the militia had bivouacked in the temple, defiling and defacing it.

Then, in October of 1848, the building had been deliberately set on fire. All of its wooden parts had been burned, including most of the roof. Elizabeth had watched the conflagration from the window of her home. The shooting flames from the fire had lit up the whole city. When it was over, only a hollow, blackened shell remained of the building.

And now this. The tornado had completed the destruction of the edifice. The Icarians had been in the midst of refurbishing it, but the building lay ravaged now. Elizabeth doubted that it would ever be restored again.

A mayfly appeared and began darting around her head as she stood silently staring at the temple. She brushed it away with her hand, but it kept coming back. She watched the insect fly about for a moment, noticing its lacy wings and slender, trailing tail. She knew the mayfly had only hours to mark its existence, and then its life would be over. She left it alone, letting it glide through the air unmolested. The sight of the temple, lying spoiled and wasted, filled her with sorrow.

Emmaline stirred in her arms. When Elizabeth looked down into her face, the baby broke into a sudden bright smile. She waved her arms and wiggled her legs. Elizabeth watched her without changing her own solemn expression. A wide, open-mouthed grin lit Emmaline's face, and her blue eyes crinkled with mirth. She gurgled, chortled, and blew slobbery bubbles. She kept grinning at her mother until Elizabeth couldn't help responding. She gave the child a broad smile and cuddled Emmaline against her cheek. The baby's softness and the sweet, clean smell of her little body were soothing.

As Elizabeth lifted her eyes again to the silent, broken temple, she felt a measure of peace return to her. The structure standing before her appeared desolate, but

Elizabeth knew its legacy was still very much alive and flourishing in the hearts of the Saints. She suspected that the Saints dwelling in the valleys of the Great Basin would raise another temple, probably an even larger and more magnificent temple than the one they had left behind in Nauvoo.

Without consciously realizing it, Elizabeth sensed her own life mirrored in the birth and destruction of the temple. Because of her choices, Elizabeth, too, had suffered a certain amount of destruction to her spirit. But Emmaline was her legacy; Emmaline could carry on all that was worthy and good in Elizabeth. Perhaps she would be stronger in spirit than Elizabeth had been.

That thought comforted Elizabeth. She turned away from the damaged temple and returned to the carriage where Alexander sat impatiently waiting for her. His smile was scornful as he took Emmaline from her arms and helped her into the carriage. He whistled and jostled the reins, and the sleek thoroughbred sprang forward. The animal held his head proudly, lifting his feet in quick, precise movements as he trotted down the dirt road.

Elizabeth cuddled Emmaline against her breast. She glanced at Alexander, who was gazing straight ahead in silence. The handsome horse, the beautiful carriage, the dashing figure Alexander cut in his stylish coat and trousers—all of it stirred up the pride in Elizabeth's heart. She looked over her shoulder at the temple as the carriage moved away. In the spot where she'd been standing, the mayfly darted in the air.

"It is necessary for us to be faithful and humble, and if we listen to counsel we shall prosper."

HEBER C. KIMBALL,
MEMBER OF THE QUORUM OF TWELVE APOSTLES

CHAPTER TWENTY-THREE

As Odysseus crested a small rise, James caught his first glimpse of the Mississippi. He sucked in his breath with sudden emotion at the sight of it. Sunlight glistened on the river, turning it into a shimmering, silver string. The ribbon of water curved around the banks of what had once been a thriving city. But now, Nauvoo looked quiet and forlorn as James sat astride his horse on a ridge overlooking the riverside town.

James touched his heels to Odysseus' flanks, and the gelding immediately started down the rise toward town. The stout horse had traveled the exhausting distance between Utah and Illinois without balking. The ride from Chicago to Nauvoo had taken four days, and James had felt apprehensive the entire time, wondering what kind of reception he would have from Elizabeth and Alexander.

He entered Nauvoo at the top of Mulholland Street and began searching for Camden Street, following the directions Elizabeth had written out in her letter. He was surprised by the number of new houses built on the bluff; the town had apparently moved away from the flats and concentrated itself on higher ground. The streets here seemed more narrow than the ones in the old part of the city, and they were laid out in a disorderly fashion. Roads were not bounded by large lots as in former times. Few public buildings met his view. The new Nauvoo presented a decidedly different look.

If he followed Mulholland, he would see the gray limestone temple erected by the Saints and completed just before they were driven from Nauvoo. In his mind, he envisioned the structure built in perfect symmetry. His mind's eye recreated the thirty pilasters ringing the outside of the edifice, with the base of each slender column resting on blocks of stone sculpted into moons, and the tops crowned with sunstones. Above these were stone engravings of stars. A gilded angel weather vane fluttered atop the stately tower. The temple's noble bearing had defined the city's skyline. For James, the temple had always symbolized in a physical, tangible form his faith in the Lord Jesus Christ and his commitment to the gospel.

But James would save his actual visit to the temple for tomorrow. Today, he was concerned with seeing his sister and renewing family ties. He found Camden Street without difficulty and turned onto it. Dozens of homes lined the dirt street, some more imposing than others. Near the end of the road he spotted the white, two-story frame Elizabeth had described in her letter. He reined Odysseus to a stop and sat staring at the home for a moment. It was a handsome building with its Greek features, shuttered windows, and fan-shaped gable ornaments. The style fitted Elizabeth, he thought. Functional, yet slightly pretentious.

He jiggled the reins, and Odysseus moved forward with a lively step. James guided the horse into the yard and dismounted, tethering Odysseus to the post near the front door. Then he unstrapped his leather-bound traveling trunk from the back of his saddle. He'd just taken a step toward the house when the front door opened and a woman, carrying a young child in her arms, came out onto the porch. James halted in mid-stride.

"James?"

His sister's voice lit a spark of joy inside him. "It's me, sis," he replied, breaking into a smile. He hurried toward her, carrying his trunk in his hand.

She didn't speak again until he was face to face with her on the porch step. "Let me have a look at you," she finally said in a quiet voice. She gazed into his face while he stood grinning at her.

"You look wonderful, Elizabeth," said James eagerly. "And this is Emmaline?" James stroked the baby's chubby cheek with his finger. "She's beautiful, sis. Hello, Emmy. My, you're a pretty little girl, aren't you," he said to the baby, lowering his head next to hers.

"This is your Uncle James," Elizabeth smiled to the child. Emmaline shrank back in her mother's arms. She nestled her little head in Elizabeth's bosom, but kept one eye trained on James. Elizabeth laughed. "She'll warm up to you, James, when she gets acquainted. Come inside. It's awfully good to see you." Elizabeth leaned over and kissed his cheek.

"I'm pleased to be here." James put an arm around his sister's shoulder and hugged her. He felt a bit ill at ease making the gesture. Elizabeth was obviously glad to see him, but he sensed her reticence. He followed her inside the house, deciding she was just as nervous about seeing him after a four-and-a-half year absence as he was about seeing her. "I wasn't sure you'd received my letter from Chicago telling you when I'd be here," he said.

"Yes, it arrived several days ago. I've been looking forward to your visit."

James smiled at Emmaline whose eyes focused on him as he followed Elizabeth into the front hallway. She led him past a spacious parlor. As he glanced into the room he saw a collection of graceful furniture, luxuriant draperies on the windows, and expensive-looking paintings adorning the walls. A handsome walnut tall clock stood against one wall of the parlor, and a matching secretary squatted beside the opposite wall. The secretary held an assortment of bulky leather-bound books.

"Alexander is still at the mill, but he'll be home soon. Are you hungry, James? I've fried chicken and fruit in the pantry."

"Thank you, Elizabeth. I'll just wait until supper to eat with you and Alexander, if that's all right. How is Alexander? Is his work going well at the mill?" James asked as he trailed Elizabeth past the richly furnished parlor and down the hallway.

"Yes, he's fine. His work at the mill keeps him busy."

James noticed that his sister didn't mention whether her husband would be pleased to see him. He and Alexander had never shared much in common, and they weren't on the best of terms when James and his family left Nauvoo. "This is a lovely home, Elizabeth," he said as his sister led him up the carpeted staircase.

"Thank you. We like it. You'll be staying in Emmaline's room, if you don't mind, James. We've moved her cradle into our room so you won't be disturbed at night with her fussing. She thinks three a.m. is a choice time to wake up and play."

James smiled. The child was staring solemnly at him from her mother's arms as they walked along. James pulled a silly face, trying to get her to smile, but she didn't change expression in the slightest. "She's such a little doll, Elizabeth. Mother gave me strict instructions to relay in detail every aspect about the baby."

Elizabeth turned into the first room off the hallway. The walls were painted a light pink, and a pink and gray rag rug covered the floor. A variety of children's toys were stacked neatly on an open shelf. A small rocking horse, with a tail and mane fashioned of red yard, sat in one corner of the room. A fireplace with a screened hearth occupied the far wall.

"I hope you'll be comfortable in this room," Elizabeth said. She went to the window and drew up the shade.

Sunlight flooded the room, heightening the color of the pink walls to a warm, rosy hue.

James set his trunk on the floor at the foot of the bed. "This will be perfect, Elizabeth. Thank you."

The two of them stood facing each other, and an uncomfortable silence echoed between them. James cleared his throat. "Mother and Father said to give you their love. They sent gifts with me for you, Alexander, and the baby. Milly and Roxie sent gifts, too."

"How is the family, James?" asked Elizabeth in a soft voice.

"Everyone is fine, sis. Mother is busy with the house—cooking, cleaning, all those things—like usual. Roxie has grown into a beautiful young woman. She has a dozen beaus."

Elizabeth smiled as she listened to James' description.

"Milly is . . . well, you know Milly. Energetic. Out-spoken."

Elizabeth chuckled.

"And Father is working at the newspaper office. The brethren have started a paper called the *Deseret News*. In fact, the first issue is set to roll off the press this month. It's probably already out." James relayed this information about Christian in a hurried voice. He didn't know how Elizabeth felt about their stepfather after being away from him these past few years.

Elizabeth nodded. "It's wonderful to hear about them. I want to know everything in detail after you've had a chance to eat and rest up a bit from your trip. And I want to hear all about your experience in Chicago at medical college."

"All of that could take me several days to relate," James chuckled.

"Good. Then we can plan on your staying with us for at least that long."

Emmaline began to squirm in Elizabeth's arms. She shifted the baby into a different position and kissed her cheek.

James eyed the child fondly. "How old is she now?" he asked.

"Five and a half months. Here, let's see if she'll go to you yet." Elizabeth held the child toward James' outstretched arms.

"Will you come see me, Emmy?" James cooed. "Come on. Uncle James wants to hold you."

Emmaline kicked her legs and struggled to return to the security of Elizabeth's bosom. Her mouth twisted into a crooked shape, and she whimpered plaintively.

"You don't want to go see Uncle James?" Elizabeth said to the child. "Come on, Emmy. Just for a minute." Elizabeth smiled at her daughter and tried again to pass her to James. Emmaline clutched the collar of Elizabeth's satin dress and let out a loud bellow.

"Whoa," James exclaimed with a grin. "She undoubtedly is a girl who knows her own mind." *She takes after her mother on that count,* he almost added. He was glad he caught himself before uttering the words. They would have come out sounding offensive, and he certainly didn't want to say or do anything to slight his sister. He was determined to make this a pleasant visit. He'd already promised himself to be on guard against saying anything that might be construed as antagonistic to either Elizabeth or Alexander.

"I'll take Emmy downstairs and give her a bottle while you unpack, James. Come down to the parlor when you're ready," Elizabeth said with a warm smile. James grinned in return. He was pleased with the fact that the two of them had gotten off to an amicable start.

Elizabeth left the room with Emmaline wriggling and wailing in her arms. James smiled as he grasped his traveling trunk and hauled it up onto the bed. He unbuckled the straps and opened the lid of the trunk. He removed the clothing packed inside, as well as the wrapped gifts his parents had sent for Elizabeth and her family. The medical books he had purchased at the college in Chicago he left stacked in the bottom of the trunk.

He went to the mirror fastened on the small chest of drawers and pulled a comb through his hair. He wiped away a smudge of dirt streaked across his cheek from the hot, dusty ride into Nauvoo. Then he changed into a fresh shirt. He thought about Elizabeth as he replaced his few items of clothing in the trunk. He was glad to see her, happy to be in her home. She looked good, he mused—a little thicker in the waist and broader in the hips than he remembered, but she was dressed as lovely as always and had her hair arranged in a stylish fashion. And Emmaline was an appealing child. Her eyes were a clear blue, and the little bit of hair she possessed was the same dark shade as Alexander's.

He closed his traveling trunk, set it back down on the floor, and went downstairs to join Elizabeth in the parlor. Emmaline was lying on the couch, sucking happily on her bottle. Elizabeth sat next to her in a leaf-green upholstered chair. James chose a comfortable-looking cushioned chair for himself, across from the windows facing the street. While Emmaline dozed on the couch, he and Elizabeth enjoyed a long, quiet chat together. He told Elizabeth about the family's activities, their home in the valley, and his plans for his and Inger's forthcoming marriage. Elizabeth made a few comments and asked a question or two, but for the most part she seemed content to silently absorb every word James said.

They waited for Alexander to come home from the mill, but when he didn't arrive by the expected hour, Elizabeth and James ate supper without him. The evening wore on, and soon shadows began to fill the corners of the house. Elizabeth lit the oil lamps in the parlor and then went upstairs to put Emmaline to bed for the night. When she returned, James was standing at one of the windows, watching dusk settle on the housetops and along the tree-lined street.

"Why don't you ride down to the mill and see what's keeping Alexander," Elizabeth suggested. "You remember where it's located? It's still in the same place."

James was grateful for the invitation. Although he had enjoyed his conversation with his sister, he was becoming restless sitting in the house. He wanted to get outside where he could see the town. Travel the old familiar roads. Perhaps get a glimpse of his former home on Durphey Street. "Yes, I remember where it is," he answered. "Alexander won't be surprised to see me, will he?"

Elizabeth smiled. "I told him you were coming to visit. Did you think I hadn't?"

"I wasn't sure. To be honest, I wasn't sure how happy he'd be about my stay here."

Elizabeth snaked an arm around James' waist. "You and Alexander may have had your differences, but he harbors no ill feelings toward you."

"Nor I toward him."

"Good. Then you have nothing to be concerned about. Go on down to the mill. Alexander will be pleased to show you around. He's added a few new structures since you saw the place last."

"All right. I'll be back in a while, then." James kissed his sister's cheek, clamped on his hat, and left the house.

He walked the few yards to the barn behind the house where he'd stabled Odysseus earlier in the afternoon. He put on the horse's saddle and bridle. "Want to stretch your legs a bit, boy?" he said as he climbed into the saddle. He reined Odysseus out of the barn and set off in the direction of the river. Night was rapidly closing in. He decided to take a direct route to the stream where Alexander's sawmill was located, rather than making a circuitous ride to some of the landmarks he wanted to visit. There would be time enough for that tomorrow during the daylight hours.

He urged Odysseus into a trot, and in a few moment's time he drew abreast of the sawmill. Alexander's place of business sat beside a stream feeding into the Mississippi. James noticed immediately the new structures Elizabeth had mentioned. The existing shed-like building where the lumber was cut and stored was now joined by a small stone structure and a two-story frame building. James reined his horse toward the stone structure and dismounted. The building inside was dark. James glanced about, but the grounds seemed deserted. "Alexander?" he called. He walked Odysseus to the frame building and tied the reins around a long, horizontal hitching pole. "Alexander? Are you here?" he called again as he walked toward the two-story frame.

When he reached the door of the building, he found it ajar. He slowly pushed open the door and peeked inside. The room was dim in the oncoming night. He could see the shadowy outlines of a desk, several chairs, and odd pieces of lumber leaning up against one wall. Evidently, this was the office where Alexander transacted business.

He was about to turn and leave when he noticed a strip of light underneath a closed door on the opposite side of the room. He wondered if Alexander might be in the next room, working on his accounts or doing some other task in connection with his work. James decided to knock on the door of the adjacent room to see if Alexander was inside.

He strode across the office, and as he was ready to lift his hand to knock on the door, he heard muffled voices coming from the next room. He paused and put his ear to the door. The voices sounded agitated, as if in heated argument. James began to retreat from the room, but then a man's escalating voice and the sound of a loud thud against the wall of the room, followed by an audible groan, changed his mind about staying out of whatever business was taking place. He grasped the door handle and yanked open the door.

Alexander turned a startled face toward him. His fist was gripping the collar of an older man with black, shaggy hair and black eyes. The man was shoved up against the wall, obviously at Alexander's mercy.

"Alexander?" James queried. His eyes raced from Alexander's surprised face to the face of the man under attack.

When Alexander realized James was standing in the doorway, he loosened his hold on the other man, but didn't release him entirely. "Well, look who's come to pay a call," Alexander said sardonically. "I'm afraid it's not a very good time for me, James. As you can see, I'm in the middle of some unfinished business here."

The other man wrenched free of Alexander's grasp. He stood beside the wall, his eyes blazing. James saw that the man's cheek was bruised, and the corner of his mouth trickled blood. "What's going on here, Alexander?" he demanded.

"Benjamin and I were just doing a little reckoning of our business affairs. Oh, but you haven't been properly introduced to Benjamin yet, have you? Where are my manners?" Alexander sneered.

James' eye darted to the dark-haired stranger, who was wiping blood off his mouth with the back of his hand.

"James, I'd like to present your uncle, Benjamin Dawson."

James' jaw fell open. "What? What are you talking about, Alexander?"

The man Alexander had introduced as James' uncle stepped a pace away from Alexander and glared at him.

"This has turned out to be a real nice family gathering," Alexander said with sarcasm. "Come on, Benjamin. Say hello to your nephew."

The man gave James a brief look, then his eyes returned to Alexander. "We'll settle this later, Scott," he growled.

Alexander grabbed the other man's shoulder. "I want that money in my hand by noon tomorrow—not a minute later. Do you understand me, Benjamin? And you'd better have every penny of it."

James watched the altercation unfolding before him in astonishment. He stared at the man being assailed by Alexander. This man was his uncle? James didn't know his natural father had living brothers. And what business did he have with Alexander? Was Elizabeth aware that their uncle was here in Nauvoo? A dozen questions swirled in his head. He took a step toward Alexander and his uncle.

Alexander whirled on him. "Stay out of this, James. It doesn't concern you."

"Let him go, Alexander. Whatever is going on between you two can be handled without violence."

Alexander released his hold on Dawson's shoulder. He made a pretense of straightening the other man's shirt.

"James is right. We can take care of this matter amicably, Benjamin. You come round to my office tomorrow and we'll settle our account then."

Alexander spoke the words without malice surfacing in his voice or in his eyes, but James knew his brother-in-law well enough to recognize the threat behind them. As soon as Alexander relaxed his grip, Benjamin started toward the door. As he passed James, he lifted his eyes briefly to his nephew's face. There was no sign of warmth in that quick expression, or any hint of interest directed toward him. James stepped aside so Benjamin could pass through the doorway. His uncle left the building without another word. James turned back to Alexander.

"It's too bad you had to walk in on that, James. I would have preferred welcoming you to Nauvoo under different circumstances."

"Was that man actually my father's brother?" James asked coldly.

"Yes. And your uncle is a thief. He stole a large sum of money from me some months ago, and I've been trying to find him ever since. One of my employees finally flushed Dawson out of the woods."

"Does he have your money?" James followed Alexander as he walked from the room and into the adjoining office.

"If he doesn't have it, he'd better get it." Alexander gathered some papers from his desk in preparation to leave for the night.

James stood beside him, eyeing him critically. "And if he doesn't get the money, were you planning to take it out in blood?"

Alexander looked up at him. "Don't be ridiculous, James. I'm not a violent man." His gray eyes flicked over James' face. They were as hard as slate. He finished scooping up his papers, then opened the door of the office to the outside and gestured for James to pass through.

As he bent to lock the door, Alexander said, "Say, James, it probably would be better if you didn't mention anything about Benjamin Dawson to your sister. She doesn't know he's here, and it would only upset her to find out."

James frowned. He disliked being a party to Alexander's deception. "I hear what you're saying, Alexander."

"Thanks. Did you come down to the mill on horseback?" Alexander asked cordially. The whole incident seemed to abruptly vanish from his mind.

"Yes. My horse is tethered over there." James pointed to the hitching pole.

"Then I'll get my mare and we'll ride home together." He put a hand on James' shoulder. "Good to have you here, James."

It took all of James' self-control to avoid shrugging off Alexander's hand. He had always disliked his brother-in-law, and tonight's episode intensified those feelings. In his estimation, Alexander Scott was an odious scoundrel.

"I presume you've been to the house already," Alexander commented as James mounted his horse. "Elizabeth was glad to see you, I'll wager."

"Yes. She was," James answered without expression. He sat astride his horse, watching Alexander through slitted eyes.

James watched the muddy waters of the Mississippi glide by. He leaned over the side of the ferry, shifting his gaze downriver where the Mississippi wound around a bend and disappeared from sight. Near that point was the fishing hole he had frequented as a young boy. The ferry slipped past a tree-covered island located in the middle of the river. The bank on the Montrose side of the water was fast approaching. James drew a deep breath. It felt good to be on the river again; he had missed the mighty arm of water that ran half a continent to the ocean.

The morning was impeccable. Sunlight blazed on the Mississippi, and white puffy clouds floated in the blue stretch of sky overhead. James' collar was open against the summer heat, and his sleeves rolled to his elbows. He wore a pair of comfortable-fitting brown cotton trousers. Over one shoulder he'd slung an empty knapsack. He had left the house shortly after Alexander went to work at the mill, telling Elizabeth he had an errand to do. He was glad he hadn't had to endure much conversation with Alexander that morning. Last night's scene at the mill had haunted his sleep.

When he and Alexander returned to the house the evening before, Alexander behaved as if nothing out of the ordinary had occurred. But James couldn't erase from his mind the image of Benjamin Dawson's bruised cheek and cut lip. James had squirmed in his chair while Alexander told his wife about some of the events of his day, deliberately leaving out any mention of Dawson. He wondered if Alexander made it a habit to lie to his wife. Finally, sitting in the parlor with Alexander became so unbearable that James had excused himself and gone up to bed.

James felt the ferry slow, then bump against the shallow landing of the bank. He followed the few other passengers off the boat and found himself standing on a dirt footpath leading to the main street of Montrose. The street ran parallel to the river and was bordered with homes. James had been to Montrose only a few times as a boy. He glanced at the homes fronting the river. Many of them had fallen into disrepair, and were obviously uninhabited.

His eye traveled along the row of houses until he located the one he sought. The home was constructed of timber, and its shingled roof was faced along the outer edges with faded blue tiles. James strode to the house. He saw at a glance that it was unoccupied and in a dilapidated condition. The wooden shutters were cracked, and one hung askew on its hinges. Several windows were broken. Weeds had taken over what once was a garden and orchard. The appearance of the place caused him sadness. He bent down and pulled several fistfuls of dry, brittle weeds growing beside the porch and tossed them aside. Although his action accomplished little in restoring tidiness to the premises, it made him feel better.

He tried the knob on the front door. It was locked; but when he pushed against the door with his weight, the lock gave way easily. He stepped into what used to be a comfortable parlor, but now shards of glass lay on the floor where they had fallen from the window frames, and a thick coating of dust covered what little furniture remained in the room—a table, a few broken chairs. Leaves and other debris cluttered the floor. James felt a wave of dismay as he looked around him. This room had once rung with laughter and conversation, prayer and singing. He could almost hear the echoing voices of husband and wife, sons and daughters. Inger's own melodious voice seemed to permeate the air as he stood silently in the abandoned house.

James shook himself from his reverie, remembering the purpose for which he'd come. He left the ruined parlor in search of the pantry Inger had described to him. He passed through a second room where an oak bed, stripped of its straw tick and blankets, stood forlornly against the wall. Another room opened directly in front of him. He entered the room and glanced about. He spied a chair overturned on the floor, with its seat cushion lying nearby. James picked up the chair and righted it, then he gently replaced the cushion. Although the embroidery on the cushion was faded and water-stained, he could still make out the pattern. It was sewn in the likeness of a deer bounding through a wooded forest. The green, brown, and blue threads must have once been brilliant, but the embroidery was ruined now.

This room had obviously been used as a cooking and eating area. A large fireplace was fixed in one wall, and a circle of bricks set in the floor indicated where a cookstove once rested. The pantry must be close by. He turned to one side and spied a small, closet-like alcove. A few quick steps brought him into the alcove. Shelves lined the walls of the tiny room. A few pieces of crockery and a tin washtub sat on one of the shelves. On the floor near his feet was the outline of a double door, with two iron handles protruding from it.

James smiled. He removed the knapsack from his shoulder and set it down on the floor. Then he grasped the handles on the double doors and pulled upward. The doors opened with a creaking groan, revealing a ladder descending to the cellar below. James put one foot on the ladder, testing its strength. Then he climbed down it.

The cellar was damp and dim, with a musty smell. He stepped off the ladder onto the earthen floor and glanced around. A large barrel squatted in one corner of the cellar, and a wooden rack with trays stood near the far wall. Other than that, the cellar was empty. He wished he'd questioned Inger more closely about exactly where in the cellar she'd hidden the porcelain dishes. She'd specified only that she'd buried them in a safe place. A safe place. James studied every nook and corner of the cellar. He dug the toe of his boot into the damp earth. Had Inger buried the dishes in the dirt floor of the cellar? No, he didn't think so. There was too much danger of water seepage to justify the ground as a safe hiding place. James decided the china plates and saucers must be secreted someplace else.

He walked to the wooden rack and pulled out the top tray. The tray was made of wire meshing and had probably been used for drying fruit. He pulled out each tray, but the china dishes were not in the rack of trays.

He gazed about the cellar again. A waist-high ledge, or shelf, extended out from one portion of the cellar wall. The shelf was lined with straw. Perhaps the dishes were concealed in the straw. James went to the ledge and sorted through the moldy straw with his hands. His searching uncovered a single discolored egg; the straw-lined shelf had apparently been used to store eggs and other perishables.

James frowned in exasperation. Where had Inger put the china? Perhaps some thief had already come inside the house and robbed what few possessions the Johanssens had left behind. But if that was the case, he would have taken the flour barrel sitting in the corner of the cellar, wouldn't he? Large, well-made barrels were expensive to buy. And if flour still remained in the barrel, he would have taken that, too, for flour was a precious commodity.

James strode over to the barrel and stared at it. It was one of the biggest barrels he'd ever seen—too large for the Johanssens to have taken with them in their wagon across the plains. Too large, in fact, to easily haul up the ladder from the cellar to the floor above. James blinked with a sudden thought. He rocked the barrel, feeling its weight. It was heavy. He felt his heart skip a beat. He tried to remove the lid, but it was fastened tight. He pulled a jackknife from the pocket of his trousers and attempted to pry it open. The lid finally gave way with a squeak. When he peered inside, he saw that the barrel was filled nearly to the top with flour.

James thrust his hands inside the barrel, the powdery substance sifting through his fingers. He reached in deeper until the flour came up to his shirtsleeves, rolled at his elbows. Then suddenly, his fingertips nudged something solid. He held his breath, struggling to grasp the object, but it was just out of reach. James withdrew his hands and searched for a container or receptacle of some sort to scoop the floor into. There was nothing at hand. He rocked and tugged at the barrel, inching it along the dirt floor to the shelf-like ledge jutting from the cellar wall. When he had the barrel in place, he began dumping handfuls of flour onto the straw lining the shelf.

The flour was old and spoiled, useless for consumption. His excitement mounted as he emptied the flour from the barrel. Half way down, he found what he was looking for. With bated breath he wrapped his fingers around a delicate china cup. He withdrew the cup, covered with a layer of fine white flour, and wiped a section of it clean with his hand. A lovely design of curling vines and curving leaves emerged, painted in colors of lavender and gold. James chortled aloud. He set the cup carefully on the ground, then dug his hands into the flour barrel again.

Within a few moments he had eight flour-dusted cups and eight saucers sitting beside him. Not one of them was cracked or broken. Inger had chosen an ideal hiding place. He tipped the barrel on its side and rummaged around the bottom of it to make sure he'd retrieved all the pieces of china, then he climbed up the ladder to get the knapsack he'd left on the pantry floor. When he came back down to the cellar, he removed several cloths from the knapsack. He picked up the first cup and examined it more closely in the dim light of the cellar. The pattern of leaves and vines were painted in pale lavender. Each delicate leaf was edged in gold paint, and the veins in the leaves were also painted gold. The lavender vines curled and twisted among the leaves, creating a beautiful design. The rims of each cup and saucer were gold, and a translucent sheen emanated from the fine porcelain. James carefully wrapped a cloth around the cup he held in his hand, and placed it inside the knapsack. He did the same with each remaining piece of china. He smiled with satisfaction as he imagined Inger's astonished expression when she removed the cloths covering the precious treasure.

James gave a moment of thought to what should be done with the discarded flour heaped on the shelf, and decided to leave it for the mealworms to feast on. He climbed back up the ladder with his knapsack tucked securely under his arm, and closed the double doors in the floor behind him. Then he strode out of the house whistling a cheerful tune.

CHAPTER TWENTY-FOUR

Elizabeth replaced the bootie Emmaline had pulled off her foot. The baby sat in her mother's lap, squirming and wriggling while Elizabeth tied the ends of the pink yarn into a bow at the ankle on Emmy's crocheted bootie. "So you took a ride past our old home on Durphey Street?" she asked James, who was sitting beside her watching her wrestle Emmaline.

James took hold of Emmaline's chubby little leg so Elizabeth could tie on the bootie securely. "Yes. The outside of the house and yard look nice. The people who own it must be taking good care of the property."

"I suppose so." Elizabeth gave the yarn bow a final tug, then readjusted Emmaline on her lap. "Did it make you feel melancholy to see the house?"

James nodded. "I couldn't help recalling the good times we had in that house. I remember helping Father build it, and Mother's satisfaction in moving from the small log cabin we had been living in."

Elizabeth felt a flicker of impatience. "Those times weren't always good ones, James. Or have you forgotten that?"

"No, I haven't forgotten. I haven't forgotten the hostility we were subjected to as a people. Or the loss of our properties and homes. Or even the persecution the Prophet Joseph suffered, and his death. But all those things have made the Saints stronger—have made me stronger."

Elizabeth frowned. James hadn't changed over the four years since she'd seen him last. He was still self-righteous and sanctimonious.

"Here, let me take Emmy," he offered. James held out his arms, and Emmaline went to him without hesitation. "You've finally gotten used to me, haven't you, Emmy?" he crooned to the baby. Emmaline favored him with a wide-mouthed grin. "And you're getting some teeth, too, aren't you?" James chuckled. "What a big girl."

"She has four teeth," Elizabeth reported, silently scolding herself for being disagreeable. She didn't wish to argue with her brother; there had been enough of that in years past. She hoped to enjoy this visit with James, and not let any of their past differences interfere with her pleasure in seeing him.

When she'd caught her first glimpse of him, dismounting from his horse in the yard, she'd been surprised by how much his looks had changed. He was no longer the gangly teenager she remembered. His face was more angular and firm now, and his shoulders broader. His dark hair was parted and worn off his brow; the style emphasized his brown, expressive eyes. There was an air of self-assurance about him that Elizabeth had never noticed before. Perhaps it came with maturity, or as a result of his experiences away at school.

James began bouncing Emmaline on his knee, and the baby giggled and waved her arms. Elizabeth smiled at the picture of the two of them. She tried to think of something conciliatory to say. "You haven't told me much yet about your semester at medical college. The course work ran twelve weeks?" she asked in a honeyed voice.

James shifted the baby onto his lap and put an arm around her tiny waist. "Yes, twelve weeks—April through June. For the most part it consisted of listening to lectures, but we also gained practical experience by working in a Chicago hospital. We studied anatomy, physiology, chemistry, pharmacy, obstetrics, operative procedures, and a bit of dentistry."

"It sounds difficult," Elizabeth conceded.

"Some things about the training were difficult. A lot of reading was required. I enjoyed that part of it, but it took a good deal of time to digest the information. I was glad I'd had as much experience in medicine as Dr. McCaffrey had given me. Some of the students at the medical college had spent most of their apprenticeships observing, rather than assisting, the doctors they worked with."

Emmaline sat calmly in James' lap, sucking her thumb. Elizabeth patted the baby's foot. "Did you learn anything new about the medicines you doctors dispense?" Elizabeth asked her brother.

"Dr. McCaffrey practices homeopathic medicine. It's similar to herbal medicine in that he uses herbs and other natural substances to compound his drugs. At college, I learned more about traditional medicines and treatments."

"You mean like bleedings and purges?" Elizabeth asked, wrinkling her nose.

"No. Most physicians today don't believe such measures do a lot of good. Doctors still don't know exactly what causes disease, but we have a much better idea of how to treat it than we ever had before." James glanced at the little girl in his lap. She looked up at him and smiled.

"I'm glad to hear that. Blood-lettings, sweatings, and purges—it seems barbaric to me," Elizabeth remarked.

"Many people would agree with you about that. Doctors have managed to earn the public's distrust. It's going to take time to change that attitude and gain public confidence." James scooted Emmaline onto one knee. "Medicine has come a long way in the last few years. A great many new drugs have become available, and the discovery of ether gas has made more complex surgeries possible. The field is really exciting right now. Discoveries are being made at an incredible pace."

Elizabeth listened without comment. James' enthusiasm for his subject was evident; it showed in his expression and in the tone of his voice. He could hardly keep still in his seat.

"New drugs have been proven effective in treating illness, and doctors have learned more about existing drugs. Uses for morphine, quinine, iodine, ergot, antimony, and a dozen other drugs are more clearly understood now, and hence more successful in treating disease."

"I know laudanum and calomel have been used extensively in the past," Elizabeth observed.

"Yes. Laudanum is a medicinal tincture of opium, used to control pain. And calomel is administered as a purgative. But I'm talking about a whole new array of compounds."

Elizabeth arched her back and stretched her arms overhead. She gazed at James wordlessly.

"Not only are new medicines available, but a number of modern, sophisticated instruments make diagnosis more accurate," James continued eagerly. "The clinical thermometer has been improved, as well as the monaural stethoscope. And the general adoption of medical record-keeping is becoming a boon to theoretical and practical research."

Elizabeth was tiring of the topic. "It must have been interesting for you, James. I'm glad you had the opportunity to go to school. How did you like Chicago?"

Emmaline sat quietly, sucking her thumb. She reached up with her other hand to grasp James' hair. James returned her arm to her side and patted it. "Chicago is a fascinating city. Sprawling. Populous. Practically every building houses two or more businesses, and street peddlers are busy hawking newspapers, firewood, and loaves of baked bread. The streets are a maze of confusion with buggies and coaches, horses and wagons, and people on foot going every which way at once. Everything is in commotion."

Elizabeth laughed. "It sounds as if you didn't like it much." She lifted Emmaline from James' knee. The baby was fussing and rubbing her eyes with her fists. It was nearly her nap time.

"I didn't dislike it. It was exciting to be there. But the clamor and the fast pace of life in the city were jarring. I'll be glad to get back home to the quiet peacefulness of the valley."

Elizabeth unexpectedly envisioned a broad, green valley surrounded by towering mountains whose peaks were threaded with silver streams, much like that described in her family's letters from home. For an instant, she longed to be there.

James reached over to tickle Emmaline's chin. The baby smiled briefly, then puckered up her face and began to whimper.

"She's tired. It's time for her nap. I'm going upstairs to put her to bed. When I come down, I'll fix you something to eat," Elizabeth offered. "Alexander said he'd be home to join us for supper."

After Elizabeth tucked Emmaline into her cradle, she started supper. She and James visited about inconsequential things while she prepared the food. James put the silverware on the table and filled the glasses with water. Elizabeth set a wine glass at Alexander's place.

A few minutes later, Alexander arrived home. Elizabeth immediately noticed his irritable mood; he was obviously upset over something. "Sit down here, sweetheart," she said, pulling the chair away from the table for him. She hoped to mitigate his ill humor before he expressed it in James' presence.

"Hello, Alexander," James said in greeting. "How was your day at the mill?"

Alexander slid into his chair. "Well enough. And you? What did you do today?"

Elizabeth took the seat next to her husband. "James went to see some of the old sights in town," she answered for her brother. "We've been talking a bit about the years we spent together growing up in Nauvoo."

"Did you ride down Durphey Street?" Alexander asked. He shook out his linen napkin and laid it across his knee. Elizabeth poured a quantity of claret into his wine glass. The fluid sparkled in the belly-shaped crystal goblet. She caught the quick, disapproving glance James cast at the glass of wine.

"Yes, I saw the house and grounds. The orchard looks like it's doing well."

Alexander and Elizabeth started on their supper. James hesitated for an instant. Elizabeth knew her brother preferred to say a blessing on the food before he partook of it, but such prayers were never said in her household.

"So. What else did you see while you were down on the flats?" Alexander asked, cutting the roasted meat on his plate with a gleaming silver-plated knife and fork.

James picked up his napkin and spread it across his lap. "I stopped outside the Mansion House. Young Joseph Smith happened to be working in the yard, and I had a nice chat with him."

Alexander forked a piece of meat into his mouth.

"I visited some of the old public buildings on Main Street—the Cultural Hall and the printing complex where my father worked."

"Ah, yes. The printing office of the *Nauvoo Neighbor,* wasn't it?" Alexander replied.

Elizabeth stiffened. She heard the scorn in her husband's voice. She hoped James hadn't noticed, too.

"That's right. The *Nauvoo Neighbor.* It was a fine newspaper. Until a few overzealous men forced the closure of the printing house."

A bead of sweat broke out along Elizabeth's brow. James *had* noticed, and he wasn't going to let Alexander's sarcasm pass unchallenged. She hoped to head off what she knew would be Alexander's snide reply. "Have some more creamed potatoes, Alexander. They're awfully good," she said quickly, holding the serving bowl out to him.

"No, thank you, Elizabeth. If my memory serves me correctly, James, I believe it was the mayor and the city councilmen who first took matters into their own hands by terminating the printing of the Mormons' rival paper, the *Expositor."* Alexander leisurely took another bite of meat.

Elizabeth put a hand on Alexander's arm. "Please, Alexander," she whispered. She knew James' anger would be kindled if Alexander pursued the topic. The seizure of the printing office and destruction of the *Expositor*'s press was the pivotal event leading to the Prophet's martyrdom. Joseph Smith had been mayor at the time. He and members of the city council carried out the council's order to dismantle the *Expositor*'s printing press because the antagonistic paper was deemed a public nuisance. They were subsequently arrested on a charge of riot, brought against them by the publishers of the newspaper. The Prophet went to appear before a justice of the peace in Carthage, where he was detained and committed to the Carthage jail. A mob with blackened faces stormed the prison, and shots were exchanged. As he tried to escape through the window of the jail, Joseph was shot and killed. James had loved and revered Joseph Smith. Elizabeth knew he would not countenance any derogatory remark from Alexander concerning the Prophet.

James' eyes flicked from Alexander to Elizabeth. "It's all right, Elizabeth. This conversation isn't really about the printing house or the newspapers. Is it, Alexander?"

Alexander's slate blue eyes narrowed. Elizabeth was confused. Some unspoken communication was passing between Alexander and her brother, and she didn't know what it concerned.

"Did your customer keep his appointment this afternoon, Alexander?" Elizabeth heard her brother ask in a cold voice.

Alexander put down his fork. "As a matter of fact, no, he did not. I probably have you to thank for that. I could have finished my business last night if you hadn't interfered." Sparks flew from Alexander's eyes, like flint striking steel.

"What are you talking about, Alexander? What business?" Elizabeth asked. Her throat was dry and the palms of her hands itched.

"Go ahead, Alexander. Tell her." James' voice was icy.

"If you wish to spend another moment under my roof, I advise you to keep your mouth shut."

"Alexander!" Elizabeth was shocked by his words, and appalled by his behavior toward her brother. Her whole body began to tremble with emotion.

James glared at Alexander for an instant, then he slowly pushed himself away from the table and stood up.

"Where are you going, James? Sit down and eat your super," Elizabeth cried.

"I believe I need a breath of fresh air," James answered without expression. He set his napkin on the table, turned, and walked out of the room. Elizabeth heard the front door close behind him.

"Alexander, I can't believe what I just heard from your lips. How could you speak to my brother in that manner—ordering him from the house! I'm ashamed and embarrassed . . ."

Alexander's fist slammed down on the table. "Silence! I'm not in the mood for your whimpering, Elizabeth. Your brother had it coming. He's been strutting around here like a bandy rooster ever since he arrived. Poking his nose where it doesn't belong."

Elizabeth numbly watched the water in the glasses dance from Alexander's blow to the table. Alexander snatched up his wine goblet and drained it in a single gulp. "You shouldn't have spoken so rudely to James. I doubt he'll be back except to collect his trunk. I don't know whether I can forgive you for this, Alexander."

"Forgive me?" Alexander repeated incredulously. "Do you think it matters to me whether you do or not? Come, come, Elizabeth. You forget yourself. Your job is to back me up and do as I say—that is, if you want to continue living in the comfortable manner to which you've become accustomed."

Elizabeth's eyes filled with tears. "You're an evil man, Alexander. You attack people in the areas where you know it will hurt them the most." She wiped away a fallen tear, leaving a smear on her cheek. "I am going upstairs. I can't abide looking at you."

Elizabeth reined the mare to a stop and peered through the gathering darkness. The ruined temple and its grounds were swathed in shadows, but it was still light enough for her to see the hunched figure sitting on the grass in what used to be known as the West Grove. The clearing where the Saints had once sat to hear the Prophet Joseph speak was now occupied by a field overgrown with weeds.

Elizabeth dismounted her horse and tied the reins to a tree branch. She walked toward the still figure sitting on the ground beneath the leaves of a large oak. "I thought I might find you here."

James looked up. "Elizabeth . . . I didn't hear you coming."

"I know. I could tell you were deep in thought."

James glanced wordlessly at her. Elizabeth tucked the folds of her skirt underneath her and sat down beside him. Neither of them spoke for a moment.

"I apologize for Alexander's boorish behavior. I don't know what gets into him sometimes," Elizabeth offered quietly.

"Thank you, Elizabeth. But you don't need to make excuses for him. He's the same man he's always been. He has an abiding hatred for the Saints."

"That's not altogether true, James," she replied.

"Well, it doesn't matter." Elizabeth watched her brother stare out into the shadows gathering across the temple grounds. "I've been sitting here thinking about the many times we came to this grove for Sunday meetings. I used to listen to the brethren speak and watch the sunlight play on the stone face of the temple. What happened to the temple, Elizabeth? Look at the destruction of it."

Elizabeth's eyes followed in the same direction as James'. "A tornado passed through here about six weeks ago," she answered in a quiet voice. "The Icarians were in the middle of refurbishing it. They had purchased the whole temple block. But I don't know if they'll do anything with the building now because of the extent of the damage."

James sat silently staring at the edifice. "I'm not talking about just its outward appearance. There's no heart in it anymore. No spirit. With the Saints' removal from Nauvoo, the temple no longer serves the purpose for which it was constructed."

"It can be rebuilt, James."

James shook his head. "No."

Elizabeth's eyes returned to her brother. "Come back to the house with me, James. I don't want the incident at the dinner table to ruin our visit."

James shifted his position on the weed-infested ground. "I'm leaving for Salt Lake City tomorrow . . ."

"Please, James, don't do that." Elizabeth felt tears pricking her eyes.

"It's not just because of what happened tonight. I was planning to leave in a day or two anyway. I'm anxious to get home—anxious to put into practice what I've learned at school. And I miss Inger."

Elizabeth bit her lip, trying to control her emotions. "You're really planning to marry Inger?"

"Yes, of course. Why do you ask?" James turned to look at her, and Elizabeth could see the solemnity in his brown eyes.

"It's just that I never imagined Inger as someone you might be interested in—someone you might marry," Elizabeth answered lamely. She couldn't tell James she considered Inger to be plain-looking, and without charm or humor.

"Why not? Inger is a tremendous girl."

"I'm sure she is," Elizabeth answered quickly. "I guess I felt that way because we've always known the family.

In your vocation as a physician, I thought you'd meet someone from a wealthy family, or perhaps a girl who'd had a little experience beyond the sheltered family life we knew."

James turned to face her squarely. "There's not a finer woman than Inger. What you really mean is that you find Inger's humble and spiritual nature unappealing. Don't you?" James' eyes were like two black pits in the shadows shrouding his face.

"No. That's not what I mean. I just thought a girl with a little broader background might enhance your role as a physician. Forget it, James. It's none of my business, anyway." Elizabeth put on a frown and sat stiffly on the dry, lifeless grass.

James said nothing for several seconds. "It's those very qualities I love most about Inger. Her sensitivity to the spiritual side of life. Her devotion to the gospel of Jesus Christ." James stared Elizabeth in the face. "You used to be like that."

Elizabeth gave a short, harsh laugh. "I was never like that, James."

"Yes, you were. What happened to cause your heart to turn from the teachings of the gospel?"

Elizabeth didn't reply. She pressed her lips together in a hard line. She didn't want to discuss this topic with James.

"Don't you believe the gospel to be true anymore, Elizabeth?"

Elizabeth's heart began throbbing in her chest. The harsh pounding made it difficult for her to draw a breath.

"Answer me, Elizabeth. Do you believe the gospel of Jesus Christ to be the truth?"

"I don't know!" Elizabeth blurted out. She could feel the throbbing now in the veins in her neck. They felt as if they would burst with the rush of blood coursing through them. "I don't think about it one way or the other, James. All I know is that being a member of the Church brought me nothing but persecution, fear, and suffering. Why should I embrace a religion that brings only unhappiness?"

James was silent for a moment. "It's true that God requires sacrifice from his Saints. But if abiding by the commandments were easy, then there would be no test of faith."

Elizabeth lifted her head to stare at her brother, but she didn't speak.

"Living the principles of the gospel brings happiness, Elizabeth. It's disobeying the commandments that brings sorrow and misery."

Elizabeth rose up onto her knees. "You and Mother and Christian were obeying commandments when you sold our home and left Nauvoo to travel across an empty continent because Brigham Young told you to do so. And Zachary died because of it. Do you call that happiness? Do you call that a blessing?" Elizabeth's voice was hoarse with emotion. "And what about Zachary's choice? Was he happy to give *his* life for the gospel's sake? He was just a child, James! A small boy who had no choice but to comply with his parents' decision, whether he wanted to or not. And he lost his life because of it," she concluded bitterly. She sank back onto the grass, her breathing rasping in her throat.

James took her hand into his. "I don't know the reason why Zachary's life was taken. Only God knows that. But I do know it was for a purpose."

Elizabeth looked up into her brother's eyes. They were gazing steadily into her own.

"It's necessary that we experience some suffering, some sorrow, in this life. That's what makes us grow and become stronger people. And sacrifice is part of it. We may not understand all of the reasons why in this life, but sacrifice, faith, and obedience are necessary to our salvation. And if we endure them well, God will reward us in the life to come." James spoke the words softly, reverently.

"Sacrifice brings forth the blessings of heaven. Is that what you're trying to say?" Elizabeth asked, giving her brother a wry smile. His words had a curious effect on her. They seemed to calm her spirit.

James smiled. "I see you haven't forgotten everything you learned about the gospel."

"No, I haven't forgotten everything. Though I seldom think on them, James."

James let go of her hand and lay back on his elbows in the dry grass. "Do you remember how we used to sit here in this very spot and listen to the words of the Prophet Joseph? And how we watched the temple rise skyward a few inches every day under the workmanship of the brethren's hands?"

Elizabeth smiled back into her brother's face. "Yes."

James leaned forward, and his expression took on an earnestness Elizabeth had seldom seen before. "Elizabeth, I know you believe in Jesus Christ. You know Christ is our Savior, our Lord and Redeemer. He stands at the head of the Church." James' eyes almost glowed with the intensity of his words. "And Christ loves us. That's why he gives us commandments and laws to follow. Those commandments are the gateway to happiness and joy in this life and in the life to come. Christ wants us to return to him. And that's where Zachary is today—in Christ's loving arms."

Tears pushed against Elizabeth's eyes. James' words touched a chord deep inside her. "I wish I had your faith, James. Maybe if my circumstances were different . . " Her voice trailed off into the still night.

"Father once told me something I've always remembered. He said our circumstance matters little; what matters most is what's in our heart."

Emotion welled inside her, squeezing the tears from her eyes. She let them trickle down her cheeks unchecked. "Christian is a wise and good man. I've come to realize that." She paused, trying to get her emotions under control. "But I can't change the past, James. And I haven't strength enough to change the present. I can only look to the future. Perhaps my children will be spiritually stronger than I am."

James was silent for a few moments. Then he covered Elizabeth's hand with his. "I like to think life is like a fallow field. There's a season for sowing, and a season for reaping."

He patted Elizabeth's hand. "The entire crop hasn't been harvested yet, Elizabeth."

Elizabeth sat on the floral-patterned velveteen couch, staring at the pencil drawing she held in her hand. Her eye followed the contour of the sweeping lines sketched on the page. She stroked the drawing tenderly with her fingertips, her thoughts far from the elegantly-furnished parlor where she rested.

"I think I have everything."

Elizabeth looked up to see her brother standing at the foot of the staircase with his traveling trunk in his hand. She smiled at him. "You haven't forgotten to pack the gifts I'm sending home to the family?"

James patted the trunk. "They're right here."

"That's good."

James walked to Elizabeth's side and set the trunk down on the floor. "What do you have there?" he asked.

"I was just looking at this while waiting for you. Sit down for a minute." Elizabeth patted the seat next to her on the couch.

James took the seat offered him. "What is it?"

"The drawing Christian made of Mother when she was a young woman living in Missouri."

James took the framed drawing into his hand and studied it. "Oh, yes. I remember seeing this. He sketched this portrait of her before they were even married, didn't he?"

Elizabeth nodded. "Mother gave me the drawing before all of you left Nauvoo for the Great Basin. She said she wanted me to have it to remember her by." Elizabeth felt a lump forming in her throat.

James handed the drawing back to his sister. "She was a beautiful lady, wasn't she?" he commented. "She still is."

"I wish I could see her. And Millicent and Roxie."

"Then come with me back to the valley, Elizabeth. I can wait a few days for you to prepare for the trip. We could go a good part of the way by stagecoach, and you can bring Emmaline. Mother so wants to see Emmy."

Elizabeth followed the lines of the drawing with her finger. "I'd like to do that, James. But I can't." She looked up at him. His eyes were solemn on her face. "Perhaps some day."

James put an arm around her shoulders. "I hope so, Elizabeth. In the meantime, you'll think about the things we spoke of last night in the grove?"

"I'll think about them, James," she answered, "but I can't promise you I'll make any changes in my life."

"Well, you hold on to this drawing of Mother, and keep the gospel light flickering in your heart. Perhaps some day your testimony will catch fire."

Elizabeth laughed softly. "You never give up, do you, James?"

"Not when something important is at stake."

"And that is exactly why you will make a wonderful doctor. Go home, James. And give Inger a hug from me."

James grinned at his sister. Elizabeth's heart felt lighter than it had in a very long time.

James stood and reached for his trunk. "Tell Alexander goodbye for me."

Elizabeth nodded. "I will."

James bent down and gave Elizabeth a kiss on the cheek. "Be happy, sis," he whispered. Then he turned and strode to the door.

Elizabeth set aside the drawing and followed James to the front door of the house. She stood on the porch, watching him strap his trunk on the horse's rump behind the saddle. Then he carefully laid a bulky-looking knapsack across the pommel of the saddle. "What's in the knapsack?" she called to him with a grin.

"A little something I dug up for Inger."

Elizabeth chuckled. She didn't know what James had stowed in the knapsack, but she guessed it was something with which Inger would be pleased.

"Goodbye, James. Have a safe trip," Elizabeth said to him.

James swung into the saddle. "Take good care of my favorite niece," he said as he raised a hand in farewell.

"Yes, I will." Elizabeth watched her brother snap the reins against the gelding's neck. The horse started forward in a brisk trot. Elizabeth stood on the porch, waving, until James rode out of sight.

CHAPTER TWENTY-FIVE

"So when I showed the publishers of the magazine your drawings, they were favorably impressed. They want you to send more of your work to them in Chicago as soon as you can. The editor said you showed great talent and promise."

"Whew," Lars whistled. "I never expected that. Thank you, James. I have other drawings, and a couple of watercolors, already completed. I guess I can send those and see what happens."

James smiled at his friend. "You're going to be a famous naturalist, Lars. Not only are you a scholar of the plant and animal life in the valley, but you can render their likeness on paper like no one else I've ever seen."

"He's absolutely right, Lars. I've been telling you that all along." Inger leaned across the table to give her brother a hug. Then she cuddled next to James again, slipping her arm through his.

James had ridden Odysseus out to the Johanssens' place earlier that evening, eaten supper with Lars and Inger, and then taken a private stroll with Inger in the moonlight. The August night was soft and warm, and the moon burned in the sky like a lighted lamp. He had missed Inger while he'd been away in Chicago even more than he'd realized. And he knew he never wanted to be separated from her again.

He'd returned home from Nauvoo two days before, and since that time he'd spent every moment he could with Inger. He'd told her about his experience at the medical college, and his visit with Elizabeth and Alexander in Nauvoo. He'd confided in her about the altercation between Alexander and Benjamin Dawson at the mill, and his own argument with Alexander at the dinner table the next day. Inger had expressed the same dismay and frustration over the incident as James himself had felt. She'd asked a dozen questions about Elizabeth and Emmaline. She wanted to know everything about them. She'd told James how disappointed she felt about Elizabeth not being with them to share the joy of their wedding day.

"The Eastern papers and magazines pay well for that kind of art work, Lars," James commented. "You can sell your drawings and gain a reputation at the same time."

Lars laughed. "I'll be content just to wander the valley with my sketchbook and pencil. If I can earn a little money by selling my drawings, I guess I wouldn't complain too much."

James chuckled at the other man's words. He and Lars were as close as brothers. And they would be brothers in very fact with his marriage to Inger.

"Just remember to stop in occasionally to see your family," Inger remarked.

"Hey, you're not talking to Jens here. No matter how far away I might roam, I'll always keep in contact with Johanna, Kirstine, and you," Lars said to his sister.

"Speaking of Jens," James interjected, "did you hear from him at all while I was away at school?"

Inger shook her head. "Not a word. I thought he might contact us, at least concerning the bag of gold dust he left behind, but he didn't. Who knows when we'll see him again."

"Whenever he does show up again, it will be too soon for me," Lars muttered.

"You don't mean that, Lars," his sister chided gently. "Jens is our brother. Father and Mama would want us to be forgiving and loving toward him. No matter what he did."

"You're right, sis. I guess I just feel angry with him for coming here and putting you in danger."

"What happens if he does come back looking for his gold?" James asked, frowning. "I've worried about that possibility ever since the two of you gave me his money."

"Well, if he does come back wondering about his gold," Lars replied with a mischievous gleam in his eye, "we'll tell him the money went toward payment for the loan of your horse."

Inger giggled, and with it the frown eased from James' forehead.

"And if that doesn't convince Jens, then you can show him your physician's certificate." Lars grinned broadly. "It looks professional enough to intimidate the most callous of criminals."

James smiled. He appreciated Lars' efforts to put him at ease concerning the money he and Inger had given him for medical school.

"Have you told Lars yet about Dr. McCaffrey?" Inger asked, fixing her smile on James' face.

"What about him?" Lars' flaxen brows raised in question.

"Now that I have my certificate, Dr. McCaffrey has officially turned his practice over to me. He's planning to leave Salt Lake City at the beginning of next week. So I guess I'm on my own." James made a pretense of gulping with fright.

"Oh, you're not the least bit afraid of that, Dr. James Kade." Inger grinned at him. "You can hardly wait to be on your own."

"I am looking forward to it, I confess. But I'm not without some fear and trembling. I intend to practice a more traditional type of medicine rather than the homeopathic methods Dr. McCaffrey used. I'm a little nervous about that. But I'm thrilled and excited, too. If it weren't for the two of you, I might never have had the opportunity to finish my medical training."

"Well, I'll give you my sister in marriage to even out the debt. How does that sound?" Lars teased him.

"I accept," answered James promptly. He looked into Inger's eyes and felt his heart racing. He kissed her tenderly on the lips. Then he kissed her again.

"Okay, okay," Lars laughed. "Can't you two wait for the wedding to do that?"

James took Inger's hand into his. "Ten more days, and you'll be Mrs. James Kade. That will be the happiest day of my life, Inger."

"And mine," she answered softly.

James smiled into her face. Her eyes were bright with joy, and her cheeks glowed. He ran his hand along her soft, yellow braid. It was like a beam of sunlight. "I have a gift for you, Inger," he said quietly.

He stood up from his chair and went to the peg beside the door of the Johanssens' cabin where he'd hung his knapsack. He took the bulky sack in hand and returned to his seat near the table. "This is for you, sweetheart."

Inger took the knapsack from him. "What's this? You've already given me several gifts you brought from Chicago. You spoil me, James."

"This one's not from Chicago."

Inger began to undo the strap on the outside of the knapsack.

"It's from Montrose."

She looked up at James with a startled glance.

"I planned to give it to you on the day of our wedding, but I can't wait until then. So I brought it tonight." He watched Inger's face to savor her expression.

She glanced from James to her brother, who was seated across from her at the table. Lars shrugged his shoulders to indicate he didn't know anything about what was inside. Inger unfastened the strap of the knapsack and folded back the flap. A puzzled frown flickered across her brow as she looked inside.

"What is this, James?" she murmured. She lifted out the soft cloth wrapped around a flat-shaped object. She laid the object in her lap and slowly uncovered it.

James held his breath in anticipation.

The cloth fell away, revealing a beautiful, shimmering porcelain plate. The plate was edged in gold, with a pattern of curling vines and lavender leaves threaded in gold. "Oh, James," whispered Inger. Her hand trembled as it tenderly brushed the plate. She looked up at him, and James saw tears glistening in her eyes.

Lars leaned forward for a closer view of the plate resting in Inger's lap. "Isn't that a piece from Mother's set of dishes from Denmark?" he asked.

Inger nodded without speaking. She reached into the knapsack again and withdrew a second piece of china, wrapped in a square of clean cloth. When she removed the cloth, a delicate china teacup of matching design gleamed in her hand, "James . . . I'm overcome. You went to the house in Montrose and got these from the cellar?"

James nodded. A huge grin lit his face, and joy filled his heart.

Inger stared at him with tears brimming in her eyes. "Thank you. Thank you, my darling."

"All eight plates are there, Inger. And all eight cups. And not one was cracked or broken. You hid them in an excellent place." James' smile reached from ear to ear.

Inger wiped away a tear rolling down her cheek. She dipped into the knapsack again and again, until all the porcelain plates and cups were sitting in a shining row on the table in front of her.

"Look at that." Lars whistled under his breath. "Mama would be glad to know that something she valued from the old country actually made it all the way to the valley of the Great Salt Lake."

"Yes, she would," Inger agreed. She sat motionless, staring at the china in wonder.

James picked up one of the thin china cups and eyed it thoughtfully. "This will make a fine family heirloom for our children, Inger. You can tell them the story of how you hid the china in a flour barrel in the cellar of your house when the Saints were forced to flee Illinois. The children will realize they have a very brave and clever mother."

Inger slipped her hand into James'. Across the table from them, Lars rested his fingers on one of the glistening china plates and watched the joy radiate from his sister's face.

"You can tell our children what a beautiful city Nauvoo was, and how you could see the temple gleaming on the hill from your home across the river in Montrose," James continued. "You can bear witness of Joseph Smith, the Prophet. You can explain the principles of the gospel of Jesus Christ to them as they sit around your knee in the evenings beside the hearth, and share your testimony with them."

Inger's eyes lingered on James with loving tenderness.

He bent over and whispered softly in her ear. "And I'll be there, in the home we share together, to tell them of the love I have for their angel mother."

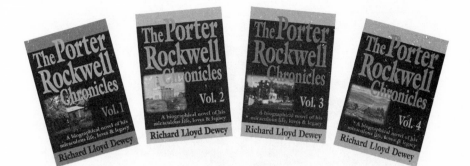

The Porter Rockwell Chronicles
by Richard Lloyd Dewey

This best-selling, historically accurate biographical novel series renders Porter's life in riveting story form, bringing it alive for adults and teens alike.

Volume 1 begins with his childhood years in New York where he becomes best friends with the future Mormon prophet Joseph Smith. The story continues through Porter's settlement with the Mormons in Missouri, where he fights against mobs and falls in love with and marries Luana Beebe.

Volume 2 covers the turbulent first four years in Nauvoo, where he continues to fight mobs and becomes Joseph Smith's bodyguard.

The Nauvoo period of his life draws to a close in Volume 3 as his best friend Joseph is murdered and his wife Luana leaves him and remarries, taking his beloved daughter Emily with her. Porter must bid a heartbroken farewell as he and the Mormons are driven from Nauvoo and flee west.

Volume 4 continues with his first ten years in Utah, where he is joyously reunited with his daughter Emily, takes on the U.S. Army in a guerilla war, and enters a new phase of adventures as U.S. Deputy Marshal.

Volume 1 (ISBN: 0-929753-16-X)   Hardcover, $26.50
Volume 2 (ISBN: 0-929753-17-8)   Hardcover, $26.50
Volume 3 (ISBN: 0-9616024-8-1)   Hardcover, $23.88
Volume 4 (ISBN: 0-9616024-9-X)   Hardcover, $24.88

*Look for them in your favorite bookstore,
or to obtain autographed copies, see last page.*

Or order online at:
www.stratfordbooks.com

Porter Rockwell: A Biography

by Richard Lloyd Dewey

The epic biography that traces Porter Rockwell from turbulent Eastern beginnings to battles with Midwestern mobs to extraordinary gunfights on the American frontier. Quotes hundreds of journals, letters, and court records. Illustrated by western artist Clark Kelley Price.

Hardcover, $22.95   ISBN: 0-9616024-0-6

Look for it in your favorite bookstore,
or to obtain autographed copies, see last page.

Or order online at:
www.stratfordbooks.com

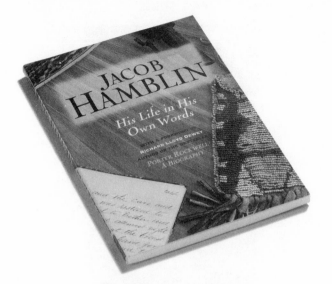

Jacob Hamblin:
His Life in His Own Words

Foreword by Richard Lloyd Dewey

Far from the gun-toting reputation of super-lawman Porter Rockwell, Jacob Hamblin was known in early Western history as the supreme peacemaker.

No less exciting than Porter's account, Jacob's adventures encountered apparent Divine intervention at every turn, a reward seemingly bestowed to certain souls given to absolute faith. And in his faith, like Porter, Jacob Hamblin was one of those incredibly rare warriors who are absolutely fearless.

His migrations from Ohio to Utah with life-and-death adventures at every turn keep the reader spellbound in this unabridged, autobiographical account of the Old West's most unusual adventurer among Native Americans.

In his own words, Jacob Hamblin bares his soul with no pretense, unveiling an eye-witness journal of pioneer attempts to co-exist peacefully with Native brothers, among whom he traveled unarmed, showing his faith in God that he would not be harmed.

Easily considered the most successful — and bravest — diplomat to venture into hostile territory single-handedly, Hamblin takes the reader into hearts of darkness and hearts of light.

Softcover, $10.95   ISBN: 0-9616024-5-7

Look for it in your favorite bookstore,
or see last page for ordering info.

Or order online at:
www.stratfordbooks.com

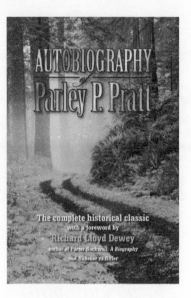

Autobiography of Parley P. Pratt

Foreword by Richard Lloyd Dewey

Parley P. Pratt's riveting autobiography has thrilled generations of Latter-day Saints. More than just a biography, it is also one of the richest sources of amazing facts from early church history and a treasure trove of classic passages frequently quoted to this day in lessons and over the pulpit. It deserves a place on the bookshelf of every Latter-day Saint and the attention of every student of Mormonism.

Elder Pratt's death was as colorful as the rest of his life. It is generally known that the apostle was assassinated in Arkansas while on a mission, but the fascinating details surrounding this crime of passion are not widely known. In the foreword, bestselling author Richard Lloyd Dewey pulls together the long-obscure historical facts to tell the rest of the story.

In this new edition of Parley P. Pratt's renowned autobiography, spelling, grammar and punctuation have been corrected and modernized so that Pratt's narrative is now easier than ever for readers to enjoy.

Softcover, $19.95   ISBN: 0-929753-12-7

Look for it in your favorite bookstore,
or see last page for ordering info.

Or order online at:
www.stratfordbooks.com

Hübener vs Hitler

A Biography of Helmuth Hübener, Mormon Teenage Resistance Leader

REVISED, SECOND EDITION

by Richard Lloyd Dewey

Nobel Laureate author Günther Grass said Hübener's life should be held up as a role model to every teen in the world. Regional best-selling author Richard Lloyd Dewey (*Porter Rockwell: A Biography*) holds up Hübener's life as a light not only to all teens, but to adults as well.

As an active Latter-day Saint, young Hübener recruited his best friends from church and work and established a sophisticated resistance group that baffled the Gestapo, infuriated the Nazi leadership, frustrated the highest judges in the land, and convinced the SS hierarchy that hundreds of adults—not just a handful of determined teens—were involved!

While other books have told the story of the group of freedom fighters Hübener founded, this is the first biography of Hübener himself—the astounding young man who led and animated the group. The inspiring, spell-binding, true story of the youngest resistance leader in Nazi Germany.

Hardcover, $27.95   ISBN: 0-929753-13-5

Look for it in your favorite bookstore,
or to obtain autographed copies, see last page.

Or order online at:
www.stratfordbooks.com

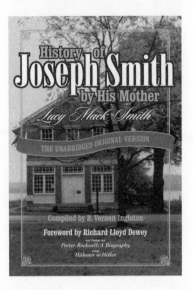

History of Joseph Smith by His Mother

THE UNABRIDGED ORIGINAL VERSION

by Lucy Mack Smith

compiled by R. Vernon Ingleton
with foreword by Richard Lloyd Dewey

Of all the versions of Lucy Mack Smith's remarkable history that have
appeared since its initial publication a century and a half ago, this is by
far the best. For the first time ever, the complete original version is
presented, plus the corrections added later by church historians, plus
all the facts from the rough draft that have until now been missing from
published versions. R. Vernon Ingleton has done a superb job of putting
all the elements together to allow Lucy at last to tell her story in its
entirety in an easy-to-read format. This is a masterpiece!

Hardcover, $27.95   ISBN: 0-929753-04-4

Look for it in your favorite bookstore,
or see last page for ordering info.

Or order online at:
www.stratfordbooks.com

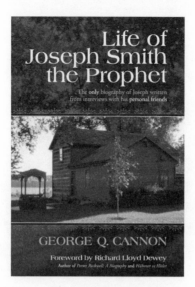

Life of Joseph Smith the Prophet

by George Q. Cannon
with foreword by Richard Lloyd Dewey

This is the *only* biography about Joseph written from personal interviews with his friends! The author served as First Counselor to four prophets, all of whom knew Joseph. Having full access to Church archives, Cannon weaves the intricate tale of Joseph's intriguing biography in a mesmerizing manner. He stays focused, keeping the reader spell-bound as Joseph has to flee time and again for his life. The reason? Apostates and bigoted religious leaders seek his blood. Seen from an insider's view of what really took place in Nauvoo, Cannon shows how the conspirators worked, even recruiting the governors of two states to get Joseph taken down. But in the end it was Joseph who prevailed spiritually—proven in part by the success of the restored church and its twelve million members today. This must-read biography gives insights, humorous stories and anecdotes with suspenseful plotting rarely seen in this long-out-of-print book that has been republished in clean, modern type for easy reading.

Hardcover, $27.95   ISBN: 0-929753-09-7

Look for it in your favorite bookstore,
or see last page for ordering info.

Or order online at:
www.stratfordbooks.com

New Evidences of Christ
in Ancient America

by Blaine M. Yorgason, Bruce W. Warren, and Harold Brown

In 1947 California lawyer Tom Ferguson threw a shovel over his shoulder and marched into the jungles of southern Mexico. Teamed with world-class scholar Bruce Warren, they found a mountain of evidence supporting Book of Mormon claims. Now the reader can follow their adventure as they unearth amazing archaeological discoveries and ancient writings, all of which shut the mouths of critics who say such evidences do not exist. In this volume, the newest archaeological evidences are also presented.
    Endorsed by Hugh Nibley.

Hardcover, $24.95   ISBN: 0-929753-01-1

Porter Rockwell Returns
by Clark Kelley Price

This classic color print of the painting by renowned western artist Clark Kelley Price depicts Porter Rockwell coming home at night in a lightning storm through downtown Lehi, Utah.

In this vivid scene, Rockwell is returning from a hard day's work, with an outlaw draped over the horse he has in tow.

36"w x 24"h, $30.00   ISBN: 0-929753-0-6

*Add $10.00 shipping and handling for first print
and $1.00 for each additional print sent to same address.
Utah residents, add 6.25% sales tax.*

Send check or money order to:
Stratford Books, P.O. Box 1371, Provo, Utah 84603-1371

Or order online at:
www.stratfordbooks.com

Prices subject to change.

ORDERING INFORMATION

The Porter Rockwell Chronicles
by Richard Lloyd Dewey.
Volume 1	Hardcover, 490 pp. ISBN: 0-929753-16-X	$26.50
Volume 2	Hardcover, 490 pp. ISBN: 0-929753-17-8	$26.50
Volume 3	Hardcover, 490 pp. ISBN: 0-9616024-8-1	$23.88
Volume 4	Hardcover, 490 pp. ISBN: 0-9616024-9-X	$24.88

Porter Rockwell: A Biography $22.95
by Richard Lloyd Dewey.
Hardcover, 612 pp. ISBN: 0-9616024-0-6

Jacob Hamblin: His Life in His Own Words $10.95
Foreword by Richard Lloyd Dewey.
Softcover, 128 pp. ISBN: 0-9616024-5-7

Autobiography of Parley P. Pratt $19.95
Foreword by Richard Lloyd Dewey.
Softcover, 426 pp. ISBN: 0-929753-12-7

Hübener vs Hitler (Revised, Second Edition) $27.95
A biography of Helmuth Hübener, Mormon teenage resistance leader,
by Richard Lloyd Dewey. Hardcover, 594 pp. ISBN: 0-929753-13-5

History of Joseph Smith by His Mother: $27.95
The Unabridged Original Version
by Lucy Mack Smith, compiled by R. Vernon Ingleton.
Hardcover, 548 pp. ISBN: 0-929753-04-4

Life of Joseph Smith the Prophet $27.95
by George Q. Cannon.
Hardcover, 615 pp. ISBN: 0-929753-09-7

New Evidences of Christ in Ancient America $24.95
by Blaine M. Yorgason, Bruce W. Warren, and Harold Brown.
Hardcover, 430 pp. ISBN: 0-929753-01-1

FREE SHIPPING & HANDLING ON BOOKS
Utah residents, add 6.25% sales tax.

Send check or money order to:
Stratford Books
P.O. Box 1371, Provo, Utah 84603-1371

Or order online at:
www.stratfordbooks.com

Prices subject to change.